Drawn West

By Arline Fisher

Dear Readers,

Those of you who read my first novel, "The Corner Saloon," will recognize some familiar characters here, including Kathleen who fled San Francisco to return to her native Ireland, and a little girl named Viola who was traveling with her aunt and uncle on the same ship. Even the mysterious Vicente makes a cameo appearance along with his apprentice, Philip. But this is Viola's story as she grows from a budding young artist into an accomplished, but anonymous, famous painter. Her journey through the American West of the late 1800s and early 1900s is romantic, passionate and revealing.

Enjoy!

Arline Fisher

Chapter One

"Look at her sleeping there, the little lamb." Viola heard someone sniffle and felt her blankets being adjusted. "What's to become of her now do you think?" Someone brushed a curl off her forehead.

"The conductor said he would send a cable to her father's brother, in London I believe he said," another voice answered. "I suppose he'll have to come and take charge of her." This woman sniffled also. Viola heard them leave the room, taking the candle with them. Before she drifted back to sleep she wondered who the women were talking about, but only for a few seconds before she was back in dreamland where she was a powerful queen.

In the morning Viola awakened not to her mother's usual greeting but instead to see the conductor of her papa's orchestra and two of the ladies who played violins, an instrument similar to what her papa played, the viola. The conductor looked stern, as he always did, but the women were red-eyed and holding handkerchiefs tightly in their hands. At first no one said a word, but finally the conductor cleared his throat. "Child, you must listen to me now," he intoned. "There has been a terrible...accident, and your parents..." His voice trailed off and the women both began to cry.

The younger of the two women, whom Viola had come to know as Mary, moved to Viola's bed and hugged her tightly. She continued, "Your parents are in heaven now, Viola."

"Heaven? Well, when I shall I go to meet them? When will they return?" Viola asked, uncomprehending. "Mommy promised to braid my hair today." The woman hugged her all the tighter, but Viola struggled to push her away. "And my daddy said we would go to the park again." This set off another round of sobbing on the part of the women, and the conductor again attempted to explain.

"Bad men attacked your parents last night, on their way home from our concert. I'm afraid they were both killed." It was clear from the look on the eight-year-old girl's face that she still wasn't understanding. "Your parents, young lady, have gone to be with God...forever." He hastened to add, "I have written to your uncle Arthur this morning and I expect to hear from him soon as to where you will go."

"Go? But I..." and now Viola began to cry as well. "I want to go with them." She squirmed out of Mary's hold and pulled the covers over her head. "I won't go anywhere until you bring them here."

She heard the adults murmuring until finally one of them said, "Leave her be for now, poor thing." The conductor left the little bedroom in the rooming house where the Viennese orchestra members were staying in New York during their tour, but the women stayed behind for a moment. "Let's give her some time and then bring a little breakfast." They left Viola, covers over her head, crying silently as understanding slowly dawned. She refused the breakfast they returned with and the dinner after that. But the following morning when her mother was still not there to awaken her, Viola relented and accepted a few spoons of oatmeal. She later heard them arguing out in the hallway.

"It's all his fault," one said angrily. "If he hadn't insisted on bringing us to this barbaric place, this never would have happened!" Another person tried to hush the speaker, but she had more to say. "The fact that he thought we could bring some culture to these imbeciles is ridiculous. Did you see that some of those barbarians actually brought *food* to the concert!" They wandered away from Viola's door and she heard no more for the rest of the day.

Across the ocean, Viola's uncle, Arthur McDougall, was equally incredulous. His hand shook as he read the cable again, this time aloud to his sister. "Well I had absolutely no idea! I can't think of the last time I've seen Thomas or heard a word about him," he said, referring to his late brother. "And now to learn that he became a musician in Vienna, was married and had a daughter. Well, it's just too much to comprehend, I say." His sister was only two years older than he but Thomas had been a fully twenty years younger.

Vivian nodded her agreement. "It's astonishing. It truly is. Thomas was an uninspired musician at best, as I recall, and now to hear that he was touring with the Vienna orchestra." She shook her head. "And what of his wife's family? Why aren't they taking in the girl?" She looked sternly at her brother. "It's too much to expect of *us*, surely."

"Hmmm. There are questions to be answered, certainly, but I suppose we must at least..."

She stopped him in midsentence. "We must write back and say that the responsibility is not ours to assume."

Arthur looked at the cable again and placed it in his suit pocket, leaving the parlor for his office where he could at least have a glass of port and contemplate this turn of events. His brother was dead and he had a niece he never knew existed who was now waiting in New York City — for him.

Chapter Two

Arthur spent the rest of the afternoon in his office rewriting drafts of several cables, one to New York, of course, but others to Vienna. With his connections in the world of music as an agent for opera stars, Arthur hoped to learn more about what kind of a man his brother had been and also more about his wife. Perhaps Vivian was correct in suggesting that his late brother's wife's family would want to take the girl in. When he was satisfied that the cables conveyed the appropriate gravity of the situation and his overall concerns, he donned his hat and topcoat and prepared to leave for the cable office. "I shan't be long," he called out to Vivian, "simply going to the bank." He didn't share the content of any of his missives with her, knowing in advance what her reaction would be.

When he posted the cables he added a few extra schillings, asking that no runner be dispatched to his home as soon as any responses were received; rather he would call for them himself. There was no point in alerting Vivian to his strategy at this early stage. He had learned that the orchestra would remain in New York for at least another six weeks, so he had time to arrange a booking there, or cable the orchestra funds to support the girl and her passage back to England.

The smell of a roast beef greeted him when he returned home. The lamps had been lit and it was quite cozy. Arthur was already imagining how a little girl might view his home when Vivian interrupted his reverie. "And how was Mr. Entwistle?" she inquired as he passed the parlor door.

Arthur was confused. "Mr. Entwistle?"

"The banker, obviously."

He hastened to cover his mistake. "Oh, yes, quite. No he was in a meeting and I didn't have a chance to speak with him." Vivian looked doubtful but Arthur quickly continued on to the kitchen to have a word with the cook. He hoped it wasn't too late to ask her to make some bread pudding for tonight.

The dinner conversation was quite subdued, with Vivian mostly reviewing correspondence they had received from their various clients and proposed bookings for each. The subject of their newfound niece never came up, about which Arthur was surprised but profoundly grateful for the moment.

He didn't have to wait long for the answers to his questions. Within days he had received cablegrams from Vienna. Everyone was sad to hear of Thomas' death. He had been a valued and respected member of the community. His musical prowess on the viola had impressed all who heard him play. His wife would also be missed. One respondent wrote to Arthur, "She was but a girl herself when Thomas rescued her from the streets. She, like many others, had fled the poverty of Ireland only to find more poverty and hardship. Thomas took her in and theirs was a true love story." Another wrote that, "Their little girl was a beauty and bright as a shiny penny already." They inquired, "Was the girl gone as well?" They hoped not.

What Arthur heard from New York was not as encouraging. The tour was not going well, the orchestra members were very unhappy, and they would soon be moving on to Philadelphia. She was a sweet young girl, but the atmosphere was really not conducive to taking care of Viola. When would Arthur arrive to collect her? He sighed when he read the cable and knew he could no longer put off the inevitable.

His sister, Vivian, had never married and had instead devoted herself to taking care of Arthur, her younger brother by two years. It was not entirely selfless, however, Arthur realized. Vivian had been able to attain a position in the rather glamorous world of the arts that would never have been available to her otherwise. She was Arthur's gatekeeper, as it were, determining which invitations he would (or they would) accept to performances, which promising stars he would meet with, and the like. In addition, she ran the household although in recent years she had hired a cook and housekeeper, so it was merely their supervision that required her attention. Where Arthur was pleasant and relaxed, Vivian was dour and constantly on guard for any imagined slight or insult. That, added to her appearance, with her gray hair always tightly in a bun and the dark voluminous dresses she preferred, made her a formidable sight indeed. Arthur cringed when he thought of the impression Vivian would make on a newly-orphaned young girl.

That night at dinner he began slowly. "I have made some inquiries about our brother's situation, and it seems..."

"And why would you do that? Do you intend to stir up a hornet's nest of creditors perhaps that will soon come after you?" Vivian put down her fork and gave Arthur one of her most fearsome stares. "Or is there more to it?"

Arthur was used to this technique but it still unnerved him. "Well, of course there's more to it. There's our niece to think of." He pushed the cables over the table to Vivian. "Just see. She has no one but us."

"I'm sure there are orphanages in America," Vivian said, tossing aside the cables without reading them.

"I will hear of no such thing!" Arthur stammered, quite astounded at Vivian's proposal. "I shall make the necessary arrangements in the morning to go to New York and rescue our niece." He resumed attacking the rather dry chicken which threatened now to stick in his throat.

"I hope you will have a pleasant sailing then," Vivian said in a low tone. "While you are gone I will vacate my rooms and instruct the staff to prepare them for *your* niece then."

Oh, Arthur thought, it just goes from bad to worse with this difficult woman. "That will not be necessary and you know it. You will come with me on the trip and Viola will return with *both* of us. You are correct in saying that the staff can make rooms ready for her, as the house is certainly large enough." Vivian said nothing and Arthur thought he had gained a victory. "After all, you can't expect me, a single man, to properly care for such a young girl."

"Perhaps you should marry then!" Vivian stormed away from the table and Arthur could detect that she was close to tears. He pushed the chicken away and reached for the sherry. It would be a long journey to America.

Chapter Three

Viola was indeed a very smart little girl, but she was also headstrong, willful, and in short, as stubborn as a steadfast mule. It fell to Mary and one of the seamstress' assistants to take care of the orphan and within just days they both agreed: Even the biggest diva on the stage was easier to be around. "I will not wear that dress. It's itchy and I don't like it," Viola announced, stamping her feet for emphasis when Mary tried to slip a jumper over her head.

"You will wear it or you'll stay in your room all day in your bloomers!" Mary challenged her.

"That will suit me just fine," the little minx retorted. "I don't care for the music all of you play. And, I do not like Herr Stormer," she said referring to the imperious conductor. Mary hid her own smile.

"Very well then. You must stay in your room until we return from rehearsal later today." Viola said nothing in return and merely turned her back on Mary to look out the window. Mary would have gone to the little girl to give her a reassuring hug, but ever since Viola had accepted the news about her parents she resisted any such attempts to comfort her.

When at last the musicians returned from their lengthy rehearsal, mealtime became another battle with Viola. "I don't care for potatoes that way. My mommy never made them that way. They look like someone else has already chewed them," she pronounced, turning her nose up at the mashed potatoes. "I believe I will just have meat and maybe pie later."

The cook was incredulous. "Oh, you will, will you?" She towered over Viola. "I *believe* you will eat what I put on your plate, young lady." Viola turned her plate upside down and glared up at the cook. The others at the table were secretly amused by this nightly melodrama, but under the stern eyes of the conductor, no one said anything.

"Herr Stormer, I should like to be excused," Viola said, adding a slight curtsey, which she had discovered he rather liked.

"With as little as you have eaten, I hope you won't waste away during the night," he replied in a rather menacing tone, but Viola was not to be intimated. "I hope we find more than your bones in the morning," he added. "You are excused, young lady." He looked at the cook and shrugged his shoulders. "The dinner was excellent tonight, as always." Viola trudged out of the dining room and the cook collected her empty plate. Herr Stormer couldn't suppress a smile of his own, thinking about the challenge Arthur McDougall had ahead of him. He had met Arthur and what he thought of as his battleax of a sister on several occasions and wondered how the rather on-in-years couple would cope with such a precocious child. He had received a cable earlier in the day from Arthur indicating their expected arrival in New York three weeks hence. Somehow he thought they would all survive three weeks with the girl until she was no longer their problem.

The next morning Mary was surprised to find Viola already dressed for the day, although her hair was a shambles, something Mary endeavored to fix with only limited success. The girl's massive blonde curls were as stubborn as their owner, escaping even the tightest braid. "Does the fact that you're dressed mean that you are going to rehearsal with us?" Mary gently inquired.

"No. I have been watching the people coming and going out on the street and I believe some of them are school children," Viola thoughtfully explained. "I think perhaps I can go with them." Mary realized that Viola must have been extremely bored just sitting by herself in her room all day, and she hated to throw cold water on Viola's plan. Still.

"I don't think you can just decide to go to school, dear," she began. "I think your parents have to take you."

Viola immediately became angry. "So, I shall never go to school because I have no parents?"

"No, no, that's not what I meant." Mary hoped one of the other orchestra members would come by to rescue her from the conversation. "I'm sure when your aunt and uncle arrive, that's the first thing they'll attend to — your education."

Viola had been listening to all the conversations about her aunt and uncle and knew their arrival would be weeks away. She also knew there was every chance they wouldn't remain in New York or return to her home in Vienna. No one had seen Viola cry since her parents died, but now she did. "I can't be here by myself all day," she wailed. "Mommy and daddy used to take me places and talk to me, especially mommy." She made no effort to halt her tears. "I used to have books and dolls and friends. Now I have no one."

It broke Mary's heart, too. "You have all of us." She hastened to add, "I know it's not the same, but you need to have faith that a good life awaits you with your uncle. People say he's a very kind man."

"Yes, and they say his sister is a shrew!" Viola challenged. Mary had heard the same.

Finally Mary had a sliver of an idea. "Let's see if we can get some paper and a pencil for you so that you can draw pictures of your parents, or your dolls, or whatever you see out your window." Viola stopped crying, mostly, and seemed to brighten at the idea.

"Yes, I do like to draw very much," she conceded. "Very much."

Chapter Four

Arthur had campaigned tirelessly over the days following the cables and finally believed he had succeeded in convincing Vivian to accept Viola. Retrieving her was another matter. "You can't expect me to send fare for her passage and then just tell the concert master to just put her on the next ship." Arthur was exasperated. "She's just eight years old for Christ's sake!"

"It just seems that it shouldn't take two of us to go fetch her," Vivian responded. "After all, she is only an eight-year-old girl, as you so wisely point out." She felt very satisfied with herself but Arthur was having none of it.

"The little girl must be bereft and we must seek any way we can to comfort and reassure her," and he glared at his sister, "and that means both of us!" He gathered up some papers and prepared to leave the study where they had been arguing for the better part of an hour. There were times when he wished he had an office to go to, like most professional men, instead of working out of his home. But, his home made entertaining so much easier and his clientele definitely expected a certain level of sophistication.

"Well, there could be one benefit to our going to New York," Vivian began slowly. "You always say that we need to be more familiar with the opera houses there, so I suppose we could use part of the trip to assess them."

Arthur seized on the idea although he knew it was far from spontaneous on Vivian's part. Although he had been to the United States several times, she never had but would be loath to admit it. "That's a capital idea, Vivian, really." He poured it on. "You're so astute at judging just which of our clients would do best in a given theater setting." Vivian smiled and allowed him to continue. "And while we're there it will give us a good opportunity to meet with Herr Storm. It seems he's rather adventurous taking an orchestra on tour when no one else ever has."

"Adventurous or foolish remains to be seen," Vivian said. "I don't think the ticket receipts have been anywhere near expected." She assumed her usual haughty tone. "You know we really can't expect those people to appreciate any level of true culture, even the most well-to-do among them. After all, they're only one generation from living with the savages — and like the savages, I dare say."

Arthur didn't want to lose his small victory so simply said in his most bland tone, "Well, I'm sure you're right, dear sister. You know so much more about those things." He didn't tell her he had already booked passage for both of them on a ship leaving within the week. "I think it's best now that we've made our decision that we act without delay." He put down his papers and gathered up his coat and hat. "I'm off to the wharves then and shall book us suitable accommodations to leave in a few days hence." He didn't have to pretend to be excited as he truly was. He was to be an uncle, something he never foresaw!

Across the pond, as the English liked to call it, Viola was enjoying a certain level of excitement as well, but it did not derive from the news of her aunt and uncle's imminent arrival. She found that the days simply flew by when she was sitting in her window sketching the street scenes below. She drew the flower cart that was often parked outside the theater across the street. In the early mornings she waited for the arrival of another cart laden with cuts of meat, and she perfectly captured the insouciance of the mangy dog that often lingered there begging for treats. In the evening she looked forward to the arrival of the theater patrons and wished they would stand beneath the marquee for just a bit longer, but if she couldn't capture their poses exactly, her imagination filled in the missing details. Just before the sun set, Viola saw her own reflection in the window and set out each day to refine her self-portrait. She didn't think she was exactly pretty, but there was definitely something unique about her eyes, and of course, her tumultuous hair.

When Mary and the others came back from rehearsal, Viola was eagerly awaiting them. "Mary, please, I must have more paper and at least two more pencils," she pleaded. "I have asked the cook to sharpen mine, but you can see it's barely big enough to hold onto now." She plaintively held out an inch of wood encasing a nubbin of pencil lead.

"I will ask the conductor. You know, child, all of these things cost money," Mary said gently.

"Oh, don't worry about that. My uncle has lots of money and he'll certainly pay you back," Viola said triumphantly.

"And how do you know he has lots of money?" Mary inquired, genuinely curious.

Viola looked a little embarrassed and out of earshot of the others said, "My daddy always complained that his brother could have done more to help him, been more generous." Viola started to tear up at the mention of her father but suppressed it. "He said my mommy was as poor as a church mouse but when he sent a note to my uncle about helping us, he never heard a word from the old man." She stamped her foot. "I hate him!"

"Oh, now you musn't say that," Mary chided her. "He's coming all the way from England to meet you and take care of you, and I'm sure you'll have so many lovely things." Viola was not to be mollified so Mary simply told her to come downstairs at the usual time for dinner. She didn't know when she would have time to speak to the conductor about such a frivolous expense.

It turns out she should have spoken to him immediately. The next day at rehearsal several of the musicians frantically flipped through their sheet music. Some had the introductory notes, others the middle section; no one seemed to have the entire score, and that included the conductor. When it was discovered that everyone was missing sheets of music, the conductor berated the young woman in charge of the music, reducing her to tears. One of the male French horn players endeavored to save the girl some of the humiliation by volunteering to the conductor, "Sir, respectfully, many of us know these scores so well we could simply…"

The conductor cut him off with a roar. "We will not rewrite our own scores! You will find that music and you will do it now!" The girl scurried off the stage and the red-faced conductor dismissed the other musicians. Mary returned to her room every bit as dismayed as the other musicians. She hung up her cloak and decided to check on Viola.

"You're back early," Viola observed, taking a second to look away from her sketching. Mary's eyes nearly popped out of her head.

"Girl, what on earth are you drawing on!" She snatched Viola's sketch away and saw that it was on the back of the violin interlude. The floor around Viola was littered with similar sketches, all on the back of the orchestra music. "You have no idea the trouble you have caused us."

Viola smiled in her slightly wicked way. "And to think that it all could have been prevented so easily, and certainly less expensively than buying new sheet music." Mary was too shocked to respond. "Shall I tell Herr Stormer that you refused to buy me a pad of paper?" Viola taunted Mary. "Or perhaps I should just let you tell him where you found the music? I wonder which would be more difficult for you?"

Mary's patience had been tested by Viola on a number of occasions, but this truly was the ultimate. "I want you to put those drawings away," she said, gesturing to the pile on the floor, "immediately, and I will get you paper and pencils tomorrow. In the meantime, we say nothing about this." Viola at least knew not to gloat over her victory.

Chapter Five

Vivian and Arthur argued all the way across the ocean about what they would do once they arrived in New York and met their niece. Vivian was in favor of spending as little time in New York as possible, after seeing the theaters and what New Yorkers boasted of as fine restaurants. They would then collect their charge and return immediately to England where they would enroll her in a private boarding school. She stressed the boarding aspect to Arthur. But Arthur had more of a grand adventure in mind for all of them. To keep the peace as much as possible on the sailing, he said little and appeared to demur to Vivian as much as possible.

At last the ship docked in the bustling New York harbor where Arthur had arranged transportation for them to the relatively new Fifth Avenue Hotel. The hotel initially suffered its share of scorn because of its location, considered too far from the center of the city, but by this time it was considered the center of the city's social, cultural and political life. Even Vivian couldn't help but be impressed by the brick and marble façade. Arthur had stayed there on a previous trip and pointed out that a writer for *The Times* of London had described it as "a larger and more handsome building than Buckingham Palace," something Arthur thought should impress his peevish sister.

The true surprise awaited them inside. The Fifth Avenue Hotel had the first passenger elevator ever installed in a hotel in the United States. Arthur endeavored to explain its workings to Vivian. "There is a steam engine in the basement that powers a large screw that passes directly through the passenger cab." He was clearly excited and hurried her along to the contraption. She was clearly a little frightened of the whole experience but got over it quickly when she saw their sumptuous suites. Every room had a fireplace and a private bathroom, unheard of at the time. The rich green curtains and carpets accented the rosewood woodwork beautifully. "Do you suppose you can survive here for a few days?" he teased his sister. Vivian sunk comfortably into an upholstered chaise and promptly dropped off to sleep.

Arthur took the opportunity to go back down to the lobby and inquire about arranging a carriage to the hotel in the theater district where he had been told to meet Viola. He had decided that their initial meeting would not include his sister, even though he knew it was inevitable.

Viola had been told to expect the arrival of her uncle and aunt, and Mary had made every effort to make her presentable, although, of course, Viola fought her at every turn. "Sit still and let me braid your hair, girl," Mary said as Viola squirmed.

"You don't do it right! My mommy never pulled on it like that." Viola had been fussy and agitated ever since the news of their arrival. "I don't want to go with them anyway."

"Well, I suppose if you act like some kind of savage, which is what you look like now, maybe they won't even take you!" Mary threatened then immediately regretted her statement. "I mean, they have to take you, of course, but you could put your best foot forward and make them realize what a nice little girl you could be if you would only try."

"I'll put my best foot forward and kick him right in the shins," Viola said under her breath.

Mary stood back to admire her handiwork and Viola seized the opportunity to escape, but Mary had the door blocked. "You sit back down and keep your dress and your hair tidy until Mr. McDougall arrives," Mary said as sternly as she could muster. "And when you meet him, you will curtsey and then shake his hand. And smile, Viola, please try to smile."

Viola shook her head, hoping the tight braid would come undone. "Nobody can make me smile!" Mary believed her; thus far, no one could make the girl do anything she didn't want to do. All of Viola's belongings, precious few of them at that, had been packed into a small valise and stood ready by the door. Even though the little girl had been difficult from the start, Mary couldn't help but feel a little sad at the thought of her leaving, and she knew many of the other orchestra members felt the same way. The two sat staring at each other, waiting.

Finally, a light knock on the door signaled the arrival of Viola's uncle. Mary took her hand and half-walked, half-dragged her to the hotel lobby where a tall, distinguished man stood holding his top hat in his hand. He looked nervous but smiled warmly when he saw Viola. Mary pinched her to make her curtsey, but Viola stood her ground until her uncle came forward, bent down to her level and solemnly put out his hand. "I am Arthur McDougall, your uncle, and I am most pleased to meet you," he said formally, then winked at Viola who smiled despite herself. "Let me also tell you I am very sorry about your parents, but we can talk about that another time. Let's get your things together and go to our hotel, shall we?"

Mary was astonished to see Viola link her hand in her uncle's and accompany him toward the door. At the last minute, she turned back to Mary and hugged her quickly. "Thank you. I'll never forget how kind you were to me." That caused Mary to erupt in tears and she quickly handed over the girl's valise to the waiting carriage driver.

Just as they were about to climb into the carriage, Viola suddenly turned and ran back into the hotel, taking the stairs two at a time. "Wait, wait, I've forgotten something." Mary just assumed it was Viola changing her mind, but in a minute the little girl emerged with her precious sheaf of drawings, which Mary had tied up with a ribbon earlier in the day. With those in hand she skipped happily out to the carriage and clambered in without a backward glance.

Chapter Six

Arthur and Vivian settled into their rooms at the hotel and awaited the arrival of their niece. Arthur was nervous but excited. Vivian barely suppressed her annoyance, and then only because her brother warned her about it. Finally, Arthur suggested they wait for Viola in the lobby, hoping the distraction of other guests would cover ease his anxiety. But he needn't have worried once they saw the little girl enter the hotel.

Anyone who had just met Viola after her parents' deaths would have been surprised to see how quickly and warmly she attached herself to her uncle Arthur. The instant she saw him, she saw her father's kind eyes and courtly manners and knew that her uncle was somehow sent by her father to take care of her in his absence. She felt safe and comforted, just what Arthur had hoped for all along.

Her aunt Vivian was another matter entirely, and Viola felt certain she, Vivian, must have been from an entirely different branch of the family. She was waiting for Arthur and Viola in the ornate hotel lobby, all stiff and starchy in her flowing black dress. Viola released her uncle's hand and moved unsteadily to hug her aunt, but Vivian recoiled almost in horror. She put her hand out, but not to take Viola's, to push her away. Viola stood uncertainly and looked back to her uncle who appeared equally shocked at Vivian's response. Nevertheless, he gathered his composure and formally introduced them. They settled at a small table and were immediately set upon by waiters, the hotel being famous already for the number of people it employed to see to their guests. Arthur desperately wanted a sherry but Vivian interrupted his request and indicated they would all have tea — English tea!

Viola was rarely at a loss for words but now all she could do was sit and stare miserably at her feet, which Vivian immediately chided her about kicking back and forth. "Cross your legs at the ankles, dear, like any lady would." Whatever Viola did, Vivian criticized. "Have you no manners whatsoever?" Arthur attempted in vain to intervene and finally resigned himself to the fact that his sister would establish her dominance over their niece much like she had over anyone else in her sphere. Later, after an uncomfortable dinner in which Vivian had scrutinized Viola's table manners, they rode up in the elevator and Arthur watched the huge screw turning, pushing the passenger car higher and higher. He thought to himself, "That kind of pressure can go both ways." Vivian could just as easily grind Viola down as he could try to raise her up.

Of course, Viola couldn't have her own room in the hotel so she was forced to stay in Vivian's suite. While Vivian took the large feather bed, she indicated to the staff that they should bring a blanket and pillow for Viola to use on the hard little settee in the living room. At least she was nearer to the fireplace. She huddled under the blanket and allowed herself a few tears, but when she heard the old woman begin to snore, she got up and retrieved her bundle of sketches, looking for an unused piece of paper. She drew her aunt from memory, but adding horns and a curving tail, drawing dark circles under her eyes and long talons at the end of her fingers. The activity calmed her enough that she felt ready to creep back to her makeshift bed, and her aunt's snoring finally lulled her to sleep.

The next morning began as awkwardly as the evening had ended. Vivian clearly hadn't considered who would help Viola bathe and dress, so Viola more or less pulled herself together and was relieved to see that they would be having breakfast in their room. The humiliating scrutiny she felt was certain to come was better suffered in private, after all. Arthur joined them and kept up a lively stream of conversation, hoping to deter his sister in her criticisms, and for a while it worked. However, when he announced that they would all be touring the city, visiting a few of the new theaters, Vivian flatly declared, "I'll not have some ragamuffin as this," pointing to Viola disdainfully, "trailing along as we go to places where visitors are expected to exhibit at least a modicum of dignity."

Arthur patted Viola's hand. "This is no ragamuffin. This is just a little girl who needs her face washed and her hair tied up," and he looked at his sister, "something I'm sure you can do quite handily for her. Go on now, tidy up."

While he was awaiting the ladies, Arthur spied Viola's sketches and was quite astonished at how good they were! He enjoyed a guilty laugh as he came across the drawing of his sister, thinking it didn't take long for the little girl to capture her personality exactly. Vivian nearly scrubbed Viola's face right off of her head, and she was a little too firm with the hair ribbons, but Viola did emerge fresh-faced and presentable by anyone's standards.

"All right then ladies, let's go begin our adventure for the day, shall we?" He linked his arm through his sister's and grasped Viola's hand, winking at her when the older lady hesitated to enter the elevator. He had noticed that many people used the stairs, fearing perhaps that the steam engine would quit, sending the metal box crashing to the ground. Viola showed no hesitation, however, and smiled all the way down to the lobby where a carriage man was awaiting them.

The trio spent the morning riding through the city until Arthur suggested they leave the carriage and walk for a while through the city's shopping district. Viola was mesmerized by every shop window, as was Vivian, although she was careful not to show any enthusiasm. When they came to an art gallery, Viola refused to budge. "Please can we go inside, please uncle?" Arthur consented but Vivian had to control the moment, admonishing Viola not to touch anything! The paintings were largely what was known as impressionist works and Viola was wide-eyed. After studying each and every one, she finally let herself be nearly dragged out of the gallery and back to the carriage to begin touring some of the theaters as they opened their doors for rehearsals.

Vivian and Viola sat quietly in the seats while Arthur introduced himself to stage managers, conductors and producers, depending on the production being mounted at each. Finally, after a very long day they all headed back to the hotel, but just as they were about to enter, Viola pulled Arthur aside. "Uncle, please, could I ask you to get me one thing?"

He knelt down, "Of course, what is it that you desire?" He suspected it would be a new dress or a doll, knowing that's what most little girls wanted.

But Viola was not like most little girls. She was wise beyond her years and utterly focused. "I should like to have a pad of paper and some pencils." He gave her a questioning look. "I like to draw, very much, and I have nothing to draw on or with." She pulled her tiny piece of pencil out of a pocket, holding it out plaintively.

He smiled and led her into the lobby. "Vivian, wait up, will you? I must go run an errand very quickly. Will you settle Viola in your room and order us some tea?" She scowled but grabbed the girl's hand as Arthur rushed back out the door, stopping briefly to ask for directions from the doorman.

Chapter Seven

When they met later for dinner, there was a brightly-wrapped package sitting on Viola's chair. She looked questioningly at her uncle but he smiled benignly and then told her to "open it with great relish!"

"Relish? But we don't have any relish," Viola said uncertainly. Her uncle's laugh could be heard throughout the dining room.

"I just meant, dear girl, to proceed with enthusiasm."

Viola did, trying to spare the colorful paper but excited nonetheless to explore the package's contents. Inside were three different sizes of sketch pads, a box of pencils which Viola recognized must be of fine quality, a dedicated pencil sharpener (no more going to the cook to ask for the use of a sharp knife), and, most wondrous of all — colored crayons. Viola squealed with delight and jumped down from her chair so as to give her uncle a hug and kiss. She knew better than to approach Vivian thus, but did give her a wan smile.

"I don't believe I approve of just giving gifts for no purpose," her aunt said grimly.

"Why, it's not for no purpose, sister. It's so Viola can entertain us with her drawings."

"Still, it's not a special occasion or the like," Vivian sniffed.

"Oh, yes it is!" Arthur would not have the gaiety ruined. "Viola whispered to me just this afternoon that today was her birthday, so celebrate it we shall!"

Viola's back was turned to her aunt and she winked at her uncle. Truth be told, she had no idea when her birthday was; her mother usually told her a week in advance that she had to be especially good because that would determine if she got a present—or extra chores—for her birthday. But from this day forward, July 18 would be Viola's birthday. Being the precocious child that she was, she decided to press her advantage. "And will we have cake, too?"

"Of course, we'll have cake," Arthur chuckled. "I'll speak to the chef myself about it." Vivian, uncharacteristically, had no more to say on the subject but she doubted that any of it had been the truth. She would have to watch this girl quite carefully indeed.

After a sumptuous dinner and the promised cake, Arthur cleared his throat. "And, we have more to celebrate tonight." His sister brushed a few crumbs off the table and raised an eyebrow at him. "We are going to continue our adventure not back to London forthwith, but instead to San Francisco!"

"San Francisco? What? All three of us?" Vivian looked aghast but Viola just looked confused.

"Of course, all three of us," Arthur said, determined to hold onto the moment. "I have booked passage for us on the railroad, all the way to the beautiful city by the Bay, as the local residents are calling it."

"What could possibly interest us in San Francisco?" Vivian demanded.

Arthur spent the next twenty minutes patiently explaining to his sister about how the influx of money from the discovery of silver in the Comstock and gold in California had created a new echelon of society, a society that demanded entertainment at least as good as New York City offered, and Arthur had determined to provide it through his opera stars and theater actors. Viola listened to it all silently even though Arthur was careful to use terms she understood. It was clear that Vivian didn't want her around and also that she didn't relish the trip to this San Francisco place, which must be very far away. And then what, Viola wondered?

Arthur seemed somewhat deflated after the long discussion, but he brightened when Viola gave him another hug. "Tomorrow, uncle, I would like to draw your picture."

"Oh, me?" He laughed then leaned in to whisper in her ear. "As long as you don't put horns and a tail on me." Viola was embarrassed that he had seen her sketch but couldn't help but laugh. "We shall see about that. I don't know if I could sit still long enough, and we have much to attend to before our trip."

"Much, indeed," Vivian snorted. "I suppose it will be left to me to arrange for the proper clothing and whatnot for *all* of us."

"Well, you're so good at it, dear. I wouldn't entrust it to anyone else," Arthur said, enjoying his small victory.

The next few days were spent in a flurry of shopping for more clothing, larger trunks to put it in, and even a few household sundries. Vivian fretted that even though the train advertised dining cars, what if no such dining were to be had for miles on end? Arthur reassured her that they would have their own car for sleeping at night and could remain there or visit with the other passengers during the day in one of the common cars. "Common, I'm sure," was her withering reply.

Chapter Eight

The week flew by and soon they were standing at the grand train station in the center of New York City, ready to depart on their journey west. A half-dozen cables had been sent to Paris, London, Vienna, and even Istanbul, advising Arthur's most important clients that he had extended his stay away from London in order to "pursue other venues that might appropriately accommodate your vast talent." As the train whistle was heard, he couldn't help but reflect on his first journey across the vast country:

Arthur had started his career as a young barrister in London, and using a small inheritance left to him, his brother and sister, he was able to establish his own independent office in a stylish townhouse near the courts. His brother, Thomas, took his share of the funds and left for parts unknown, and it wasn't long before his sister, Vivian, came to the townhouse one day asking if she could live there with Arthur until such time as...well, until. Arthur consented and assigned her a variety of duties to keep the household running and to manage his accounts as his practice grew.

Within just a short time of practicing, Arthur began to see a trend, and that was that most of the disputes brought before the courts were over contracts, and the breaches thereof. Often they were simple landlord/tenant issues, but an area that interested Arthur greatly was entertainment. He rarely missed an evening at the opera, a performance of a small chamber music group, or the opening of a new gallery, although the musical arts were his preference. Arthur was often invited to the small, or sometimes large, galas that accompanied these opening nights, and gradually his circle of acquaintances expanded to include a number of highly sought-after performers. Even though it was considered unseemly to solicit business, Arthur often looked for an opportunity to present his card, either to the entertainer of the moment, or to the host of the event. "Yes, he would be very interested in negotiating a better long-term contract." Or, "Of course, I could be happy to represent you when you meet with the London Symphony." Business flourished.

Arthur was interrupted in his reflections by a tiny tug on his coat. "Are we to spend the entire time in one of those coaches?" Viola asked, pointing to the dark green railroad cars. "What if we have to…use the facilities? Will the train stop then?" Arthur recognized how nervous she was and realized Vivian would have been no help as she also had no experience with long-distance train travel. Vivian's stoic expression ever since Arthur had announced the trip had been disappointing to him and almost frightening to Viola.

"There are facilities on the train, my dear," Arthur said. "Imagine how slow our progress would be across the country if we had to stop every time someone had to…well, as you say, use the facilities." He laughed and sought to reassure his niece. "The cars are quite lovely and we can move amongst them, perhaps to visit with our fellow passengers. Don't worry, child, I'll show you how to manage." He couldn't help but add, "And to have fun, too!"

Vivian was at that moment barking out orders to the porters loading their baggage, insisting on a certain order and placement, and Arthur supposed that's what made her happy, being in charge. In retrospect, he didn't know if he had done his sister a favor by allowing her to move into his townhouse all those years ago. Perhaps if she had moved into a rooming house for young ladies she might have acquired a suitor and by this time been married with children herself. But, as quickly as that thought entered his mind, it vanished hearing her shrill, "No, that's not what I said! I said put the satchels in last. Honestly!"

The flip-side of this coin was, however, that Arthur himself had remained a childless bachelor, a state he never envisioned for himself. There had been numerous young ladies working in the courts or in the theaters and galleries that had let him know they would be interested, but every time he thought of bringing one home to Vivian, the romance died on the vine. Now, however, he had an opportunity to remedy at least part of what was missing in his life, a child. He would draw on his great reserves of patience and kindness and try to give Viola the childhood he imagined his brother would have wanted for her.

Every night this past week when she was supposed to be asleep, Viola had heard her aunt and uncle arguing about the trip, and specifically about taking her. Vivian wanted to hire a "keeper" to take her back to England on the next boat and enroll her in a boarding school there. For her part, Vivian would grudgingly accompany her brother to San Francisco, but when they returned to London she made it very clear, she was not going to become the girl's nanny or anything close to it. Viola didn't know what she had done to make her aunt dislike her so, but she knew she would have to be very careful around her.

The first time Arthur determined to go to America it was because he had heard of the new opera houses being built in New York City and Philadelphia. When he saw them, he was indeed impressed, but then he became more intrigued about a new phenomenon, the desire for refined entertainment in even the most difficult outposts of the country. There was even an opera house being constructed in Virginia City in the Nevada territory, thousands of miles from New York City, and it was rumored that the great Caruso would be the first performer! Arthur resolved to be there when the opera house was completed.

He was shocked to learn that the cost of such a passage would be in excess of $1,000. A short part of the journey would be on a train, but then the passengers would be transferred to carriages, where the roads allowed, and ultimately to covered wagons where barely a trail existed. It would take at least a month to reach the West Coast of the vast new country.

Arthur looked at his pocket watch. The train was right on time. Over the years he had earned back that thousand dollar investment many times over and was now truly prosperous. Their tickets for this trip were only a hundred dollars each, and they would arrive in San Francisco in little more than a week. He allowed Vivian the extravagance of reserving two cars, one where they could spend their days (and where he would sleep at night) and a separate sleeping car for the ladies. Their luggage would be stored in the sleeping car, and they could take their meals where they chose, in the dining car with "who knows who," as Vivian had disdainfully put it, or in their own car. Arthur had been reassured that the train had plenty of porters to see to their needs. Having two cars, of course, meant that Arthur could always escape to the other car, so it may not have been as much an extravagance as a necessity, as he saw it.

Chapter Nine

Viola hadn't slept at all the night before they were scheduled to depart, although she had pretended to be sleeping when Vivian returned to their room after her nightly argument with Arthur. Viola had been told to pack all her belongings in the bag Vivian had provided her, but she still worried even as they stood in the train station whether a "keeper" would arrive to whisk her away to England instead. But finally the conductor stepped from the train and shouted, "All aboard! All aboard the Transcontinental Railroad, final destination San Francisco." He drew out each syllable so that it sounded like four destinations, "San, Fran, Cis, Co." Arthur took Viola's hand and helped her up the steps to their car, then turned to extend his hand to Vivian. She was clearly irritated and spurned his help, gathering her voluminous skirts up around her and stepping onto the train unassisted.

Vivian had insisted that Viola wear a bonnet, something Viola detested, preferring to let her hair do as it would. "You'll think so until you get a spark from the engine in that rat's nest, and then there goes that hair you're so proud of," Vivian had warned. As the conductor shouted his final admonitions to the passengers to say their goodbyes to friends and family and step lively to their cars, Viola tied the bonnet down tighter and found a seat near the window. She felt sad leaving the city where her parents had died, and she wondered what they would think about her setting off with two people she didn't know at all to travel all the way across the country. She remembered her trip to America not so many months ago:

"The ship was gleaming, all the brass fixtures polished and the wood on the decks so highly-polished Viola could see her reflection. The little cabin she would share with her parents was small, but it had a window (her father told her later it was a porthole) where she could watch the ocean and keep her eyes peeled for flying fish. She wondered if her daddy was teasing her about that. When the sailors unfurled the massive white sails and raised the flags, it was a thrilling sight.

But then the ship began to move and Viola wanted desperately to go back to the docks. The back of the ship moved up, the rear moved down. Viola had never ridden a camel but imagined that's what it would be like. She could have adjusted to that, but then the ship also rocked side to side at the same time. She peered out the porthole wondering what could be causing such motion and saw waves coming toward the ship that threatened to swallow it whole. She couldn't stand to watch but couldn't stop either, and the more she saw the horizon go up and down, the more she felt certain they would all die. That feeling passed in a fit of the most extreme nausea she had ever felt (and this included the time her father insisted she try to eat a snail, although he had a fancy name for it). Her mommy held her hair back as she vomited and vomited and vomited into the bucket provided in each cabin. And it would be the same every day for weeks. Viola wept when she finally saw land.

The motion of the train was not nearly as unsettling, Viola discovered, and within minutes of leaving the station she had drifted off to sleep. Vivian busied herself with finding everything that was wrong about their cars and about how their trunks had been stored, but Arthur watched the little girl sleep and wondered about the responsibility he had so easily accepted. Clearly the child had artistic ability, even at her young age, and he wondered, should he encourage that? In fact, should he encourage anything or just let what talents she had emerge on their own and find their own roots? He knew instinctively that he had to protect Viola's sensitivity from Vivian's practicality, or at least try to temper the two. He sighed. Really, what did he know about any of it?

When Vivian had first come to live with him, Arthur thought it best just to keep her occupied with the household arrangements and for a time that worked out fine. But Vivian increasingly interjected herself into Arthur's business life and soon his social life as well. After a number years Arthur came to realize he was the husband Vivian would never have, and probably vice versa. Vivian had never been an attractive woman and became less so as the years wore on, but still Arthur wondered, had he done her a disservice by allowing her to make his life her own? And giving up an important part of his own in the process? If there were a definition of Hell, Arthur often thought, it would be this: rethinking every decision one had ever made and seeing a different outcome each time.

The train pulled into another station and only a handful of passengers departed, but many more boarded and Arthur was interested to see a variety of mining and farming implements stacked on the platform to be loaded into the cargo cars. These were people setting out for new lives on the prairies or in the gold fields. He had to admire them but wondered how many would be re-boarding the train a year hence, or even sooner. The hustle and bustle awoke Viola from her nap and she once again grew apprehensive. Perhaps this was the place they would leave her off? She examined every person standing on the platform looking for anyone who might be her potential keeper. But, the train pulled out of the station once again to Viola's vast relief.

Vivian made the decision that they would take dinner in their own cars that night, and as the sun dipped over the horizon white-jacketed porters wheeled carts bearing silver-domed dishes into their car. The food was at least as good as any they had enjoyed in the hotel and Viola ate everything served to her. At the end of the meal the porters cleared all but one dish away and Viola was delighted to see an assortment of little pastries much like she'd enjoyed in Vienna. Arthur was equally delighted to see the porter approach with a glass of sherry for him and one for Vivian, and he offered Arthur a cigar which he declined with a wink; the porter instantly understood to bring it to Arthur's car later in the evening.

The sleeping arrangements were quite comfortable, even for Viola who scrambled up a ladder to a spacious bunk with velvet curtains of its own. She could still see out a window and thought she might count the twinkling lights of far-off farmhouses until she fell asleep; it didn't take long.

Chapter Ten

It didn't take long for most of the passengers on board to know Viola's story, and they went out of their way to befriend the shy little girl who gradually began exploring other compartments on the train, sketchbook always in hand. Several of the passengers, even the toughest ranch hands and would-be prospectors, agreed to pose to have their portrait done, and to a person they were impressed with Viola's obvious talent. It hurt Viola to give up the drawings when they requested them, mostly because of the loss of a piece of paper, but Uncle Arthur assured her they could always get more.

One afternoon well after the midday meal had been served, Viola wandered up to the dining car where the conductor was enjoying his lunch in the relative quiet. Viola knew he was the conductor from the badge on his chest and from hearing him yell out, "All aboard" at every stop, but he looked nothing like any train conductor she had seen in Vienna. There, the conductors favored shiny suits with gold epilates and gold braiding down the sides of their trousers. Plus, they all seemed to have beards or mutton-chops and full moustaches. This conductor was of medium height with a full head of brown wavy hair, but he was clean shaven and wore a plain blue suit. His only concession to his position was a burgundy brocade vest where he stowed his gold pocket watch.

Viola had watched him draw the watch from his pocket, then scan the horizon for some landmark.

Having found it, he would either advise his engineman to, "Pour on the coals there, we don't want to be late," or, more rarely, "Let's back off on the steam a bit and just let 'er roll easy into town." She finally got up the nerve to ask him about it.

"Well, missy, the trains have to run on time so folks can depend on them." He saw that she wanted further explanation. "I know when I see that there farmhouse," and he pointed at one a mile or so off the tracks, "we should be twenty minutes from the next stop, and I know just how fast—or how slow—we have to be going to get there just so." He clearly prided himself on this skill which he said he had honed over eleven years as the conductor on this very train.

"What's your name?" Viola finally asked him.

"John James Forrest Nulty, at your service," the conductor said formally.

"How come you have so many names?"

He laughed. "Well, I guess my mam wanted to keep as many Irish saints happy as she could."

Viola looked a little downcast. "My mommy was Irish, too, but she's dead now."

The conductor had already heard the story, but patted her hand. "Well, if she was Irish then she's in heaven for sure, probably singing in the choir when she isn't watching out for you!" He winked. "And that makes you half-Irish, doesn't it?"

Viola allowed that it did, but then a new worry surfaced. "What about daddy? He was English, like my aunt and uncle. Where is he? Is there a separate heaven?"

"Goodness no, I'm sure your parents are together, all right, especially since your daddy had the good sense to marry an Irish girl." He laughed to try and lighten the moment, but Viola remained quiet.

"Not everyone likes the Irish, you know," she said softly. "Mommy said it was very hard when she left her home and that some of the English, not daddy, but other people were mean."

The conductor had stepped to the door to the engine to shout out a command, but he clearly heard Viola and seemed to think about what to say. "Your mommy told the truth, she did. Ireland was terribly poor and people were forced to eat dirt to survive, and even then they couldn't." He scowled. "And the English didn't help them like they could have." He thought about tales he'd heard of huge stockpiles of grain rotting on the ground because the English felt somehow the Irish should buy it—even though everyone knew they had no money to buy anything.

"My daddy said that about my uncle," Viola confessed, "that he didn't help as much as he could have."

"Well, I wouldn't know about that, but he's helping now, isn't he? And he seems like a right fine gentleman," although he couldn't help cringing when he said it, thinking of the girl's aunt. "So, miss, you haven't told me your name."

"My name is Viola McDougall on account of my father played the viola in an orchestra," she answered proudly.

"Oh, I don't think that's true at all!" the conductor said, teasing her.

"No, he did! I heard him play many times."

"Oh, he might have played that viola, but that weren't why he named you Viola, no sirree."

"Is so!"

"Nope, I think your parents probably had quite a row when they first saw you. They knew they had the prettiest baby in the world, but when your mommy saw those purple-blue eyes of yours, why she would have wanted to name you Violette." Viola seemed to consider this. "But let me tell you something," the conductor said confidentially. "There's somebody the English like even less than the Irish—and that's the French. So, Violette would have sounded too French to your daddy."

"Violette. Violette." Viola practiced saying it several times, clearly liking the sound of it. "I think when I am older I shall call myself the Irish Violette," she pronounced.

"Here comes the next station, miss, so I'm back up to the engine now. You come back this time tomorrow and we'll take lunch together, how about that?" He winked. "We Irish have to stick together, you know." Viola beamed and went back to their compartments happy that she had a new friend in the world.

Of course, it didn't take Vivian long to try to disabuse Viola of that notion. "You've been talking with the conductor, have you?" when Viola had explained her absence. "Those Irish are all drunks and conductors are the worst of the lot!" She turned to her brother for support but he sensed how crestfallen Viola looked when Vivian told her she would not be having lunch with the conductor on the morrow.

"I think he's a good chap. Perhaps I'll join you two for lunch tomorrow, how's that?" Arthur said. "That way we'll know everything's on the up and up, now won't we?" he told Vivian plainly, asserting himself once again and knowing, once again, there would be a price to pay.

Chapter Eleven

Most of the train's stops were just 'whistle stops,' little more than an opportunity to offload a sack of mail and maybe exchange one or two passengers. Fresh food supplies were loaded in the caboose and the train was on its way in minutes. But at one such stop, just after dusk, one very distinguished-looking passenger boarded the train and asked to be directed immediately to the dining car while his private compartment was being prepared. The gentleman sported black slacks, a lavender shirt that was obviously silk of the finest quality, and a black velvet jacket, worn long in the European style. Not a speck of dirt was seen even on the cuffs of the beautifully tailored slacks, no small accomplishment considering the town's muddy streets leading to the depot.

He told the attentive porter his name was Vicente and that he would require very little attention during his brief stay on the train. But the attention he would require, he told the porter, must be provided exactly as he requested. From his bag he produced a very old bottle of port and two delicate glasses. "Please decant this very carefully at my table and provide a sampling of whatever little treats—sweet or savory—your chef might provide," he asked in an accent the porter couldn't quite discern.

Vicente was escorted to his table in time to glimpse the beautiful little girl with the massive blonde curls and violet eyes and the dreadful dowager who was clearly stealing every moment of the girl's happiness.

Vicente had thought to share his port with the conductor perhaps, in exchange for information about the towns along the train route, or, failing that, at least capture the eye of an unattached young maiden, perhaps a young lady on her way west to be a school teacher (and capture a husband in the process). But what he saw intrigued him more than either of those two options. He beckoned the porter again. "Please, tell me who that woman is," he asked, pointing to Vivian.

The porter followed his gaze and groaned. "Oh, sir, that'd be Miss Vivian McDougall and that gentleman with her is her brother, Mr. Arthur. The little girl is their niece traveling with them on account of her parents being murdered." He shuddered. "Miss Vivian, she don't put up with no nonsense," and he winked at Vicente, "and she don't like nobody."

"Hmmm, no nonsense, hey? We'll see about that," thought Vicente. He watched as the uncle tenderly took Viola's hand and led the downcast child out of the dining car, leaving the wicked aunt behind. He swirled the port in the crystal glass and watched its blood-red tracks down the side. He believed the wine connoisseurs called that "good legs." There was so much to know about wine, he mused, although it was nothing to him since he no longer drank or ate anything.

When the next waiter passed by, Vicente stopped him. "Would you be so good as to ask that woman if she would care to join me for an after-dinner glass of port?" He inclined his head toward Vivian but the waiter looked everywhere else.

"You mean *that* woman there?" he asked incredulously. "Miss McDougall?"

"None other."

"Beggin' your pardon sir, but there's prettier women on the train — and nicer ones, too," the waiter said. He leaned closer to Vicente. "If'n you want to wait until the next little stop I could go fetch you a woman'd be happy to ride the rails with you as long as you'd like."

"No, thank you," Vicente said stiffly. "It's her or no one." The waiter shuffled off to do Vicente's bidding, looking back over his shoulder twice to give the gentleman a chance to change his mind.

"Miss McDougall, uh," the waiter stammered. "The gentleman in the..."

"What are you prattling on about!" she barked at the waiter who jumped back a foot and once again looked beseechingly at Vicente.

"That gentleman there," and he pointed emphatically, "wishes that you would join him for an after-dinner glass of port, Miss."

Vivian eyed Vicente. He was a little too oily for her taste with that longish black hair, but she had to admit his skin was like alabaster so he was clearly no common sort to stand around on street corners or work outdoors, God forbid. She looked around her. Perhaps this was a joke? No one else seemed to be watching. Perhaps he was an opera singer hoping to ingratiate himself with her in order to work his way to Arthur. He did have that look, in fact. Well, she could put him in his place handily enough if it came to that. "If the gentleman wishes to share a glass of port, he should bring it to *my* table," she instructed the waiter who was only too happy to scurry off and deliver her message.

Vicente expected as much from the imperious old cow. He directed the waiter to gather up the wine decanter, glasses and 'delectables,' as the waiter described the scant offerings of cheeses, olives and something that was probably jerky, and deliver them to her table. He spent a moment straightening his string tie and shooting his cuffs before walking languorously to her table. When he arrived, he bowed low before her, took her hand and gave it a light kiss and a bit longer caress. "Miss McDougall, so charmed you would have me as your guest." He folded himself into a chair and straightened the crease on his slacks. "You may call me Vicente."

"I don't know that I shall call you anything," Vivian huffed, but she allowed him to pour her a generous glass of the port. "Why this is lovely! We've gotten nothing but swill on this train." She stuffed two pieces of cheese in her mouth and reached greedily for her glass. "Train travel is just so common, don't you think?"

"Common? Hmmm. It certainly surpasses the alternative of spending weeks and weeks in a dusty wagon subject to the...elements," he said slowly.

She took another deep swallow and allowed a little belch to escape. "Yes. It is somewhat cleaner, I suppose." She added, "Still, it's nothing like being on one of the grand ocean liners, as we ourselves were just a few weeks ago." She brushed a crumb off her ample bosom. "And you, what is your purpose in being aboard?"

"I have no purpose per se, Vivian. May I call you that? I feel like I have always known you." She blushed and suddenly the train car felt very warm, but she listened raptly to his silken voice. "I am a gentleman of means and I would simply like to spend my time traveling and seeing this brave new country." He leaned a little closer to Vivian while pouring her more of the expensive port. "But I don't care to be by myself at night."

Vivian wished she could undo the top button of her dress. "Of course, of course, yes I completely agree," she stammered, not knowing what she was agreeing with actually.

"I have my own carriage that travels alongside the train route so I may disembark when I choose, but at night I feel it's better to be in the company of others."

She didn't realize when he had taken her hand, but there it was in his and he was stroking it gently. "There are things that happen out there at night," and he looked meaningfully out the window, "that we are best not knowing about." He shook his head back and forth slowly. "A sensitive woman like yourself...well, I hate to think what they might do."

"They? Who they?" Vivian was quite beside herself to use such poor grammar. It must be the wine, she reasoned, yet she accepted another glass and drank down half of it.

"I shouldn't have even raised the subject. Where are my manners?" Vicente cooed. Abruptly he straightened himself in the chair and continued. "But really, one should be aware of one's surroundings and the danger that lies therein, don't you agree?"

She nodded vigorously, spilling a few drops of the wine on the tablecloth.

"Why just this evening I heard you warn your charming little niece about the conductor. One never knows, does one?" Vicente hastened to add, "Although I'm sure the conductor is completely trustworthy. Still...there may be others on the train who are not." He peered out the window at the inky blackness. "But, it's the savages out there who concern me."

Vivian was gripping her glass tightly and had finished all but one piece of the questionable jerky. "Savages?"

"They are savages—the whole lot of them, I tell you," Vicente answered forcefully. "Indians. They seem determined not to allow us a minute's peace on our land. And the cavalry seems powerless, completely powerless, to stop them. Oh, the terror they have struck into the hearts of settlers who simply want their own bit of land." Vicente managed to look both sad and strong. Now Vivian was holding his hand. "You know they scalp white men?" He grabbed the back of her hair and pulled her head back, mimicking a knife slicing along her forehead. She gasped. "And the things they would do to a lovely white woman like yourself."

"Things?"

"May I come closer?" he whispered. She nodded and bent her head toward his ear. "Sometimes they just...touch you, but other times it can be more than that, much more indeed," he whispered, slightly licking her neck in the process. She was spellbound. "And you know, with their fast ponies they're able to ride right alongside the train, and we can't even see them. Then, when we're fast asleep, they slip aboard."

Vivian thought she would faint but Vicente had an arm around her shoulders, steadying her. She was well and truly frightened and she knew she'd had too much port. "I must retire at once," she announced and rose unsteadily to her feet.

"Yes, of course, I've kept you much too late already." He kissed her lightly on the cheek and beckoned one of the porters. "Please escort Miss McDougall to her compartment and remind her to draw the shades and lock her door." He watched the cowering woman make a hasty retreat. He laughed wickedly to himself, "That will teach you, you old witch, to frighten a young girl for no reason other than jealousy." He slipped off the train at its next stop.

Chapter Twelve

The train was due to arrive in Cheyenne in the Wyoming Territory right at daybreak and would remain there until noon, "and not a minute later," admonished the conductor. The engines would be changed out, a fresh set continuing on to Ogden and ultimately California, while others returned back East.

Viola had barely slept. She had so many questions to ask her new friend, about the train, about the Irish, about being a conductor. She sensed her aunt didn't sleep well either, hearing her toss and turn in her bunk, whimpering. It was probably the 'digestion, Viola concluded, recalling the rich dinner her aunt had consumed, beef with gravy, boiled potatoes in a sauce, vegetables in a different sauce, and bread pudding with cognac. Viola's parents had always said it was important to eat like a king at breakfast but a pauper at dinner, something Vivian had clearly never heard, although Viola reflected, her aunt pretty much ate like a king at every opportunity. Viola remembered the delight her father took in sneaking up behind her mother, his hands totally encircling her fine waist. "Look at this, such a beauty and all mine!" Her mother would bat his hands away, but Viola could see her happiness reflected in her eyes.

It seemed all the passengers were looking forward to being off the train for a few hours. The men planned to find the saloons and perhaps a "house of ill repute," as the whorehouses were sometimes described. The women were advised of the chance to peruse locally-made arts and crafts. Viola was up and dressed, waiting at the door to their cabin for any sign that her uncle was also up and about. When she finally heard him stirring, she burst into his compartment. "Oh, uncle, we're getting off the train aren't we?"

Arthur wasn't used to being assaulted by such energy at an early hour. "Yes, yes, of course. We'll see what Cheyenne has to offer us." He ran a comb through his hair and beard. "Is your aunt ready as well?"

"She slept poorly and was still abed when I came here," Viola said, "but she could catch up with us later couldn't she?"

Arthur smiled to himself. "Or not at all," he supposed. "All right, let me make myself presentable for the citizenry. Five minutes," he intoned, knowing it would seem like an hour to his niece. Viola scampered back to her cabin to check on her aunt's progress and to collect her sketchbook and pencils, all encased in a handsome cloth bag one of the ladies on the train had made special for her. Her aunt was at least out of bed but still in her dressing gown and looking the fright.

"Uncle and I are leaving the train in just five minutes," Viola announced. "He said you could meet us later," she added in a small fib.

Vivian appeared not to hear her at all and just motioned her out of the sleeping compartment. Back in the aisle she bumped into her uncle and began dragging him toward the train doors. The train whistle had been sounded and they could feel it slowing down as it approached the frontier town. While they waited, Arthur endeavored to tell Viola a little history about Cheyenne. "The settlers that came West in wagon trains rarely came to Cheyenne. And do you know why?" Viola shook her head. "Do you see any grass out there?" Arthur asked, gesturing toward the wide, flat plain. "There wasn't enough grass, or water, to feed the oxen and mules, so they had to find another way, farther south." Viola seemed to consider the situation. "But this relatively flat land was perfect to build the railway on, and when coal was discovered here, it was that much better. You've seen the men shoveling coal into the train's engine, I know." At the mention of the engine, Viola brightened, thinking of her planned lunch with the conductor once the train got underway again that afternoon. But now she was anxious to disembark and anxious to resume their journey, both.

At last the doors were opened by the porters and the steps rolled down. Viola fairly spun out of the train but then stopped dead in her tracks, nearly being run over by her uncle behind her. She had never seen anything like them! Indians! They were very tall and thin with deeply-lined brown faces, black or gray hair often in braids like her own. They were dressed in leather leggings, some with beaded decorations, others plain, with leather vests over bare chests or flannel-type shirts; all wore moccasins on their feet. Viola stood rooted to the spot staring. The disembarking passengers divided around Arthur and Viola, clearly annoyed at the bottleneck the girl had created. "Now, Viola, dear, you know it's impolite to stare," Arthur said, taking her hand and trying to pull her to the side. Some of the Indian women had spread blankets on the ground where they were displaying jewelry, small baskets and other trinkets that the women from the train were eagerly snapping up. Viola didn't even glance at them, and when Arthur suggested she might want a pretty necklace she ignored him completely. She couldn't have described what she felt, but there was an instant visceral connection, nearly a kinship. She had to find a few minutes to herself just to think and watch these awe-inspiring people.

Viola got the opportunity she needed when her aunt Vivian finally showed up at the door to the train. She took one look at the crowd of Indians and let out a blood-curdling scream followed by fainting into a heap next to the tracks. Arthur rushed to her side, letting Viola slip away on her own. She found a stack of packing crates and climbed up on them, withdrawing her sketchpad and situating herself to best advantage to watch the marketplace activity. She began sketching with a fury, especially one man who stood apart from the others but seemed to be watching everything, just as she was. Viola had seen portraits of the king of England but even that man didn't possess the sense of absolute grandeur and power that the Indian standing before her did. She drew his profile and the way he folded his arms over his chest, standing ramrod straight. His black braids had red ribbons interwoven and his vest was beaded in red and black. He must be the chief, Viola reasoned, and she was determined to meet him and present him with her sketch.

She looked to see that her uncle was still busy getting her aunt back on the train, and she knew it wouldn't be long before the conductor blew the whistle announcing their departure. She had to act now, on her own, or not at all. She believed she had captured the man's likeness exactly and was proud of her work but still uncertain of how to approach him. She hadn't seen anyone else try. She tore the sketch out of the pad and put everything else back in her bag. She climbed down from her artist's roost and made her way through the crowd until she was directly in front of him. He ignored her completely until she tugged at a strand of rawhide hanging from his side. He still kept his arms folded but glanced down just slightly. Viola held the sketch out for his inspection.

"Aieee!" he yelled, snatching the sketch and throwing it in the dirt at his feet, stamping on it until it was in shreds. Viola was horrified and very close to tears. The sketch had been so good and so perfect. Finally, she could hold back her shame no longer and turned to run back to the train, sobbing as she went. The conductor had witnessed the scene and his heart broke for the little girl. He'd explain it all to her later. He checked his pocket watch and blew the train's whistle.

Chapter Thirteen

Arthur was unprepared for dealing with two hysterical women. Vivian was still shaken from her fainting episode and insisted Arthur stand guard at his compartment door lest the "savages" attempt to break in and carry her off. "Now, sister, there's not much chance of that," he said in hopes of soothing her, but, of course, she interpreted it in entirely the wrong way. Viola, meanwhile, was sobbing uncontrollably about the Indian who had rejected her drawing. "I'm sure he was just surprised by your kindness," Arthur tried. "I'm sure it was quite a good likeness of him." That set off another round of sobbing as Viola recalled just how perfectly she had captured his cheekbones and his brooding, dark eyes. Finally Arthur resorted to the one thing that always seemed to calm him, a little sherry, a full glass for Vivian and even a half-glass for Viola. He abstained for the moment until he was sure both were settling down. He requested that the porter serve their lunch in their own compartment, and he tipped him an extra fifty-cent piece to do it quickly and with as little fanfare as possible. Vivian avowed that she couldn't possibly eat even a bite, as upset as she was, but when the porter took the lid off the chicken pot pie, she recovered sufficiently to eat half of it herself.

Viola said nothing during the meal and continued to sniffle. "Artists," thought Arthur, "their souls are just too tender for the criticism that must inevitably come their way." He turned his attention toward his niece. "You must let your aunt fix up your hair again and change your dress. You got quite dusty out in that depot." Viola shrugged. "You know we have an important meeting very soon with the conductor, and you know he couldn't abide by any tardiness." Clearly Viola had forgotten about everything else in the midst of her drawing being stomped into the dust, but now she brightened considerably. "Yes, auntie, please, come along now," she said, dragging at Vivian's sleeve. "I want some purple ribbons in my hair and the purple dress." Vivian sighed but pushed back from the table and allowed Viola to drag her to their compartment. Arthur at last relaxed with a glass brimming with sherry.

A half-hour later Viola reappeared and the transformation was remarkable. The purple ribbons in her blonde hair set off her violet eyes, a feature Arthur had never noticed before. Her dress was clean and obviously Vivian had done her usual thorough job in washing Viola's face and hands as they glowed pink. "Well, look at you! Aren't you a vision!" Arthur sought to tease the normally serious little girl. "You're not sneaking off to meet a beau, are you?" Viola scowled and turned on her heel.

"I'm ready to meet my friend, the conductor...now."

Arthur leapt to his feet and proffered his arm to her. "Then we must make haste to the dining car where he awaits." They found the conductor seated at a table next to the window with a clean white tablecloth. He was just finishing his meal but when Arthur and

Viola entered, he dispatched the porter to find sherry and some dessert tarts.

The introductions were made. "'Tis a fine thing you're doing, sir, a fine thing, taking in your niece so," he told Arthur, shaking his hand.

"I think little Viola might be just what her aunt and I need in our lives, a little sprite like this to brighten things up," he replied generously, although the conductor detected a note of concern. "Now, Viola, you said you have many questions for Mr. Nulty here, so you two talk while I relax and have a cigar." He moved to another table a few feet away and accepted another glass of sherry.

Before Viola could begin with her questions, the conductor had something to say to her. "I see you met old Jake today." Viola blushed. "He's a tough old Arapahoe, that one, but not a bad man."

"He was bad to me!"

"No, he weren't so bad. Here's what you have to understand. A lot of Indians, not all of them, but a lot of them, feel like if they have their picture made, drawn like you did or taken with one of those new camera machines, then it steals their soul and they're likely to die and wander in the hereafter without it." Viola said nothing. "Why, I'll bet he was just surprised to see how ugly he was when you showed him!" She couldn't help but laugh. "So, the next Indian you meet, you ask them all polite and proper if they'd like their old sour puss preserved on paper, how's that?" She giggled and the incident was forgotten.

Arthur appeared to have fallen asleep at his table, but in truth he was sitting with his eyes closed, lost in thoughts of his first journey across the vast plains.

The wagon master said the trip would take a month, give or take a week or two more, weather and such depending. They left St. Louis at the end of August and hoped to be in San Francisco before any snow fell in the Rockies or the Sierras. He was en route to San Francisco at the behest of his biggest client, a notoriously difficult Italian opera singer, and as it was early in Arthur's career, he couldn't refuse the summons. There had been some trouble, the telegram said, without explanation, and Arthur must endeavor to undo the damage. The Italian was a man of huge appetites, for food, women, and trouble, it seemed, so Arthur imagined the situation might well involve a woman, or several, and perhaps a disgruntled husband, or several.

For weeks they endured heat, dust and, worst of all, unremitting boredom, watching the grassy plains roll slowly by. There were times, however, when the boredom would be broken by threats of an Indian raid. The wagons would be hastily formed into a circle and the women and children told to hide inside, staying low on the floor, while the men were issued what weapons were available and told to stay vigilant. They followed the same precautions when scouts came back to the wagon train to announce the presence of a huge herd of buffalo several miles west. The animals were famous for stampeding in mass, mowing down anything and everything in their path. The further west they traveled, the more ominous the warnings became about the Indians, but there were fewer sightings of buffalo. Any grandeur the scenery might have presented was totally lost on the frightened and weary passengers.

As often as possible the wagon train followed the route laid out by the railroad surveyors, and occasionally they would pull abreast of the "Hell on Wheels" camps set up by the railroad. Arthur still recalled being struck by the massive amounts of equipment, supplies and laborers required, and as each mile of track was completed, these camps rolled along. Not only did they have mess halls to feed the laborers, mostly Chinese and Irishmen, but there were merchants of all sorts tagging along, as well as prostitutes and preachers. Every so often a permanent station would be built, and men had to be hired to run them. In addition, telegraph operators were needed so that messages could be sent about where the trains were and what direction they were headed. "Spurs" had to be added to the main railway so that trains could pass each other, the westbound cars carrying provisions and the eastbound often carrying gold and silver from the big strikes in California and the Nevada Territory. The moving camps might have been little cities on wheels, but they deserved the "hell" description as well, particularly when faced with the challenges of building the railroad through the massive mountain ranges. When Arthur's wagon train reached the base of the foreboding Sierras, he recalled seeing what he thought at first was a stack of logs to fuel the engines. Instead, it was a stack of Chinese laborers, buried in an avalanche that killed them and simultaneously wiped out miles of rail bed.

The image jarred Arthur from his thoughts and he turned to eavesdrop on the conductor. "That thing on the front of the engine that looks like a skirt, why that's a snowplow," he was explaining, "or sometimes we call 'em cow-catchers on account of they push the cows off the tracks." Viola listened raptly.

"How did you know you were supposed to be a conductor?" she asked.

"Well, of course, I didn't start out as a conductor. I worked alongside thousands of other men, cutting logs, laying steel, and even blasting the holes in the mountains for the tunnels." The conductor was warming to his narrative. "You wait till you see those big tunnels, miss. They're a wonder." He went on to explain to Viola how the railroad men actually used black powder like gun powder stuffed into holes dug by pick in the mountains. "We'd light the powder and then run as fast as we could," he said. "Oh, boy, that was something." He allowed that the Chinese usually did that part of the job, "but they hired plenty of Irish because we knew how to do a day's work, that's all there was to it."

"Did they get along, the Chinese and the Irish?" Viola asked with what Arthur thought was a surprising amount of insight.

"Each side pretty much kept to themselves, I guess," the conductor replied slowly, "but you know they had something in common and that was poverty and violence in their home countries. They thought they could work hard here, save some money for their families back home, maybe send for them some day." He grew quiet. "It worked out that way for some of them, I guess." He stood up abruptly. "Enough questions for one day, miss. I've got a train to run." He doffed his cap and left the dining car and a disappointed Viola, but a minute later he poked his head back in. "Same time tomorrow? I'll tell you what the railroad's done for this whole country."

Arthur heard the comment and couldn't help but think that the railroad may have opened up commerce but it seemed to him that it also left a swath of destruction as the Indians were driven from their lands, the buffalo hunted to near extinction, and whole forests decimated to build the railroad ties and station houses. He collected Viola and both returned to their compartments in rather somber moods.

Chapter Fourteen

Vivian was back to her usual imperious self when they returned from their visit with the conductor. A que of porters stood anxiously in the hallway as she gave orders to each of them for food to be served, hot water to be prepared and a dozen sundry tasks to be accomplished "post haste." Arthur took the opportunity to retreat to his own compartment for a nap before dinner. He was in his late 40s which was really rather old to be embarking on such an adventure as traveling across the country and then perhaps sailing halfway around the world—with an eight-year-old girl in tow, no less. He drew the heavy curtains on his compartment, removed his jacket and loosened his tie. It wasn't long before he was in that agreeable state somewhere between sleep and full wakefulness. He smiled thinking about the "situation" he had had to deal with on his first trip west.

The opera singer was waiting for him when the wagons at last rolled into San Francisco. Even though he was lavishly attired in a burgundy velvet smoking jacket, crisply-pleated black trousers and a starched white shirt, he looked worried and disheveled. He hardly let Arthur climb down from the wagon before he started in. "You must get me out of this contract — and out of this city — before the sun sets once more!" he exclaimed dramatically. "Every night that I take the stage, I am sure I am about to be killed!"

Arthur was used to the drama, of course, but he sensed that Enrico's fear was genuine. "Now, please let us repair to the hotel and have this discussion like gentlemen instead of you flapping your arms around thus in the street." He tried to grab the singer's arm and steer him to the hotel. "We can address this misunderstanding, whatever it is, after I have had a chance to clean off six weeks' worth of dirt, I assume."

Enrico looked crestfallen but agreed that he could wait in the lobby while Arthur availed himself of some hot water and a change of clothing. San Francisco was, after all, a relatively sophisticated city and it simply wouldn't do to be sitting in the Mark Hopkins Hotel on Nob Hill with horse manure on one's shoes. Arthur had heard about the vast amounts of money pouring into the city from the Comstock silver mines and the gold strikes in the California foothills, but even he was unprepared for the level of luxury that awaited him, not only in the hotel but undoubtedly in the restaurants as well. To eat meal off china rather than from a tin dish would go a long way toward restoring his sensibilities.

The hotel provided them a private cubby off the lobby where they could discuss the "situation," and Arthur was barely seated before Enrico launched into describing his predicament. "You know I am one who loves the ladies," he began and Arthur groaned, predicting what would follow. "After a particularly vigorous performance, I must say," Enrico began, but seeing Arthur's shocked expression, explained, "on the stage, sir, on the stage. Of course, I accepted dozens of roses from many of those in the audience, but one woman in particular insisted that she show her appreciation, as it were, to me directly and privately." At this point he puffed out his chest. "How could I refuse such a request from such a beautiful lady!"

Arthur asked the waiter to leave the carafe of sherry on the table. "As there was no scheduled performance the following evening, I asked the lady if perhaps she would choose to dine with me in my rooms." Arthur rolled his eyes. "She accepted and all was arranged."

"But not quite all, was it?" Arthur inquired.

"No, not quite all," Enrico admitted. "We had a lovely dinner. You know this hotel does lamb chops in a way that, well..."

"Dispense with the lamb chops, please."

"Yes, well, we had a lovely dinner and quite a quite a lot of wine, some champagne, some brandy, and soon we were en flagrante delicto, as it were." Enrico fairly purred in describing it. "But then we heard such shouting coming from the street below! The lady...disentangled...and went to see the source. It was her husband with a whip in his hand!" Enrico tried and failed to look contrite. "Imagine my surprise that she was a married woman!" Arthur struggled to keep his disbelief from showing. "She said he was entering the hotel and would immediately be at our door. I opened the window and looked down to the street below. There were ledges and cornices that could be little hand-holds, so I beckoned the lady to the window, and I must say, I helped her out onto the ledge."

Arthur spit out his sherry. "You forced a half-naked woman out onto the ledge of the city's most famous hotel rather than standing up to the husband and taking your just punishment! Or fleeing the scene yourself?" Arthur was clearly outraged.

"Let me finish." Enrico, being Italian, had to tell every story with his hands. "So, I grab her gown from the bed and put it on." Arthur recalled that Enrico had always enjoyed the more zaftig woman. "When the husband pounded on the door, I flung it open and surprised him by accusing him of interrupting my rehearsal for next week's farce!" Enrico laughed heartily. "Oh, the look on his face!"

"He believed such an outlandish lie?" Arthur was shaking his head.

"He had no choice. His wife was nowhere to be seen," and here Enrico laughed even harder, "at least not in the room. He was forced to retreat and offered his most sincere apologies."

"If that's where the story ended, then what is the situation?" Arthur asked with some trepidation.

Enrico sighed. "My paramour was not so skilled in climbing, it appears, and it was raining that night. When she realized that she was essentially unclothed for all on the street below to see, she slipped and fell." He looked genuinely sad but then couldn't help but laugh again. "When the horses at the nearby carriages saw this white phantom fall from the sky, they quite panicked, leaving her to land in piles of fresh horse manure." He tried to stop laughing. "Unfortunately, she chose to shout out my name and a number of obscenities no lady should know."

"And her husband witnessed this?" Arthur said wearily.

"Well, not the fall, but the screaming, yes," Enrico admitted. "So you see, I must leave this city as I fear I will be shot on stage!" He was working himself up to an indignant pose. "The lady, which, of course, we now know she isn't, has told everyone that she will bring her husband's pistol to the theater and shoot me dead as I take my final bow! It's simply terrible."

At this confession, it was Arthur's turn to laugh. "So it's the wife, not the husband, who plans to shoot you!"

"The husband has left her, of course," Enrico allowed. Arthur fairly howled with laughter but then became highly indignant himself.

"You've had me risk life and limb to travel all the way here to save you from a scorned and humiliated woman! You deserve whatever punishment comes your way!" Arthur called on the woman the next day, however, and with an offer of generous compensation the matter was quickly resolved and Enrico finished his run at the opera house, chastened but not much wiser.

Arthur felt the train lurch into another whistle stop station and realized it would soon be time for dinner. Thinking back on the escapade with Enrico he was rather amazed to realize twenty years had elapsed. Maybe there was some truth in what he had told the conductor that his niece might keep him young (or drive him to an early grave).

Chapter Fifteen

Viola spent the last few afternoons of their train trip in the engine compartment watching the men feed the coal into fire, keeping it at just the right level per the conductor's instructions. One such afternoon he even let Viola sound the train whistle, but the young girl didn't quite have the force to pull down strongly enough on the chain and the conductor laughed, "It sounds more like an elephant passing wind," but seeing how much it embarrassed her, he quickly added, "'course it is only Winnemucca and that's probably appropriate."

She peppered him with endless questions about the scenery passing by, about what his life had been like back in the Old Country, as he referred to it, and most painfully, what had happened to his family. "Will you send for them? Will they live at one of the train stops? Which one?" He always tried to sidestep the issue, but finally two days before the train would reach San Francisco, he brought her out of the noisy engine car into the dining car.

"Here's the truth of it all," he told her. "My wife begged me not to leave her, to come to America, but I told her the streets were paved in gold and in no time at all, I'd be sending her a ticket for her and my two girls to come join me."

"You have two girls? Are they older than me? Younger?" Viola was eager for more information, but the conductor persisted in his story.

"Anyways, when I got to America, there was a lot of bad feeling built up already against the Irish and for a long time I couldn't get no work at all." He hung his head. "I did what a lot of men did. I just drank away any money I could come by, picking up an odd job here and there." He nervously moved a glass around on the table. "Finally, it had been about six years gone by and I still didn't have any money for those tickets. I was living in a shantytown with other men just like myself, men who had given up trying, given up hoping for anything, least of all seeing their families again."

"Had your family given up on you?" Viola asked quietly.

"Well, I suppose they had. Yes, I suppose they had." He sighed. "But one day a fellow came through and said the railroad would be hiring any able-bodied man and paying $35 a month, food and lodging included. Well, I jumped at it and a whole crew of us Irish were put together and off we went, to build this here railroad." He looked out the window. "Sometimes I look out and think, I built this mile of track. I carried those rails and pounded them spikes and now here I am, riding over them just as easy as can be." He finally smiled a little. "But everything in life has its price, don't you be forgettin' that." He cleared his throat. "My price was my family. I never saw them or heard another word about them, and I never will."

Viola laid her tiny hand over his. "You can be my family, Mr. Nulty."

"That's so, isn't it?" he said a bit gruffly. "Now I know I'll have a little girl out there being taken care of just dandy." He finally drew their conversation to a halt and escorted Viola back to her aunt and uncle. "We'll be crossing the majestic Sierras all day tomorrow, and I expect you'll enjoy that," he explained. "We'll be going through some long tunnels, and it'll get a bit dark, but then we'll be right out of them." He had already told Viola about the snow sheds and their purpose in protecting the train and the tracks from avalanches in the winter months. This time of the year, late fall, it would be unlikely to see any significant snow, however, he predicted.

Vivian hadn't paid much attention to the conductor's description of the day ahead, as she was already seeing herself ensconced in a luxury suite in San Francisco, a city many were already calling the "Paris of the West." She despaired, however, of how to make Viola even a little bit presentable, especially after her hours in the grimy engine room. She was used to the bohemians in the theater world and their less-than-rigorous grooming standards, but Viola's appearance was simply beyond the pale. "Honestly, one would think your hair was black to start with!" she exclaimed, nearly breaking a comb trying to untangle a knot while Viola squirmed. "I don't think I can bear to be seen with you at dinner, even here on the train. You look worse than some of the Indian children we've seen in the stations."

"How would you know?" Viola sputtered. "You haven't set foot off the train since Cheyenne!" She didn't know why her aunt was so afraid of Indians, but she decided to torture her with her fear. "Conductor Nulty said there's Indians everywhere in the forest of the Sierras, especially in those long, dark tunnels. And in Sacramento they'll probably be hundreds of them just waiting for the train to pull in." Arthur listened to the exchange but said nothing; he didn't understand his sister's irrational fear of Indians either. Viola ate dinner by herself in their compartment while Arthur accompanied Vivian to their last full meal aboard the train.

The train's climb over the Sierras was laborious but opened up scenic vistas that even the most jaded traveler could appreciate (although not Vivian who had once again closeted herself in their compartment with the shades tightly drawn). Viola saw the beautiful stands of pine and fir, but she also saw the scarred mountainsides where the trees had been felled to provide railroad ties and timbers to shore up the mines of the Comstock. Conductor Nulty told her she would likely be an old woman before those areas ever filled in again with tall trees. After the days of crossing the barren desert, and then the towering Sierras, the lush valley surrounding Sacramento was a welcome sight for many. In the old days, Viola had learned, the train stopped here and all the passengers and goods were put on steamships to pass through a river delta and on to San Francisco. Now, they could stay comfortably on the train until it pulled into the city.

Viola dreaded their arrival, of course, because it meant giving up her talks with the conductor. She had learned a lot about the West from him, facts she doubted even her uncle Arthur knew. She felt certain she would travel west again in her life, even though her closest friend in the world might be long retired — she hoped to Ireland, even though she doubted that would ever happen.

Chapter Sixteen

Within hours of their arrival at the prestigious Mark Hopkins Hotel, Vivian had reverted to her imperious ways and had already begun terrorizing the staff with her outlandish requests and demands that tasks be accomplished immediately! She insisted that her entire wardrobe, and Arthur's as well, be unpacked, completely laundered and appropriately placed in their wardrobes before dinner. Viola was left to unpack her own belongings into a drawer. She was wearing her one good dress, something Vivian had insisted on before they left the train, so as not to embarrass her and Arthur at the hotel.

True to his word, Arthur had secured for them a suite of rooms on the top floor, overlooking the entire city. They could stay for at least two weeks, but then it was rumored that the President of the United States was to visit and would require their suite. This sent Vivian into a pique, of course. "I don't see where a man elected by the commoners of this country has any more right to this suite then do we," she complained. "It's not as if he is the king of England, after all." Arthur rolled his eyes but made no comment, although he wondered where Viola had gotten off to.

The little girl had found a window seat that allowed her to watch the activity in the street below, and as usual, she had her sketch pad at the ready. She was fascinated by the groups of Chinese with the woven bamboo hats, often as not carrying pots suspended on poles between two of them. They were able to move carefully enough—and quickly—to ensure that nothing spilled out of the pots, which Viola imagined contained meals being delivered to workmen at projects throughout the bustling city. She knew her aunt had forgotten about her entirely, but she wasn't surprised when finally her uncle sought her out. "So, what's captured your artistic eye, dear?" She shyly turned her pad his way. "Ah, the Chinese. Very interesting people, very industrious." He thought back to how they had labored on the railroad for less money than their white counterparts. "Those pots probably contain dinner," he explained, confirming Viola's original assumption.

"Can we go out for a walk, uncle?"

"Tomorrow, certainly we shall, but tonight let's just rest and have our dinner. Did your aunt send your clothing out to be laundered?"

When Viola shook her head, Arthur became truly angry. "Honestly! That woman!" Viola shrunk away, but Arthur reassured her. "It's nothing you've done dear." He sought to cover up for his sister. "It's just that we're not used to having someone else around, but you'll see, we'll start acting like a family soon enough." He left the room immediately, however, to set Vivian straight about just who would be responsible for Viola's clothing and the like. Viola heard them arguing and once again felt the fear she had when they were in New York and she was afraid of being left behind. When it came time for dinner, she told her aunt she had a stomach ache and just wanted to go to bed, which Vivian only too easily allowed.

That only meant, however, that Viola awoke ravenously hungry the next morning. She hurriedly put her dress back on and, remembering the small hotel she and her parents had stayed in with the other orchestra members, set off on her own in search of the dining hall. What she found was a grand salon with individual tables for two or four people, covered in crisp white linens and a profusion of plates and silverware. Crystal vases in the center of each table held fresh yellow roses, mimicking the pattern of the fabric on the dining chairs. Floor-to-ceiling windows opened onto an interior atrium where there were more flowers surrounding a central tiled fountain. Conversations were muted and became even more so when they saw the somewhat raggedy-looking girl clutching a tablet of some sort. She stood at the entrance to the salon and appeared to slowly study the occupants. Was she looking for her mother who might have been one of the kitchen staff? A father who was a waiter? Those nearest the door were astonished to hear, "I should like some breakfast, please, porridge and bacon, or ham if you haven't the bacon." The maître'd didn't know whether to look horrified or amused. Viola stood her ground, however, and eventually he directed her to a small table and held the chair out for her, placing a napkin in her lap. He immediately went to the front desk to make a discreet inquiry.

Viola did receive a small bowl of porridge, nothing half as good as her mother had made, but welcome nonetheless after her long night. She attacked it and was on the verge of requesting a second when she saw her uncle in the doorway. "Uncle Arthur, over here," she waved her napkin at him. He looked clearly embarrassed and not nearly as well-groomed as he would ordinarily have been at breakfast, clearly having been roused from bed.

"Viola, you can't go off by yourself this way!" He tried to look stern, then realized the other diners were watching him closely. Why not give them a show? "Imagine the riff-raff you might have been dining with!" He winked at her and she began to giggle. The waiter hovered nearby until Arthur signaled him to bring coffee, "And I believe the young lady has asked for bacon?" They continued their breakfast as if nothing was out of the ordinary, but Arthur knew he would have to explain certain things to his niece when they were in the privacy of their suite. He shuddered to think what Vivian would have to say if she heard of the incident. But damn woman! It was really her fault, wasn't it?

After breakfast Arthur took Viola for her promised walk and they were able to see work progressing on the new cable car system that would ultimately collect the city's new residential neighborhoods over the steep hills that presented a challenge for carriages. "I'll ride on one of those one day," Viola proclaimed, clearly fascinated.

Arthur held her hand. "I'm sure you'll do that and more, much more." As they continued their stroll, Arthur had a moment of inspiration, an idea he would have to pursue as soon as they returned to the hotel. He began rushing Viola. "Let's return and see if your aunt has your new clothes ready, and then perhaps we'll go out again." When they returned to the hotel they found Vivian waiting for them in the lobby, clearly annoyed.

"Ah, just the person we were hoping to see," Arthur began in a cheery tone, hoping to head off any unpleasantness. "Viola, I know, is ready for a change of her dress before we all go shopping." At the mention of shopping Vivian temporarily forgot her complaints and dragged Viola toward the stairs. Meanwhile, Arthur asked for the hotel manager and was quickly shown to his office. When he emerged an hour later, he was clearly satisfied and settled down in the lobby to wait for his female companions. He had such a nice surprise in store for them.

Chapter Seventeen

When Viola at last emerged freshly scrubbed and in a clean dress, Arthur insisted that they all go on a stroll through the Nob Hill neighborhood where their hotel was located. Vivian protested that the shopping district was blocks away and that they should take a carriage, but Arthur insisted they walk. "It will do all of us some good to take in the air," he said. "Just look at how beautiful the sky is this afternoon, not at all like our dreary London." He was positively beaming but Vivian remained doubtful. They passed several grand houses, each set back from the street and surrounded by elaborate wrought iron fences enclosing lush gardens. Three blocks from the hotel Arthur directed them around the corner of Taylor and California Streets and there stood the grandest mansion of them all. It was three stories in height, constructed of redwood with elaborate columns and pillars and a tower that commanded a view of the entire city. The house occupied nearly the entire city block and was surrounded on three sides by a fence taller than most buildings in the city.

"Good lord, what a monstrosity that is!" Vivian exclaimed.

"Monstrosity? Why it's the finest house in the city," Arthur sputtered, "the finest in California or anywhere in the West." Vivian flicked her hand in the air as if she were swatting away a mosquito and began to walk on, but Arthur stopped her. "And, the Crocker Mansion will be our home for the next year!"

"Crocker? Charles Crocker, one of the robber barons!" Vivian was incredulous.

Viola began to cry. "Robber? A robber lives here and we are to live with him?" She remembered overhearing that her parents were killed by a robber.

Arthur was completely astounded at both Vivian's and Viola's reactions. "Mr. Crocker is no such a thing! He is a well-respected businessman who financed the railroad we just traveled on and who, as we stand here, is preparing to go to Washington, D. C. to meet with the President and from there to Europe where he and his wife will enjoy the grand tour of all of Europe's finest cities." Arthur could tell Vivian was still not impressed and Viola was still sniveling. "And we shall occupy his home, this home, while he is abroad." He threw his shoulders back. "It's all settled. We move in at the end of the week. Now, come along." They set off back in the direction of the hotel, each lost in their own thoughts. Arthur felt Vivian was just being her usual obstreperous, ungrateful self. Vivian was despairing of having to spend even another day in a country she considered backwards and barbaric. Viola was afraid of simply being abandoned and forgotten about in the big house.

In the next few days Arthur busied himself calling on the theater managers and meeting with performers who might be interested in new representation. He returned to the hotel each evening in high spirits about how well he was being received and how vibrant the city's cultural offerings were becoming. But his good mood was soon dampened by Vivian's complaints about the substandard shopping and by Viola's morose appearance; the sketch pad she was never without was scarcely in evidence. "You both look lovely in your new dresses," he began. "Tonight let's go to one of the stylish new restaurants near the theaters and perhaps take in a play. Won't that be lovely?" He was met with a stony silence but chose to ignore it. "Yes, that's what we'll do. Let's meet in the lobby in half an hour." He strode off to his room to change into an evening jacket, swearing under his breath as he went.

Their move into the Crocker mansion was met with the same grim acceptance. The mansion was truly lovely inside with bay windows, a full library, art gallery and even a billiards room which Arthur planned to enjoy. He pointed out one of the bay window nooks to Viola. "Won't that be a nice place for you to settle in with a book or your drawing papers?" Viola mutely nodded her head. Vivian was already ordering the staff around and insisting that furniture be rearranged and directing a dozen other tasks to be accomplished immediately, of course.

The head of the household staff was a woman of perhaps forty years of age. She introduced herself as Rebecca and welcomed them to the house. It would be her pleasure, she said, to see to their comfort. Viola thought she detected a certain lilt to Rebecca's voice but was too shy to ask her about it until the woman showed her to the bedroom that would be hers during their stay. The room was all done in yellow with a huge canopy bed almost entirely covered in dolls; apparently the Crockers had a daughter. Rebecca showed Viola the wardrobe where her clothes would be stored and the bathroom adjacent to the bedroom which would be for her use alone. "Is there anything else I can be telling you, then?" she asked Viola.

"Yes, well, no. Uhh." Viola hesitated then blurted out her question. "Are you Irish?"

Rebecca seemed taken aback but then answered. "That I am, miss, full Irish." She seemed offended. "I know the English don't always like the Irish, but I'll do my best to serve you and your aunt and uncle."

"Oh, no, no," Viola was crimson with embarrassment. "It's just that I'm Irish, too, and the train conductor told me that we have to stick together." She realized she sounded foolish but couldn't stop herself. "His name was Mr. Nulty and he didn't have any family, except me, well, not really me, but he told me a lot about how hard it was in Ireland and how he hoped his family would join him, but then they didn't, and, oh I, don't know why I'm telling you all this."

Rebecca started to laugh. "Well, that's what we'll do then. We'll stick together. But right now you have to wash up and come down for the midday meal." Viola looked uncertain. "Can you find your way back downstairs?" Viola nodded that she could and shyly smiled at her new friend. Maybe their stay in the big mansion would turn out all right after all.

Viola had another surprise awaiting her when she finally entered the dining room. A very stern-looking woman was seated with her aunt and uncle and gave Viola a thorough looking-over before Viola was introduced to her. She was Miss Catherine Bush, headmistress of the Bush Street Primary School for Girls, which Arthur told Viola she would be attending come Monday. Viola's mother had always schooled her in reading and writing and some history, so she had never attended school. "Well, I don't know if I want to," Viola protested, feeling tears welling up again.

Miss Bush smacked her hand down on the table. "You will not be telling your uncle what you do or do not wish to do. You will report to school on Monday and you will be prepared to study and learn." Viola shrunk back and looked to Arthur for support, but he pretended to be studying his pocket watch. School it would be apparently.

Chapter Eighteen

It fell to Vivian to take Viola to the school to pick up her uniform — an itchy, gray woolen jumper with a white blouse that was expected to be starched and clean at all times, plus matching white socks and black shoes, nothing shiny, mind you. The headmistress further told Viola that her hair must be contained at all times in a braid or a bonnet. "We can't have that mass flying around distracting everyone," she warned Viola. She would be expected to present to class with a certain number of sharpened pencils and her own composition book; the school would provide textbooks. Did she prefer to study French or German? She preferred neither but already knew better than to say so. She was therefore enrolled in a French class, at Vivian's choosing.

On the appointed Monday, Viola thought Arthur or Vivian would accompany her to school, but Rebecca came to her room to be sure she was dressed in her uniform and then proceeded to quickly braid her hair. Viola had to admit Rebecca did a nice job of weaving an intricate design with her riotous curls. "Hurry now, let's get your breakfast and we'll be off." Viola dawdled over her porridge, waiting at least for her uncle to come by and wish her well, but that was not to be, and as a result she only had half her breakfast before Rebecca snatched her bowl away. She had set her writing booklet and pencils out the night before and put them in the bag the woman on the train had made for her sketchpad, something Rebecca encouraged her to leave in her room.

Rebecca walked her the four blocks to school, admonishing her all the way. "Be sure to speak up when the teacher calls on you." And, "Sit up straight." Or, "If you're called on and don't know the answer, say, 'I don't know, Miss.'" Most of all, "Be polite but don't be so shy that no one notices you." Viola felt quite overwhelmed but at the steps of the school Rebecca knelt down in front of her. "This is a grand opportunity you have, going to school. A lot of girls don't get that chance, especially at a school as nice as this. Learn everything you can, every day." She watched as Viola trudged up the steps then hurried back to the Crocker mansion to attend to a myriad of chores for the aunt, someone she already referred to as the wicked witch of England.

Viola was met in the lobby of the school by the headmistress who looked as formidable as ever. She inspected Viola's jumper and blouse, looked at her fingernails, and counted her pencils. Apparently she passed muster as the woman herded her to a classroom and assigned her to a desk. The other girls in the class looked Viola over then giggled to each other until the headmistress commanded them all to be quiet. For the rest of the morning they read their lessons aloud, in unison. Viola already knew how to read quite well and had from the age of five, so she was bored and soon grew fidgety. Instead of copying down verses in her book, she began a sketch of her teacher, noting how tightly her hair was pulled into a bun and how her glasses perched precariously at the end of an exceptionally long nose. She was just working on shading in the wrinkles of the teacher's neck when a ruler slapped down on her hand.

"Ow!" Viola shrieked. "That hurt, and look what you've done, breaking my pencil!" The other girls murmured and looked away as the teacher snatched up Viola's drawing. "Give that back to me!" Viola demanded, making her situation so much worse. The teacher pinched her on the arm and dragged her out of the classroom down to the headmistress's office. Once there she recounted Viola's various offenses but stuffed the unflattering drawing into the pocket of her skirt. Viola was made to sit in the corner of the office until the end of the school day when she was released into Rebecca's custody with a note to be given to her uncle.

Arthur read the note that night at dinner. "So, drawing again, were you?"

"Yes, sir. Sorry, sir." She hung her head.

"And was it your best work? A very good likeness?"

"Yes, it was! But they took it from me and broke one of my pencils in the process." Viola was indignant but Arthur started to laugh.

Of course, Vivian was also indignant. "That foolishness with your drawing is hardly what we pay good money to send you to school for." She was ready to say more but Viola answered her quickly.

"Well, perhaps that's what you *should* send me to school for—drawing. I will be an artist one day, not a parrot, after all."

Vivian sputtered, Arthur laughed openly and Viola went back to her dinner, satisfied that she had made her point. But, come the next morning, Rebecca stood waiting to braid her hair and it was back to school. Viola did everything possible not to squirm and to pay attention; she watched the other girls to see exactly what they did, and she got through another day, and then the day after that until the week had gone by without another incident. But it was too good to last.

The following Monday after Rebecca walked her to school a small knot of girls were waiting for her on the steps. "Is that your mother?"

"No, she's a maid, I guess," Viola answered hesitantly. It was the first time any of the girls had acknowledged her at all.

"Oh, a maid, well, of course," a tall blonde girl giggled. "The lace curtain Irish would have a maid, after all." The other girls laughed and whispered behind their hands until the headmistress came to send them off to their classrooms.

Viola thought about the comment all day. Somehow it didn't seem a compliment and she resolved to ask Rebecca about it. "Am I lace curtain Irish then?" she asked as soon as she saw Rebecca at the school gate.

"Who told you that?" Rebecca said, looking about.

"Oh, the girls this morning said that lace curtain Irish would have a maid, like you, if that's what you are," Viola said.

Rebecca was fuming and Viola was afraid she had insulted her friend and caretaker. "To say that someone is lace curtain Irish is to say that they are trying to act above their station in life, to try to be something that they are not." She could see Viola didn't understand. "Those nasty little girls were trying to say you weren't as good as they are, because you're Irish, and you're trying to act like them." Rebecca walked so fast Viola had a hard time keeping up. "You remember what your friend, the train conductor told you, you're as good as anyone and better than many," Rebecca said, grabbing Viola's hand tightly. "Don't let anyone tell you otherwise."

Arthur and Vivian had gone out to the theater that evening so Viola didn't see them to discuss the matter, but she made up her mind about how she was going to handle the incident. When she arrived at school the next morning, and after she was certain Rebecca was out of sight around the corner, she walked up to the blonde girl and without saying a word, punched her right in the nose. "That's the Irish for you — the fighting Irish," Viola said triumphantly and strode past the shocked girls to her classroom. But, she didn't have long to wait until the headmistress came for her and took her back to the office. Her uncle would be charged with finding another school for her. And weeks after that, another, until they had exhausted the number of girls' schools in the city.

Chapter Nineteen

Arthur had committed to leasing the Crocker Mansion for the full year, so it was out of the question that they would leave San Francisco early solely on account of Viola's schooling. Over dinner one night with the director of the city's opera company, Arthur complained, "I've become my nine-year-old niece's guardian since the death of my brother and his wife some months back, and she's a delightful little scamp, but..."

The other gentleman nodded sagely, "But, you're not used to the demands of a nine-year-old girl." He chuckled, "I've raised five daughters myself, and trust me, it never gets any easier." He could see that his remarks had done nothing to elevate Arthur's mood. "What seems to be the central problem?"

"The central problem is that she simply cannot get along in school — not that she isn't smart — far from it; she's actually quite gifted. But, I suppose she is overly sensitive and can't tolerate the inevitable teasing and jealousies of the other girls." He sighed. "And there's the Irish issue as well."

"The Irish girls tease her, do they?"

"She herself is half-Irish on her mother's side," Arthur explained, "and she quite overlooks the fact that she's half English as well. She's actually gotten in fisticuffs with girls who have disparaged the Irish." Finally

Arthur had to laugh. "Can you imagine a nine-year-old girl punching another one in the nose?"

Both men enjoyed a laugh imagining the scene. The director grew serious, however. "You know, my middle child had quite a temper and was tossed out of several schools, but finally we settled on the idea of a tutor. Mind you, we had to go through several of those until we found one who was the right fit for Stephanie, but when we did she positively blossomed."

"A tutor," Arthur said thoughtfully. "That might be just the thing. How would I go about finding one suitable for a liberal education?"

The director assured him he would make some inquiries the following day. The two finished their dinner in higher spirits and then decided to make a foray into the Barbary Coast "to see what wickedness is being offered tonight." It was a late night, or an early morning, for both. But the director hadn't forgotten his pledge and two days hence a courier brought Arthur a letter listing several eligible tutors and how to contact them. One in particular interested Arthur as he surveyed the list. "Patrick Sean O'Flannary," he said in his best imitation Irish brogue. Viola could hardly have a problem with him! He hastily drafted an invitation for the man to come to the mansion for an interview "no later than Friday noon," and dispatched a courier to the man's address, requesting he specify his availability.

Mr. O'Flannary sent his reply back with the same courier. He was not available in the morning but would report to the Crocker Mansion the following day at noon. He would, of course, provide references at that time. When Arthur read the response he debated with himself over whether to tell Viola of the new plan for her education and also whether to have her present for the interview of the tutor. He decided not to do either and to meet with the gentleman first on his own; he fervently hoped that would be a time when Vivian was out shopping as she would certainly oppose the extra expense of a tutor.

At the appointed hour, Mr. O'Flannary presented himself. Arthur was relieved to hear Vivian leave a bit earlier, saying she had luncheon plans with women from the local temperance society determined to do something about the "abomination" of the Barbary Coast. The prospective tutor was cleanly, if a little bit flamboyantly, attired and presented to Arthur a sheaf of letters of reference once they were settled in the mansion's library reading room. Arthur was amused to hear that he did indeed have a rather pronounced brogue. Arthur quickly explained about Viola's orphaned state but glossed over why her schooling had thus far been unsuccessful. "She's quite headstrong, I would say, but very bright and very artistic," he informed the man.

"Well, I'll brook no nonsense, you can be sure," the tutor interjected immediately. "She'll do her lessons as I say or be sorrier for it."

"I don't think anything harsh will be required," Arthur quickly said, coming to Viola's defense. "I think she just needs focus, not so much discipline."

"Hmmm. Focus indeed." He nodded his head toward the letters. "I suppose you'll want to read those. Perhaps I can peruse the library while you do?"

Arthur pretended to read the letters, but really they meant nothing to him as he had no idea who the tutor's prior employers were or what their expectations had been. Meanwhile, the tutor pulled various books off the shelves and appeared to study them intently, finally pronouncing, "I believe you have everything we need right here." He paused for just a moment. "So, when would you like me to be starting with the lass?"

Arthur appreciated his directness and decided to take the chance. He asked Mr. O'Flannary to name his salary expectation and found that it was quite reasonable. He and Viola would work together every afternoon, four hours each day. Arthur would have a chance to review the exams Viola would take and could modify the direction of the lesson plans if he thought necessary. After coming to terms, Arthur asked him if perhaps he would like a glass of sherry. The day had become quite gloomy as the fog rolled in and even with all the fireplaces being lighted, it was still damp in the drafty mansion. The tutor accepted the sherry eagerly, and then a second. The more he consumed, the broader his accent became.

Chapter Twenty

Arthur had told Viola that she was to make herself presentable and join him in the library slightly before noon, and that he had a special surprise for her. He had no idea how she would react to her new tutor, although he had already endured a verbal flogging the night before from Vivian about the expense and the idea of a stranger coming into their home every day. And she certainly was not going to supervise their time together! Arthur listened patiently but in the end told Vivian the matter was settled, the tutor was hired and would begin working with Viola the following day.

Promptly at noon Rebecca came to the library to announce that a Mr. O'Flannary was at the door. "Show him in, please," Arthur said, admonishing Viola at the same time to sit up straight and stop fidgeting about in her chair. When the tutor entered the room, Arthur introduced him. "This is Mr. O'Flannary, Viola, and he will be your personal tutor every afternoon. You must pay attention to him and study as he directs."

"'Tis grand to meet you, miss," Mr. O'Flannary said to Viola. He set his hat on a side table and extended his hand to her. Viola was uncharacteristically shy but did shake his hand and gave a slight curtsy. "Let's get started right now, shall we?" He went to the library shelves and pulled down a slim volume, then moved one of the chairs to the desk in the center of the room and indicated Viola should seat herself there. "Miss Viola, will you open the book and read to me the first passage?"

Viola opened the book slowly but instead of reading, she blurted out, "Are you Irish?" Arthur shook his head.

"Are you Irish, sir?" the tutor said. "You must address me properly."

"Are you Irish, sir?" Viola persisted.

"I most certainly am, young lady, and my whole family before me." Viola beamed but he kept a stern expression on his face. "Now, if you will. Please read the first paragraph."

"Is your whole family here with you then...sir?" Arthur was about to intervene, but the tutor was used to inquisitive children.

He looked about the room as if inspecting every corner. "My whole family does not appear to be here with me, do they? But, that book of poetry is and fairly cries out for you to read from it. Will you do that for me, miss?"

Viola giggled but began to read, at first haltingly, then with more confidence. She used to read to her mother and father every chance she got and had known her letters since she was only about four years old. The tutor was impressed but didn't let on. Why this assignment would be easier than taking candy from a baby! Arthur excused himself after a few minutes, pleased with his choice. Hopefully, Viola would apply herself because certainly she would have to be put in school when at last they returned to London.

After testing Viola's reading ability, the tutor quizzed her on her numbers. She could count, "as high as needed," she assured him, although clearly lacked the more challenging multiplication and division skills. "And just what is your favorite subject to study?" he asked his new pupil.

Viola thought about it for a moment. "I like to study people so that I can draw them, mostly. And I like to wonder what their lives are like."

"Any people in particular?"

"Well, now just the ones I can see from my window," Viola acknowledged. "Although sometimes my uncle takes me out for a walk and I try to remember everyone I see."

"You must show me your drawings one day," Mr. O'Flannary said, and before he could stop her Viola raced out of the room and up the stairs to her room. She was back with her sketch book in a flash, holding it out proudly to him. He strode around the room flipping through her drawings until finally he came to one that had a certain familiarity to it. "And who is this?" he asked Viola, turning the pad toward her.

"Oh, that's my best friend, Mr. Nulty. He was the train conductor when we came out here." Viola looked wistful. "I don't know when I'll see him again, maybe never." He continued through the pad. "You know what he told me, sir? He said us Irish have to stick together and…"

"*We* Irish, miss, *we* Irish." The tutor laughed. "Well, then you and I shall stick together, too." He handed the pad back to her. "Your drawings are quite good. We'll have to take more walks, too. Fresh air is good for the brain, after all." They spent the rest of the afternoon with Viola reading aloud from some of the volumes of classics the tutor found in the vast library.

That night at dinner, Arthur asked Viola how she had fared with the tutor. He was astonished when she scooted her chair back and came to the head of the table where he sat, throwing her arms around him. "Oh, uncle, it was wonderful! Thank you so much for finding him just for me." Vivian was speechless as was Arthur but he finally patted Viola on the shoulder and told her she was welcome and to make the most of the opportunity. She solemnly promised she would do just that. The next morning found her sitting in her window seat, anxiously watching for the tutor's arrival. She was surprised to see him, when at last he did appear, carrying a rope.

Chapter Twenty-One

Viola groaned when the tutor announced that the lesson plan for the day would focus heavily on mathematics. "I don't see how my work as an artist will ever rely on mathematics," she complained.

"Well, do you plan to just give your paintings away?" he taunted her. "And will the store owners give you free paint, free canvases, free brushes?" Viola saw where he was heading but still stood her ground. He had made up a list of multiplications for her to complete, but she just toyed with her pencil and tossed her hair back petulantly. "All great artists are in some way mathematicians," he tried again. "If you see a portrait where the person's head is half the size of their hands, you know the *proportion* is wrong, don't you?" Viola nodded her reluctant agreement. "That proportion is really multiplication." He paused, seeming pleased with his explanation, but still Viola made no move to start her assignment. It was at this point he finally reached for the rope. "All right, outside with you, then!"

"You're not going to tie me up, are you?" she said with genuine fear. "I'll do the problems, I promise." He was already holding the front door open, rope coiled in his hand.

"Yes, you will do the problems, miss," he said, beckoning her down the steps and out to the sidewalk. He tied one end of the rope to the wrought iron fence. "Now, come along. Stand just there," he directed her to a point midway between himself and the fence, directly next to the rope. "You have jumped rope before, haven't you?"

"No, sir," Viola said, a little bit sadly. "I seen the other girls at school do it, but they never asked me."

"I *saw* the other girls," he corrected her gently. "Well, you'll learn two things at once then." He flipped the rope over her head. "Now, get ready to jump!" She was too late, so he tried it again; on about the fourth attempt, she cleared the rope. Rebecca was watching the scene play out in the window and couldn't help but laugh. She simply had to join them. She put down her dusting rag and, not seeing Vivian ready to order her about, went outside. Mr. O'Flannary nodded at her when she gave him a questioning look. Could she join in?

"Down in the valley...*jump*...where the green grass grows...*jump*," Rebecca intoned, jumping in with Viola. "There sat Viola...*jump*...sweet as a rose. *jump* Along came Johnny...*jump*...and kissed her on the cheek...*jump*. Rebecca jumped but Viola was too shocked.

At this point the tutor picked up the verse. "Now when I say a number, you must double it. Let's start!" He flipped the rope. "How many kisses...*jump*...did Viola get this week? *jump* One?"

Viola and Rebecca yelled out, "Two" in unison.

"Two?" *jump,* met with an enthusiastic "four"...*jump*..."Four?" *jump*...answered with "eight." And on they went up to doubling sixteen before Rebecca jumped out and Viola collapsed in a fit of giggles. Even Mr. O'Flannary was laughing. "See, mathematics is not so difficult, is it?" He untied the rope. "Now, back inside to do your assignment, miss." He winked at Rebecca. "And you, lassie, best be getting back to your chores."

Viola was in high spirits at dinner that night and told her aunt and uncle quite enthusiastically that she had "mastered" mathematics and learned to jump rope, too, all in the same afternoon. Arthur didn't know what to make of her story, but Vivian had seen the three of them outside. The tableau had made her a little wistful as she could barely recall being asked to jump rope or do the counting games other girls did when she was a child. Now, of course, she was much too old for any such foolishness.

Mr. O'Flannary was a good tutor and nearly every day devised some new challenge for Viola whom he found quite bright indeed. At the end of their fourth week of working together, he had an announcement. "I have spoken to your uncle, miss, and we are to be allowed to go on a little trip today. So, get your coat and gloves, and bring your sketch book, too. Quick, quick!"

Viola raced out of the library and up the stairs to her room, nearly knocking Vivian down. "Good heavens child! Is the devil himself chasing you?" Vivian never missed an opportunity to chide her about her unladylike behavior.

Viola shyly put her hand in Mr. O'Flannary's when they left the mansion and began walking down Nob Hill. She was a little disappointed when they came to the Mark Hopkins Hotel, where they had stayed when they arrived in San Francisco. "Well, I've already been here," she started to complain. "I thought we were going someplace new and special."

"Did I say that?"

"No, sir. I just thought..." The doorman held the door open and Viola trudged inside.

Once they were in the center of the ornate lobby, the tutor swept his arms out. "Now, look how grand this is and how well turned-out all the guests are." Viola looked around but still couldn't fathom how this outing would be anything special. "You, Viola McDougall, future famous artist, have an assignment this afternoon."

"Here?"

"Yes, here, the very center of civilization for this lovely city," he intoned in an exaggerated brogue. "Your assignment takes two parts. One, you will find someone to interview. Two, you will sketch a fetching likeness of that same person." Viola looked paralyzed. "Do you understand?"

"I can't just talk to a stranger," she protested. "I could sit up there," she said, pointing to the mezzanine, "and sketch somebody down here, but…"

"No, you must address yourself to a likely person and explain what your task is for this afternoon. I myself will wait patiently in the salon for your report." He smoothed his jacket down and turned on his heel, leaving the little girl looking forlorn in the center of the lobby.

Viola looked about bleakly but finally squared her shoulders and marched up to a man sitting in one of the lobby's velvet wingback chairs. He had a rather incongruous white suit on and a cane resting across his legs. He held the newspaper in one hand and absentmindedly stroked his full mustache with the other. "Excuse me, sir," she began timidly. He appeared not to even notice her. "Excuse me," she said a little louder. "My tutor has brought me here this afternoon to meet a person that will let me talk to them and sketch them as well." The man had a faint hint of a smile. "So, will you do that? Talk to me?"

"What shall we talk about, miss?" the stranger said gravely. Viola looked puzzled. "The state of the world? The color of your eyes? The weather?" The stranger was teasing her, Viola understood, but at least he was talking to her.

"Well, sir, for starters, what are you about?"

"About?"

"What do you do, sir?" Viola persisted. She sat down opposite him. "Are you a merchant visiting here?"

"Ah, no, not a merchant." He set the newspaper aside. "Actually, I am a writer, and just like you I must talk to people and find out what they're about, as you put it." He extended his hand formally. "Samuel Langhorne Clemens, miss. Pleased to make your acquaintance." Viola shook his hand, as her father had taught her to do. For the next hour, she peppered the man with questions about his home, his family, and the kinds of stories he wrote. "I'll tell you a little secret," he said, leaning forward. "I sometimes write under another name entirely, Mark Twain." Viola giggled. "That way if I have to say something critical about another person, let's say, then I can and they won't even know it was me."

"I think that's very smart, Mr. Clemens," Viola agreed thoughtfully. "I think I shall sign my paintings with another name and that way even people who don't like me, might still like my paintings." While they were talking she had been sketching him and was finally satisfied with the result. His eyes seemed to twinkle in her drawing, yet his intelligence shown through as well, and his mustache looked positively luxuriant.

"Well, that's very fine indeed," he said when she at last let him see the drawing. "You've made me look like quite a handsome fellow indeed, young lady." As he was handing the sketchbook back, Mr.

115

O'Flannary reappeared. He recognized the writer immediately and made to shake the man's hand. "You've got quite the star pupil here," the writer assured him. "We'll be seeing more of this young lady, I'm sure." Viola skipped most of the way home, quite pleased with how she had acquitted herself.

Chapter Twenty-Two

Arthur stood quietly in the doorway to the front parlor watching his niece, who as always, was engrossed in whatever was going on outside. She had grown at least three inches taller in the past year and he could tell she was going to be a beautiful young woman. Yet, she seemed to take no notice of herself unlike most young women her age. Vivian was constantly reminding her to tidy her dress, clean her nails and, "Please, do something with that hair!" Arthur supposed Viola was lonely as she had only her tutor and occasionally Rebecca to talk to, no one her own age, and undoubtedly she still grieved for her parents, but she never complained. And now he was going to have to give her more sad news.

The Crockers had completed their grand tour of Europe and would be returning to San Francisco at the end of the month. Would the MacDougalls be so good as to vacate their mansion before then? Arthur had discussed it with Vivian who was only too ready to leave San Francisco, even though she had gotten quite caught up with the Temperance League and spent many nights harassing the customers of the Barbary Coast saloons (Arthur being fortunate not to have run into her).

"Viola, dear, do you have a moment?" he began tentatively, pulling a chair up next to her window seat. "I have some news for you, well, for all of us, actually." She looked alarmed already. "The people who own this mansion, the Crockers—you know I've spoken of them before — well, they're coming home at the end of the month." He waited for the implication to set in but still Viola said nothing, just waited placidly with her hands folded in her lap. "So, we'll be moving. Rebecca will help you pack your things, of course."

In a pitiful squeak, Viola finally asked the question he had been dreading, "Where?"

Arthur did his best to smile. "Why, we'll be going back to England, of course. We have a beautiful home there with a lovely garden and library, not so large as this, but every bit as nice."

Viola's face fell. "But I...my tutoring has been going so well and..." She brightened for just a moment. "Can Mr. O'Flannary go with us?"

"Mr. O'Flannary has his life here, Viola, so, of course, he can't." Surely it hadn't escaped her notice that the tutor and the Crocker's maid had struck up more than a friendship. "Don't worry, there'll be other tutors and better schools in England." Then, to sweeten the deal, he added cautiously, "And, I have a manor home in Ireland which we can visit occasionally as well."

Viola still tried to find a bright spot in the situation. "Will we be traveling back to New York on the train then?"

He couldn't even give her this small hope. "No, dear, your aunt is still upset over that unfortunate Indian business on the train. We'll be sailing on a ship out of the city here, going round the Horn and then on to England. We leave in two weeks." Viola was clearly heartbroken and Arthur knew of no way to console her. "So, that's that, then. You shall have to say your goodbyes, such as they are, and then look forward to the sailing journey." He left the little girl leaning against the window, a few tears running down her cheeks. All he could hope for was a miracle that would make her enjoy the weeks on board the ship.

The next two weeks flew by in a flurry of organizing and packing, much of which fell to Rebecca and her small staff, although Vivian was very much in charge. When Viola's tutor arrived and saw the commotion, he didn't seem surprised, of course, Rebecca having told him of the McDougall's imminent departure. When Viola began crying at the sight of him, he hugged the little girl tightly. "Now, now, lassie. Let's remember all the grand adventures we've had." He recounted several including their first day of jump rope and the excitement of meeting the famous Mark Twain. It all served to make her cry the harder, unfortunately. He grew solemn, addressing Viola at her level. "You'll have a great many adventures ahead of you, and one day Mark Twain will read about you, instead of the other way around." He tried a small laugh. "And all because I helped you become so smart."

Viola, of course, had missed nothing. "Perhaps with all the time you've spent with Miss Rebecca, she has become powerfully smart as well!"

"That she is, miss, that she is. She's too smart for me, I'm quite certain," the tutor admitted, "though it weren't for lack of trying."

"*Wasn't*," Viola corrected him, "*wasn't* for lack of trying."

"See, just look how sharp you are. And with that fair beauty and those flashing purple eyes, aye you'll have the gentlemen falling at your feet!" He opened up the case where he kept her assignments and withdrew a small package which he placed in her lap. "Go ahead now, open it, will you?"

She plucked at the ribbon and gradually undid the striped wrapping paper. Inside was a fountain pen with a gold nib and an exquisite package of writing paper. The pen was inscribed with her name, and the whole gift must have been quite costly. Viola looked at it solemnly. "I'll use it to write to you, tell you of my adventures, tell you how my next tutor is so much more handsome." They both laughed and the tutor felt that Viola's spirit would rebound and carry her through the challenges ahead, one of the biggest being how to get out from under the oppression of her aunt who took that moment to enter the room.

"Now, don't be throwing that paper about, Viola," she said, all the while trying to see the gift. "And you, Mr. O'Flannary, isn't it time you started her lesson. After all, we are still paying you through the end of the week!" The woman was simply insufferable.

On the day when they were ready to leave for the ship, Rebecca pulled Viola aside. "I've a gift for you, nothing grand, mind you," the housekeeper said, hugging Viola tightly. She handed Viola a sketchbook smaller than she usually used and pressed inside of it were violets. "Whenever I see violets, I'll think of you and hope you are happy," she explained to Viola who was embarrassed at having nothing to give in return, or almost nothing.

Viola pulled a sheet from her book on which she had drawn Rebecca, quite finely, sitting in front of a fire. Across from Rebecca was Mr. O'Flannary and between them a crib.

Chapter Twenty-Three

At last the steamship blew its horn, the gangways were retracted, the ropes were removed holding it to the wharf and the massive anchor was slowly raised. Many of the passengers stayed on the starboard deck to wave goodbye to family and friends who had come to see them off. The McDougalls had no one, but Vivian still pressed against the railing, waving at everyone as if the entire city had come to wish them well on their month-long journey. Viola was disconsolate seeing the landmarks she had come to know fade slowly in the distance. Arthur was distracted, still going over in his mind the last-minute trip he and Vivian had made to Virginia City to inspect the progress of rebuilding Piper's Opera House. His biggest operatic star had a signed contract to appear there, but Arthur was skeptical the building would be complete, and he worried how the rotund Italian would tolerate the mining town's elevation and its dry, dusty air. Arthur must remember to cable his manager and advise them to pack extra lozenges and to always keep a warm, damp towel over the singer's throat. There were always a thousand details, Arthur reflected any one of which could derail a performance.

Vivian was turning over a thousand details in her mind, too. They were going home! Finally she could look forward to returning to their stately townhouse with its half-dozen fireplaces. She simply must remind Arthur to cable ahead and assure that the house manager has contracted for an adequate supply of wood and coal for the winter. Oh, how she yearned to sit in her parlor with a bit of handiwork in her lap and a cat curled around her ankles. When London's notorious fog would allow it, the sun streamed in the tall windows and it was the most delightful place to pass an afternoon. Suddenly her mood darkened, however, as she realized it wouldn't simply be her and Arthur sharing the townhouse. She would have to make some arrangements for Viola. Where was that girl, anyway?

Viola had found a niche between two stacks of crates that was out of the wind and away from the crowded railing; she huddled there waiting for someone to even notice that she was missing. Gradually the passengers drifted down to their staterooms or found seats in the ship's common area, referred to as the grand salon. They would be many days at sea before the next port-of-call with little to occupy them other than idle conversation, and for some, card games. The passengers seemed to be mostly men traveling alone, salesmen, probably, with a few families. Viola didn't see any women on their own and what children she saw were much younger than herself. Her aunt had made her pack her sketchbook in one of the many trunks which were probably being stowed in their stateroom, so it left Viola with nothing to do but look around at the chaotic scene. It turned out to be lucky that she wasn't absorbed in one of her sketches as a huge grappling hook mechanism dropped onto one of the crates next to her and might have split her skull in two if she hadn't jumped out of the way just in time. Strong arms tugged her out of the way and Viola was startled by a torrent of words, not quite Spanish but certainly not in English. It was one of the young sailors, gesticulating wildly at her. Viola was so startled she began to cry, and of course, that was when Vivian finally found her, appearing to struggle in the arms of a red-faced sailor.

Vivian recalled how she had admonished Arthur to be certain they would be sailing on a ship with an English crew, and while he had assured her that he would do so, she had no doubts that he only told her that to mollify her and had made no such attempt. Now it was confirmed. She had heard from some of the women in the League when she told them she would be sailing 'round the Horn that some of the crews were quite disreputable and given to bouts of heavy drinking and insolence to the passengers. One woman confided in Vivian that some of the crew members were barely better than pirates, and that the Portuguese were the worst! And that was most assuredly Portuguese the sailor was using to frighten Viola. Vivian looked about for Arthur or any other gentleman to come to their aid but was finally forced to advance upon the sailor and grab her niece out of his clutches.

As soon as Vivian had the girl a comfortable distance from him, the sailor executed a gallant bow, removing his cap and apparently apologizing profusely while gesturing at the equipment moving overhead. Vivian refused to relinquish her most intimidating stare, however, and dragged her still-sobbing niece off toward the stairway to the lower decks. Perhaps it would be best if Viola remained in their rooms until they were back in England, Vivian reasoned. After all, a petite blonde like Viola might bring a pretty penny in some exotic port. Vivian's imagination ran wild, although she said nothing of the sort to Viola, simply pinched her arm even tighter as they made their way down the narrow hallway.

Arthur was waiting for them outside their stateroom, ironically named the California. Enough already, Vivian scowled, thinking Arthur might have selected it deliberately just to annoy her. It worked. She was now quite annoyed with him, with the girl, the pirate and perhaps even the captain of the ship for selecting such a clearly unruly crew. Traveling was not the elegant experience it had once been, she observed, and might likely be the death of her yet!

Chapter Twenty-Four

Viola moped about and had to be forced to eat even one meal a day. Arthur worried she was sea-sick but finally realized she was just sad and bored. If he had given it more thought he would have realized she was also worried about what lay ahead. After three days being shut in her cabin with Vivian who rarely talked to the girl other than to admonish her about one thing or another, Arthur finally took the initiative. "Viola, dear, what do you say that we go up to the promenade deck and take in some glorious sea air, stretch our legs a bit?" Viola looked up at him sullenly and gave a long, exasperated sigh. "Come along now. I don't want to walk about alone." He winked. "You know how the ladies are with me."

She dragged her coat behind her until Vivian barked at her to pick it up and put it on properly, and gloves, too! "And you without your sketch book, I dare say I've never seen such a sight," Arthur tried. Viola trudged back into the cabin to collect it and allowed her uncle to take her hand as they left the cabin. The seas were smooth and many of their fellow passengers were "taking the air." More than one of the ladies smiled shyly at Arthur as they joined the group walking around the deck. Arthur tried to get Viola interested in the other passengers, suggesting them as possible subjects for a new sketch. "Now look at that fellow there, the interesting way he holds his pipe." Viola barely followed Arthur's gaze. "Wouldn't he make a fine subject, much in the style of one of the Dutch Masters, don't you think?" Viola sighed but made no move to approach the man with the pipe.

Arthur paused in their stroll to chat with a couple he had met the evening before at dinner, unaware that Viola had continued on her own. Viola finally had seen something she was very interested in indeed— simply the most beautiful velvet bag she had ever seen, on the arm of a young woman perhaps ten years older than herself and with a mass of flaming red hair blowing loose in the sea breeze. She watched as the young woman found a sheltered spot on the leeward side of the deck and began emptying out the contents of the bag. Pieces of velvet and silk, some kind of sparkling brocade, bits of ribbon in dozens of colors, and even feathers spilled out. Viola was intrigued about what the young woman intended to do with these treasures, but as she watched the woman did nothing more than turn each piece over carefully in her hands, arranging some pieces with others, then scattering them and rearranging them again. Viola's curiosity drew her closer, but she was too shy to approach the woman directly. She would observe her, however, over the coming days.

When Arthur finally noticed she was missing, he tried to be stern with her but couldn't bring himself to be too hard on her. "Now, really, you mustn't wander off like that, Viola. Just think what your aunt would say." Viola gave a sour smile and Arthur had to hide his own grin. "Let's go into the lounge and see what treats are in store for our luncheon. I do say that sea air has quite enhanced my appetite." Viola looked back at the woman sitting by herself, seemingly lost in thought, but she allowed her uncle to once again take her hand and lead her to the lounge where she more than made up for her flagging appetite of the previous few days.

The next day Viola left the cabin on her own and went directly to where the woman had been sitting the day before. She herself took the spot and pulled out her sketchpad. She drew a tower she remembered from San Francisco and a scene of a couple in a lush garden. She soon sensed someone watching her and steeled herself to the harangue she knew would be forthcoming from her aunt. "That's quite lovely," she heard instead. "Is that your home, then?" Viola turned to see the woman with the flowing red hair. And that voice! Viola recognized the same lilt she had heard in the train conductor's speech and in Mr. O'Flannary. The woman was undoubtedly Irish!

Viola was so flustered she dropped her pad as she jumped to her feet. "Oh, ma'am, I'm so sorry to be sitting in your place." She swept one arm out to the woman who did sit down.

"Come now. There's room for both of us," she beckoned to Viola. "I don't believe this crate has my name on it alone." Viola was spellbound and just wanted the woman to keep talking so she could absorb every syllable. "Cat got your tongue?" she asked.

Viola was confused. "I don't have a cat. No."

"It's just an expression, you silly goose!" Kathleen laughed. "But, of course, you're not a goose either, are you?"

"No, I'm an artist." Viola surprised herself by saying that and felt shy and stupid all over again.

"Yes, you are indeed. I could see that." When Viola still didn't respond, Kathleen decided to try once more. "Do you have other sketches you could show me?"

That was all it took to open the floodgates. For the next two hours Viola showed Kathleen her sketches of San Francisco and the people she had met there, explaining each sketch. When she got to the drawings she had made on the train, she embarrassed herself by breaking down in tears. "There was a mean Indian but a wonderful train conductor, and..."

Kathleen pulled a scented handkerchief from her bag and gave it to Viola. "We meet all kinds of people in this life, especially when we travel, it seems." She gave Viola a minute to regain her composure. "Now, look at us. We've just met and I don't think either of us is mean, are we?"

Viola's sense of humor rebounded. "Well, I'm not anyway." That launched into another half-hour of storytelling about just how mean her aunt could be, when who should appear but Vivian, clearly vexed.

Kathleen already recognized her, having seen her with Arthur when they were leaving San Francisco. "Oh, Miss McDougall. Your niece here has just been telling me what a grand time you have shown her in San Francisco and how she looks forward to seeing your estate in London."

Vivian was momentarily confused. "Estate? Well, it's not exactly an estate, but yes, it is rather elegant." She looked the red-haired woman over and quickly surmised what Viola's attraction to her was. "And you live just where in Ireland?"

"My situation is, at the moment, uncertain," Kathleen answered hesitantly. "That is, I'm certain I will live in Ireland, probably in Dublin." She took a deep breath. "I will be designing costumes for the Dublin Opera Company, so, of course, I shall live there." Vivian was certain her story was an exaggeration and made a note to discuss the opera company later with her brother.

"Come along, Viola. We must get ready for dinner. The captain has invited us to his table tonight," she said, more for Kathleen's benefit than Viola's. These upstart Irish. When would she be shed of them?

Chapter Twenty-Five

From that point forward on the journey, Kathleen and Viola were virtually inseparable. Where Viola had assumed that Kathleen was examining the bits of cloth and ornamentation to perhaps make a doll for her child, she learned instead that Kathleen was planning elegant evening gowns for the stage and for the women fortunate enough to attend such gala events. Like Viola, Kathleen sketched out her creations, and it was in the midst of doing one of those sketches that she attracted the attention of one of the passengers, a woman of ample girth and clearly ample funds as well.

"Let me see what you're working on there," the woman demanded abruptly, pointing to Kathleen's pad.

"Oh, it's nothing," Kathleen stammered.

"Well, then you're a foolish young woman indeed to spend so many hours on nothing," the woman replied testily. "I've been watching you," and she turned to Viola, "and you, too, but you're just a child and entitled to fiddle the day away." She held out her hand for the sketchpad which Kathleen had no choice but to surrender. "Hmmm, just so," she murmured as she flipped through a dozen or more dress sketches. "Better in blue, I would think." Finally, she handed the pad back to Kathleen. "I will take the fourth, fifth and sixth gowns, although the fourth one must be blue, not that gaudy purple you indicate."

Kathleen was speechless but Viola was not. She had heard Arthur close a number of deals in the year they had already spent together. "We shall have to agree on an advance and a time for a proper fitting and all," Viola said.

If the older woman was surprised, she didn't let on. "Well, of course, we can do that. I am in the New Hampshire stateroom. You may come to take tea with me this afternoon and settle such details." She swept up her skirt and flounced off down the deck.

"What did you just do?" Kathleen asked Viola.

"It's not what I did. It's what you did. You just got your first customer!" Viola hugged Kathleen. "And you know she'll brag to her friends about the exclusive designer she has discovered." Kathleen finally allowed a smile to escape. "Let's go tell uncle and see how we, or you, should handle this." Viola dragged Kathleen to her feet and they went off in search of Arthur whom Kathleen had yet to meet. They found him in the ship's salon, looking pensively out at the ocean. "Uncle, listen to what just happened. Oh, and this is my friend, Kathleen, who draws just like I do, but..."

"Really, child, slow down just a moment, will you?" Arthur had seen Viola and Kathleen together and was happy his niece had found someone to spend time with on the ship. "Now, this is your friend, Kathleen is it?" he said rising.

Kathleen extended her hand. "Kathleen Evans, sir."

"And you, too, are a budding artist?" he asked.

"No, sir, I hope to be a costume designer for the Dublin Opera Company and for others as well."

"But here's the most exciting part," Viola interrupted. "This woman just asked her to make three gowns and now they're going to take tea and I thought you could tell her what to do."

"Oh, you did, did you?" Arthur said while winking at Kathleen. "You thought I would tell Miss Evans here how to take tea?"

"No, not that. Honestly, uncle, do I have to explain everything?" Kathleen was mortified but Viola plunged on. "You must tell her how to negotiate a fair price for her gowns and all of that, like you do with your singers." Viola turned now to Kathleen. "My uncle, Mr. McDougall, represents opera singers and other performers and sees that they get the most money. I believe he's really quite good at it."

"Thank you for that high compliment," Arthur said. "I'm sure I know nothing about the price of ball gowns, but let's sit and have a bit of sherry and discuss the matter, shall we?" He pulled out a chair for Kathleen and one for Viola as well while signaling one of the porters. For the next two hours Arthur graciously discussed supply and demand with

Kathleen who listened intently but asked intelligent questions. He explained the fine distinction between designing for an individual woman and for a theater company. "A woman in society is only going to wear a special gown once, I believe, while a theater company will use the gown over and over." Kathleen explained that she had worked with the wardrobe mistress at Piper's Opera House in Virginia City and knew just how many times a gown could be repaired and reworked. "So, you understand completely, then," Arthur acknowledged. "The other aspect is that a gown designed for the stage must be striking at perhaps a hundred feet away while a woman at a party wants to appear more subtle, but equally stunning." Kathleen hadn't considered that distinction.

Arthur ordered more sherry for himself and Kathleen and a hot cocoa for Viola. "Now, it seems, the question becomes, do you save your most spectacular designs for the stage for thousands of people to enjoy? Or for an individual woman such as you met today? Who will pay more? The theater company that may keep the dress for years or the society matron who will wear it once?"

Kathleen pondered the question. "Well, it makes sense that the theater company should pay more."

"I don't believe so," Arthur replied thoughtfully. "The theater-going public expects a certain level of sophistication in costuming, and they assume the company gets special consideration from the designers and dressmakers because of the exposure it affords them. Because of these considerations, they often are able to buy the costumes very reasonably." Kathleen nodded her head. "The society woman, on the other hand, realizes she is getting a gown designed solely for her, and she expects to pay for that exclusivity. Therefore, you must be prepared to charge her accordingly."

"Uncle, you should see her sketches." Viola attempted to take Kathleen's sketch pad, but Kathleen was having none of it.

"We've taken enough of your uncle's time today already, Viola, and besides, I must freshen up if I am to have tea with my first customer shortly." She turned to Arthur. "I am truly grateful. You've given me much to think about."

"Never sell your talent short, my dear. It's the only thing that is truly uniquely yours." Arthur walked her to the door of the salon. "Perhaps you can join my sister and I, and Viola, of course, for dinner and tell us how your first sale progressed."

Chapter Twenty-Six

Oftentimes Kathleen and Viola said nothing to each other as each sat on the deck in "their" place drawing or just thinking. But there were other occasions when Viola just couldn't stop herself from peppering Kathleen with questions, particularly about Ireland. "Oh, lass, I'm afraid you've made it a much grander place than it is," Kathleen explained patiently. "The countryside is green and lovely, but, oh, it's such a hard place, too."

"But that's because of the English!" Viola answered indignantly.

"Not entirely, Viola." Kathleen sighed. "You have to understand. The Irish relied too heavily on one thing—the potato—and when the blight began, there was nothing to be done." Viola was not to be mollified by anything Kathleen said but also knew she didn't have the answers needed to counter Kathleen's description of events of the time. "Do you think my pa and I would have left our home if there was any way around it?"

"Well, you left your home in San Francisco," Viola said petulantly, "and there was probably a way around that!"

"You can be a wicked, hurtful little child. You know that don't you!" Kathleen did indeed seem hurt by the accusation and Viola was immediately contrite. She threw her arms around Kathleen and began to sob. "All right, all right, enough of that," Kathleen said, stroking her hair. "When you're older you'll have affairs of the heart that will drive you to do things you can't imagine." Kathleen continued to rock Viola back and forth as she thought of her own child being conceived in anger and dying in much the same state, along with her being powerless to stop either event. She thought of her first husband, Padraig, a thousand times a day and genuinely hoped he was in heaven. Those thoughts alternated with remembrances of Philip with his boundless kindness toward her after Padraig's death, but their marriage proved doomed as well after the baby's death even though he knew the child was not his own.

Viola finally stopped sniveling and apologized to Kathleen. "I don't understand why anything happens the way it does," she admitted. "My parents were so wonderful, and look what happened to them? And my aunt and uncle are old, I think. What will happen to me if they die?" Viola had finally voiced the fear that had plagued her ever since her parents' deaths.

"Oh, they're not so old as that," Kathleen said cautiously. "They'll certainly live to see you a married woman and bounce your children on their knees." Viola wrinkled her nose up at the suggestion. "And I'm sure they'll put money aside for you so you can do as you like until then."

"Uncle did say something about that," Viola agreed begrudgingly. "But Aunt Vivian would probably take it. She's a witch. And I hate her!"

"Well, I don't think she's a real witch is she?" Kathleen began to tease the girl. "You haven't seen her fly around on a broom, have you?" Viola allowed that she hadn't but felt it was entirely possible. "And she hasn't made any stews, has she, with snails and the eye of newt?" Just then the ship's horn sounded, signaling their arrival in a new port. Kathleen and Viola moved closer to the rail to watch the commotion that always accompanied a landing. "Look, there goes your aunt, probably going in search of some new newt, don't you think?" Viola collapsed in laughter. "Now, you go back to your cabin. I have to go do some shopping myself."

Viola was not allowed to venture into the port cities, even with her uncle at her side, and it pained her greatly to miss the opportunity to observe the locals up close. Vivian had decreed that it was just too dangerous as she was certain Viola would wander off and be kidnapped. Arthur didn't care to argue the point and rarely ventured into the port cities himself. They were all rather the same, he felt, shabby and filled with con artists eager to take advantage of the more affluent travelers. Many a gentleman came back to the ship minus his wallet and some had unknowingly acquired a dose of the pox as well. The ladies complained that the local men were often too friendly, although they often looked wistfully at the docks as the ship pulled away.

"When I am older I shall travel wherever I choose," Viola stated to no one in particular. Mr. Nulty and

Mr. O'Flannary both said she was destined for great adventures, and since they were Irish should be able to foretell the future, she reasoned. Still, she stayed by the railing until the passengers began returning to the ship, anxious to see what treasures they would bring aboard. Dinner that night would be more lively than usual as the guests regaled each other with what they had seen during the short sojourn in port, their last stop before the often treacherous rounding of the Horn and then the long journey across the ocean to London.

Chapter Twenty-Seven

"Now that's very peculiar indeed," Vivian thought as she made her way back to her stateroom, slightly tipsy from all the champagne at dinner, the sherry beforehand, and the port afterwards. The man she saw letting himself into his cabin just two doors down looked exactly like the gentleman she had talked with on the train, down to the smallest detail; even his jacket was the same. But how could that be? She had never seen him board the ship at any of the ports where they had called. Surely he could not have spent the entire journey in his cabin? Perhaps the poor man had been ill all this time. She hesitated before entering her room. She really should find out if he needed any assistance, she convinced herself, resolutely making her way down the hallway, one hand steadying herself against the wall.

Vicente, of course, was well aware of her presence and had been for several days since he was loaded onto the ship in his specially-made crate. Vivian was of no interest to him, per se, although he did relish the chance to torture her just a bit. It was actually Kathleen who had drawn him toward the ship. Vicente's protégé, and Kathleen's former husband, Philip, still obsessed over her, and his constant whining had driven Vicente to make promises he now had to keep. "You know you can't be with her!" Vicente had angrily reminded Philip during their last conversation in Virginia City where Philip had returned to play piano in the new opera house. "She is out of your life forever, as surely as if she had died."

"She isn't dead to me," Philip admitted morosely. "I loved her from the minute I saw her in the wings of the stage."

"Yes, and I'm sure she loved you, but the point is, life goes on." Vicente laughed at his own little joke. "She told you she was returning to Ireland and I'm sure that's just what she'll do."

"But what if something happens to her? What if she doesn't get to Ireland?" Philip was truly distraught. "What if she changed her mind and came back to San Francisco to find that I was no longer waiting for her?"

Vicente felt like shaking him but instead calmly offered a proposal. "What if I go to her, discern her plans, and return to you with proof that she is doing well? Will you leave off with this mooning about?"

Philip irritably began, "I don't know how you would do that…"

"There's a lot you don't know. That's my point entirely." Vicente waited an instant. "Deal? As they say at the Delta?"

Philip nodded his grudging consent. "Deal."

And so, Vicente found himself on a ship sailing for England, once again in the company of the annoyingly smug Vivian McDougall who clearly intended to pay him a visit this night. When she rapped on his door, he let her wait a moment then opened the door with a flourish, pretending to be surprised. "Why if it isn't the lovely Miss McDougall!" he exclaimed, touching his chest as he did so and standing aside to let her enter.

Vivian was aghast at what she saw. His quarters were twice as luxurious as her own even though Arthur had reassured her that their staterooms were among the finest on the ship. It appeared he had been sold a bill of goods indeed! All of the furniture was upholstered in a deep raspberry velvet, accented by shimmering cherry wood tables. A brocaded drapery closed off the bed chamber although Vivian could make out one side of a four-poster bed, also covered in a velvet spread with dozens of pillows piled high. The sight caused her to stammer. "Oh, Mister, uh. I realize I don't actually know your name."

He leaned forward to take her hand and bent deeply over it, kissing it lightly. "You may call me simply Vicente, Madame." He could feel the shiver that ran up her spine. "Please, do sit. Some champagne perhaps?" He pointed toward a silver bucket in which rested what appeared to be a magnum of the finest champagne served only to guests at the captain's table. She knew she had had quite enough to drink already but was nevertheless powerless to refuse.

"I must say...Vicente, that I am truly surprised to see you on board. At which port did you join our voyage?"

Vicente poured her champagne into a delicate goblet. "Oh, I've been here all along, just keeping to myself, I'm afraid." He leered at her. "Of course, now I realize my mistake as I've denied myself the opportunity to spend more time with you."

Vivian raised her hand to her mouth to hide her smile. "But you've been well on the journey, I trust?"

"Oh, quite. The sea air is so good for one's constitution, don't you agree?"

"But I haven't seen you on deck, taking in the air, that is," Vivian queried.

"Ah, I go out in the evenings only." He pointed to his face. "With this complexion, I dare say I would burst into flames if I were exposed to the sun which is so much brighter when reflected off the ocean." She nodded but couldn't think of a suitable response while he poured her another glass of champagne. "Look at you, with that lovely peaches-and-cream skin which you surely must keep out of the sun."

"I do wear a hat, of course," Vivian admitted.

"Yes, wise of you to do so and keep looking so young," Vicente cooed. "You should see how enchanting your skin looks just now in the lamplight, just a glowing pink like the faintest blush on a rose." Vivian found she was experiencing the same off-balance sensation she had when attempting to navigate the ship's hallways during stormy seas. She was surprised to see her glass empty again, although only for a moment.

Vicente leaned toward her rather urgently. "And, one must be so careful venturing off the ship into the ports. There are so many…unsavory…types just waiting to take advantage of a young woman such as yourself."

That was the second time he had called her young in as many minutes. "I generally go with my brother or another group of ladies," Vivian agreed. "But you're quite right. I have heard of encounters some of the passengers have had with very unscrupulous merchants and the like."

"Oh, but if they were only after your purse, dear lady," Vicente said, lowering his voice.

"And, I do not allow my niece to leave the ship, ever!" Vivian seemed to get her bearings back. "Of course, my brother thinks I'm being quite cruel and unreasonable about it."

"No, no, I believe you are the voice of reason, even though…" Vicente pursed his lips.

"Even though she should be seeing the world, yes I know," Vivian said irritably. "It's just what Arthur says."

"Au contraire," Vicente said, patting her soothingly on the arm. "I just meant that even here on ship there are those who would do harm to a woman, yes even to a young girl, harm." He steepled his fingers in front of him. "There are quite likely to be pirates aboard the ship, even as we sit her and talk."

"Pirates! But I'm sure the captain…"

"Oh, if the captain knew, Madame, if the captain only knew." Vicente knew he had reeled her in quite enough to inflict the final blow. "Certainly some of the sailors themselves are quite dangerous in their own right, but it's the others we have more to fear from, particularly when we are at their mercy hundreds or thousands of kilometers out in the ocean."

"Others?" Vivian found herself perspiring quite copiously.

Once again, Vicente leaned closer and in a conspiratorial tone, told her, "All those crates you see being loaded on board? Surely you can't imagine all of them contain grain and foodstuffs?" Vivian sat rapt. "No, my lady, some of them are filled with pirates whom the sailors will free one night when we least expect it. Yes, I daresay they will be at our bedsides ready to slit our throats—or worse—before the captain even realizes he has lost his ship to them."

Vivian was dismayed to find her glass empty and looked beseechingly at Vicente. "But what shall I do?" she wailed.

"You must let me come back to your cabin with you tonight and see to your safety," Vicente said quite commandingly. "I shall see that your doors and portholes are locked, and then you must remain there until the ship is safely docked in London." She looked crestfallen but he continued. "I don't believe you will be totally safe until you are in your parlor at home." That should keep the witch from spying on her niece and ruining any fun she might have with Kathleen, Vicente thought, quite proud of his strategy. He half-carried, half-walked Vivian back to her stateroom. He felt her swoon as he kissed her lightly on the cheek before she tumbled into bed.

Now he simply had to obtain reassurance for Philip that his beloved Kathleen was safe as well.

Chapter Twenty-Eight

Vicente had observed Kathleen making at least two visits a day to the stateroom of a Mrs. Turnbull, and he was curious as to what that might be about. After putting Vivian to bed, so to speak, he returned to his cabin and spent the rest of the night pondering what proof he might obtain of Kathleen's safety, and moreover, her plans for the future that would satisfy Philip. When the sun began to break over the horizon, he secured himself in his packing crate, certain he would come up with some idea by sunset that night.

However, it wasn't only Vicente who had been observing Kathleen. The captain had been showing rather too much interest in the young woman with the flaming red hair, often devising ways to be in her path as she made her way down the narrow corridors of the ship, or accosting her as she strolled above-deck. Kathleen had refused several offers to dine privately with him in his quarters, and as the ship drew closer to its final destination in London, he began to press his case more ardently. As most of the guests were making their way to the dining salon that evening, he spied Kathleen walking alone and grabbed her roughly by the arm. "So, Miss Evans, another evening dining alone?"

"Let loose of me, sir," Kathleen protested, looking around to see if anyone else was observing her detention. "I shall dine alone or with whomever I choose!"

He leered at her and pushed her deeper into a doorway. "You do realize that any number of women on this ship would be flattered at my invitations and return my attention eagerly."

"Then you should be asking *them* to dinner. Now, please, you're hurting me and embarrassing yourself!" She twisted in his grasp but he was not about to give in so easily after having been rebuffed by her for so many weeks already. "I shall scream!"

He pressed himself against her and held a hand over her mouth. "You ungrateful Irish bitch! You'll scream all right." But just as he was about to run his other hand down her breast, he found himself held in a vice grip around his neck that felt like the cold steel of shackles.

"Unhand the lady," a man whispered close to the captain's ear in a truly menacing tone. The captain had fought off pirates and contended with rebellions of his crews over the years, but this was the first instance in which he felt real fear. "I assure you, a fate worse than death awaits you if you do not." The captain was unable to move his neck even the length of an eyelash but he dropped his hand from Kathleen's arm and let it hang limply by his side as Kathleen squirmed out of the doorway recess. As she made her escape, the captain felt himself not so much dragged as carried by the neck to the open maw of the stairway down to the steam engines. The stranger released him with a shove that sent him sprawling down into the hold. When he righted himself, he turned quickly to see his assailant but saw no one at the top of the stairs.

Kathleen was too stunned to move much beyond where she had been accosted but eventually blended in with another group of passengers on their way to the dining salon. She would have liked to have thanked her rescuer, but he had seemingly vanished into thin air. Vicente, of course, was afraid Kathleen might remember him from Virginia City and he chose not to bring on those complications, or at least not yet anyway. While Kathleen went on to dinner, he made his way to Mrs. Turnbull's state room, confident that the portly woman would have been among the first to arrive in the dining salon. Indeed, her room was empty and Vicente was able to explore it for clues about Kathleen's visits.

"So, Kathleen will be designing dresses," Vicente noted to himself, admiring her drawings. "And it looks like she has even grander designs for theater costumes as well." He began rehearsing the speech he would give to Philip, although he chided himself for talking out loud to himself, something he felt only elderly people did. "Ha! But then again, I am old," he chuckled to himself, rearranging the sketches where they had been and letting himself out of the stateroom.

Vicente waited until the last diners straggled back to their cabins or went for their evening constitutionals on the promenade deck. It wasn't long before he found Mrs. Turnbull sitting near the railing smoking, of all things, a cigar! It was a shocking spectacle to see a woman smoking, but it put Vicente in mind of all the cigars he enjoyed in Virginia City, talking with his old friend Jack, the bartender-become-governor. It brought a smile to his face, but Mrs. Turnbull was quick to relieve him of it. "If you think you are coming over here to tell me to stop smoking, mister, you might as well keep right on walking!"

Vicente was taken aback. "Truly, Madame, I had no such thought in mind." He recovered and said, "In fact, I thought I might join you and suggest that we send for a nice bottle of port to enhance our experience."

She looked him up and down. "Port, eh? That used to be my husband's choice," and gesturing with her cigar, "as were these. He had one every evening and now I carry on his tradition."

"Just so. Traditions are to be respected," Vicente agreed, pulling out a chair opposite her. "Shall I get that port then?" She nodded her agreement and he waved down one of the deck porters to place his order. They made small talk about the ship and the weather until the port arrived, brought from a supply Vicente had stowed privately for his own use. He lit his own cigar and appeared to sip on the port. "Ah, lovely."

Mrs. Turnbull had relaxed just a bit and was clearly enjoying both the expensive port and her cigar, content to watch the stars overhead. "I don't believe I've made your acquaintance," she said, then waved away his attempt to answer, "but I don't know as I care very much since we shall be in port in a day's time."

Vicente was surprised to be so easily dismissed. "Well, then all the better that I've had the opportunity to speak with you tonight." He waited for her to show any interest but when she didn't he pressed on. "I understand you have retained Miss Evans to design some dresses for you." She narrowed her eyes at him. "You know, one hears things on the ship as everyone is eager for any gossip after so many days at sea." She nodded. "I wonder if I might ask you the smallest favor," he said, lowering his voice in a confidential tone. "You see, I have a sister who is quite...well, plain, I would say, to be generous, and I think if she had some lovely gowns she might be more attractive and perhaps gain the husband she so desperately desires."

"I doubt any sister of yours is plain," the dowager scoffed.

"Oh, you flatter me," Vicente cooed. "But, sadly, yes she is, although I feel compelled to add that she has a lovely personality."

"And what is it you want from me?"

"I wonder if you might write just a little note praising Miss Evans' designs and abilities so that I might present it to my sister and perhaps encourage her to also avail herself of Miss Evans' talents," Vicente said, looking imploringly at Mrs. Turnbull who continued to look at him doubtfully. "We could accomplish it this evening in just a few moments." He refilled her glass and was relieved to see she didn't drink as quickly as Vivian and would at least be sober enough to pen such a note.

"Hmm. And why not just get Miss Evans' particulars and give them to your sister directly?"

"I had thought of that, but then it would seem like too much of a sales effort, don't you think?" He added. "Coming from a woman of obvious taste such as yourself, it would seem less commercial, so to speak."

Mrs. Turnbull actually began to laugh. "Well, in years past a smooth talker like yourself could have talked me out of my bloomers, but if all you want is a letter, I can do that at least."

Vicente put his hand over his mouth and appeared to be shocked at her frank speech but also smoothly drew a piece of writing paper and a pencil from his jacket. She hastily wrote a glowing recommendation for Kathleen then stood abruptly. "Thank you for the port and for sharing a cigar with me. I certainly always enjoyed those times with George. Good night, sir."

Vicente leapt to his feet and bowed deeply as she departed. Now, he had a letter of proof for Philip that

Kathleen was on a path to at least a small success. He put it in his inner jacket pocket and made his way to his cabin, leaving instructions with the deck hand. His packing crate would be unloaded at the earliest opportunity when the ship finally docked.

Chapter Twenty-Nine

Viola's emotions were as turbulent as the scene arrayed before her on the London wharf. Porters moved cases and onto pallets which were then winched to the docks below and quickly off-loaded. Carriages competed for space while their drivers scanned the passengers pressed against the ship's railing. There was an urgency to everything. Vivian had been barking orders at anyone who found themselves in her path. She had made Viola check and double-check that she had everything packed in her trunk which had been shoved out into the hall early that morning, well before the ship even reached the harbor. Viola steadfastly refused to pack the velvet bag Kathleen had hand-sewn for her and clutched it tightly. Theirs had been a teary goodbye the night before.

"I just know I'll never see you again," Viola bawled, her arms wrapped tightly around Kathleen who herself was trying not to cry.

"You goose! Of course you'll see me again." She tilted Viola's chin up. "You're my best friend and you've helped me get my future started with your wonderful drawings." At one point Viola had secretly taken Kathleen's sketch book of dresses and added the actual bodies and faces of famous actresses and opera stars, making the dresses come alive. Even Arthur had lavishly praised them and said they would go a long way toward opening doors at the various opera companies. He had, of course, provided letters of reference for Kathleen to many such organizations and to as many individual performers as he could. Plus, he had discretely given Kathleen an envelope of English pounds which he felt would tide her over for a few months until she made suitable arrangements.

Viola was beyond consolation, however, and retreated to her room in misery. Kathleen had to leave the ship much earlier than Viola and her aunt and uncle in order to catch a steamer to Dublin. Now, hours later, she stood back from the railing and waited to catch a glimpse of her uncle who said he would collect her when it was time for them to leave the ship. Vivian had insisted that more than one carriage be on hand to meet them so that all of their belongings could be transferred at the same time. "I'll not be leaving them to sit on the dock for just anyone to pick through!" she warned Arthur.

Vivian had spent the hours waiting to disembark regaling anyone who would listen with what an awful, simply awful time they had had in their travels. "We were nearly attacked by hostile Indians!" she told one woman, pantomiming a scalping as she did so. "And then, of course, the threat of pirates is ever-present. The worry was almost too much to bear!" she declared. Viola, listening in, thought the only worry Vivian might have suffered was when the chef ran out of potatoes and the ship was two days from the next port.

Finally, both of their carriages had arrived and Arthur came to collect Viola, Vivian having already stormed down the gangplank to begin supervising the loading of their trunks and cases. Arthur tentatively took Viola's hand as they made their way through the crowd. "Well, it won't be long now and you'll see your new home," he began. "I'm sure you'll be very happy with how they've done up your room." Weeks earlier he had asked Viola what colors were her favorite and had included that information in a cable to his house manager. Viola said nothing and just allowed herself to be carried along with the other passengers eager to reach their own carriages and homes.

Although Viola had been born in London and had lived there as a little girl, none of it looked familiar as they made their way to what was clearly a very privileged neighborhood marked by wider streets and much more greenery. The houses were set back from the street behind walled gardens much like the Crocker mansion, although none were nearly that large. Finally the carriages turned through a pair of tall wrought iron gates and stopped beneath a brick porte cochere. The house staff was arrayed on the steps waiting to greet them, although Vivian pushed past them without any acknowledgement. Arthur greeted each one warmly, sharing a few words about their journey and how satisfying it was to see his home and his loyal employees. He introduced Viola to each person; she presented her hand and curtsied appropriately, accepting their compliments on her beautiful curls without comment.

"Viola, dear, there are things I must attend to in my study, so Sarah will show you to your room." He beckoned to one of the maids who took Viola's hand and led her toward a grand staircase in the center of the house. At the end of a wide hallway Sarah dramatically opened a door and stepped back for Viola to enter her new room. "It's lovely, isn't it?" she asked Viola. The room was indeed lovely and had its own window seat with plush velvet pillows and wispy lace draperies that could be drawn back and held with sashes. A four-poster bed dominated the room and Viola observed stairs she would have to use to climb up into it at night. An elaborately framed mirror stood in one corner next to a stand with a basin and pitcher. The doors to the closet stood open and Viola could see clothes her size already in place. Sarah stood expectantly, waiting for Viola to say something, but after a few minutes she began to excuse herself. "I'm sure you're tired from your journeys, then, so I'll just leave you to rest until dinner." Viola didn't even acknowledge her departure.

After the maid left, Viola went to the window seat and found that the view was partially of a garden and also of the street. She sat for a long time but saw no one on the street nor anyone in the garden. Gradually darkness began to settle in and Viola could see the reflection of lights from downstairs spill out into the garden. The smell of roast beef wafted up the stairs and into her room and she could hear chairs scraping back from a table. She waited, uncertain what to do.

After an hour she heard doors closing along the corridor and got up to close her own. No one had come for her nor brought any dinner to her room. She had been completely forgotten already. She climbed up onto the bed, still dressed, and lay her head on the velvet bag. Tomorrow she would petition her uncle to send her to a boarding school, something she had learned about from another young girl on the ship. This would clearly never be her home.

Chapter Thirty

The next morning when Arthur entered the kitchen to give the cook the daily orders, he was surprised to see Viola sitting at the table by herself eating a dish of milk and bread, still wearing the same dress from the previous day, her hair a mess of tangles and her eyes red. "Viola. Where's the cook? What are you eating?" He fired questions at her. "You didn't come down for dinner. Are you ill?"

"I didn't know to come down to dinner," she said quietly. She pointed to her poor breakfast. "But I got hungry."

Arthur was clearly furious and yelled for the cook who scurried into the kitchen. "Fix my niece a proper breakfast, will you! And call the others to the parlor afterwards, including my sister. Tell her I demand that she attend." The cook was clearly astounded but set about fixing eggs and a slice of ham for Viola who sat guarding her plate throughout her uncle's eruption. A proper English breakfast was set before her in minutes and the cook left the room to find the other staff members.

Within less than a half an hour they were assembled around the parlor table, Vivian included. Arthur was still angry and it showed. His face reddened as he slammed the table. "I will be dashed if I have to employ a governess to attend to my niece when I have all of you," he said, gesturing to the group, "who can clearly devote a moment of their day to see to it that she is at least fed and properly dressed." He started with Sarah who had shown Viola to her room yesterday. "I expect you will see to it that Viola has water for bathing morning and night." His attention turned next to a woman Vivian insisted on keeping in their employ to do nothing more than mending and ironing. "You will lay out proper clothes for her in the morning and bed clothes at night." The woman nodded her assent. "I myself shall take responsibility for her education until such time as we decide her best options." He reserved his harshest command for his sister. "Viola is your niece as well as my own, and you will see to it that she has a proper, welcoming home here," and he added in a lower voice, "just as I have provided for you all these years." Viola kept her head bowed through the entire meeting, ashamed at being the cause of so much turmoil. "Now, the rest of you, if you see my niece roaming about, I expect you to ask her if she needs anything, anything at all, from you. I'm sure I have made myself very clear, have I not?" Everyone mumbled but no one spoke up. Later two of the maids would say it was the most forceful — and the most attractive — they had ever seen Mr. McDougall act.

From that day forward, Viola's life was one of indulgence; she wanted for nothing. Unused to children as they were, her uncle and aunt had treated her as a miniature adult and she had full run of their home in London and a manor house in Ireland. When her uncle entertained various opera stars and actors, Viola would stay in the parlor listening intently until way past a child's bedtime. She also pulled books from her uncle's shelves and insisted he read to her for hours on end. Viola laughed to herself thinking about what a spectacle they made when they boarded a ship or a train to travel almost anywhere. Three porters had to be enlisted to carry Viola's trunks full of dresses, embellishments, dolls, and of course, her precious sketch books and fine pencils. It was as if the Queen herself were setting off to see her kingdom.

As Viola matured under Arthur's guidance he still thought back to their time on the ship and realized what uncertainties Viola must have harbored.

"You little monkey! Get down from there right now!"

Viola had managed to climb to a small promontory on the ship's deck right below where the captain stood at the great wheel, steering the ship and scanning the horizon. She had been sitting cross-legged, sketching him for the better part of an hour and was so close to putting the finishing touches on his beard. "But uncle…"

Arthur McDougall was adamant. "I won't hear another word." He looked exasperated but amused at the same time. "Do I have to lock you in your cabin for the remainder of the journey?"

That threat had the desired effect and Viola scrambled down the rope riggings, handing her sketch book to her uncle before she jumped the last few feet to the deck. She closed her eyes and could still see the captain's beard and the way he tilted his head, so she knew she could finish the sketch later in the cabin and perhaps present it to him that night at dinner. *"Well, all right, see, I'm here just dandy,"* she said, clasping her uncle's hand. She had drawn quick sketches of many of the sailors who, although few spoke English, thanked her nevertheless and seemed quite impressed with the ten-year-old's talent. Bestowing her sketch on the captain would be the feather in her cap.

"What am I going to do with you, young lady?" They walked hand-in-hand along the deck. Arthur never failed to tip his hat to the ladies aboard, many of whom gossiped about whether the woman he was traveling with was truly his sister. And where had they gotten the precocious little girl? *"Your mother would have already given you a royal spanking, I suppose,"* but then he regretted mentioning her mother at all and hugged her quickly. *"Now, it's nearly tea time. You go let your aunt fix your hair and clean you up like the little lady you should be. Off you go."*

Viola had inherited her mother's abundant blonde hair, thick tangles of curls that refused to be subdued by any technique her aunt attempted. Usually, she gave up and stuck a bow in it, sighing and throwing up her hands. Today her aunt would have a real challenge as Viola had spent hours sitting out in the sea breeze, the bow her aunt had placed that morning having been blown into the sea. Viola cringed at the thought of all the yanking and tugging of the comb that awaited her below deck. She wondered if her new friend, Kathleen, went through the same tribulations with her long locks.

"Please, uncle, why can't we invite her to dine with us one night," she had implored a few days earlier. *"She must be so lonely."* Her uncle seemed to consider the idea as he too had noticed the young woman traveling alone, not a

common sight in those days, and especially not on a sailing ship bound halfway around the world. The next afternoon he made up his mind after seeing her alone at dinner once again. He asked a steward to present his carefully phrased note to the woman the next morning and hoped, at least for the sake of his niece, for a positive response.

Arthur smiled to himself. Just that week he had seen a playbill on which Kathleen's name was listed as the costume designer. The young woman was well on her way to success, and in a way, his niece was partly responsible.

Chapter Thirty-One

Kathleen declined Arthur's first invitation to dine with him and his sister, but later fell victim to Viola's persuasion, and the fact that Viola had stolen Kathleen's sketch book and was holding it hostage until she came to dinner. While Kathleen was used to wearing her vivid red hair loose in curls over her shoulders, that night she took great pains with both her hair and her gown. She gathered her red mane and carefully braided it, then wove dark green velvet ribbons through it as she piled the braids on her head. It was quite an elegant style, something she had seen a woman wear in San Francisco when Philip had taken her to the club where he was playing the piano. The ribbons matched the color of her gown exactly. She clearly impressed everyone when she entered the salon for a before dinner aperitif, but no one more so than Viola. For the remainder of the journey, the two were inseparable. Each recognized the artist in the other.

And they had something else in common. Viola had no one to confide in since her mother's death; her aunt was simply too old and too detached to understand a girl of ten. While Kathleen was already twice married, widowed and a former mother, she was still in her early twenties and also had had no one to really talk to since leaving the Irish settlement in Virginia City. One morning Viola confided to Kathleen, "I hope they send me away to a boarding school when we get back to London. At least there I'd be living with other girls."

"But don't you think you'd be lonely?" Kathleen inquired.

"I'd be lonelier living with them," Viola gestured toward Arthur and Vivian who were sitting together finishing their coffees and going over lists of what would have to be ordered for the London house when they at last returned. "I know they care about me, especially Uncle Arthur, but..."

Kathleen looked pensive. "I'm not sure where I will live when I get back to Dublin, but I'm determined to make the best of it, and you must, too." Viola looked downcast, so Kathleen continued. "Have you ever heard anyone say, 'You must bloom where you are planted.'?"

Viola giggled, seeing herself stuck in a giant flower pot, and immediately set out to draw just that. Her talent was obvious and her imagination was just beginning to flourish. Kathleen hoped that if Viola were sent to a boarding school, it wouldn't be with a bunch of strict Catholic nuns who would discourage the kind of foolishness ten-year-old girls were famous for and would squelch any sort of independent thinking, likely with the whack of a ruler.

"Do you think you'll marry again when you return to Ireland?"

Kathleen was startled by the question. "Oh, I can't imagine, truly. I want to live on my own and make my own way in life."

"But who will take care of you?" Viola persisted.

Kathleen drew herself up and with her shoulders back and head held high, pronounced, "I shall take care of myself."

Viola eventually got her wish to attend boarding school, or actually several boarding schools, and then to enjoy private tutoring after that.

When the ship docked in London there were a myriad of details to attend to in getting the house in order, unpacking trunks, and for Arthur, reestablishing his business routine. Viola bided her time, however, and waited until a quiet afternoon when she could approach her uncle in his study. "Sir," she began, "I've been thinking about my schooling and such."

"Oh, I know, Viola, dear. I shall attend to it before the week is out."

"Actually, uncle, I would like to ask you to find me a boarding school where I could be with other girls my age and not be such a burden to you and auntie."

Arthur tried to mask his relief, but he knew fully well that his sister didn't relish the thought of having the precocious girl underfoot. He beckoned Viola to a chair by his desk. "You mustn't think you're any sort of burden to us," he smiled kindly, "but, of course, your happiness and your education are most important to us. If that's what you want…"

Viola smiled broadly. "Oh, yes it is! And I promise I'll study and learn so much, you'll be proud."

"We're already proud of you. Look how brave you were on our recent journey." He slid his glasses down his nose and peered at her owl-like. "I shall make some inquiries tomorrow about the best school for you, unless, of course, you already have one selected."

Viola began cautiously. "I wouldn't want to presume that your judgment would be better than mine, uncle, but given that I do want to learn about the arts, I think a school in France might be best, don't you?"

"France! Well, you'd be so far from us, we'd only see you on holiday." But, he had to admit the girl was right. France would be so much more nurturing of her artistic leanings than the staid English schools would be. "Have you heard of such a school?"

Of course, she had. "One of the ladies on the ship said two of her daughters had attended the Lycee Cevenol, and they had matured to be quite proper young ladies. I hope it's not frightfully expensive." She looked appropriately downcast.

"I suppose if it will make a proper young lady out of you, no expense should be spared," he teased her. "I will look into it and if it seems appropriate, perhaps we can make a small visit there in the coming weeks."

Viola sprang into his arms. "You're the best uncle ever. I promise I won't disappoint you."

He chuckled when she left the library. Clearly she had been planning this for some time, although he was somewhat surprised that she didn't suggest a school in Ireland closer to her only friend, Kathleen. Of course, an education by the nuns in Ireland would hardly be what Viola would choose.

Chapter Thirty-Two

Viola went off to boarding school a stylishly-dressed, always well-groomed and coiffed girl coming into her teens with all the turbulence of the age. The first school, the one she had selected in France, did indeed provide a liberal education, far broader than her uncle might have anticipated. After a few hours of classes each day the girls were free, indeed even encouraged, to roam the streets of Paris, visiting artists' studios or taking in performances. The reasoning was that they would be exposed to all kinds of art, but they were also exposed to all kinds of artists. One of them became Viola's first lover when she was only fourteen.

Alton was not an artist himself but an assistant to a famous painter, preparing his canvasses, mixing pigments, and keeping his studio orderly. When the artist was not in residence Alton had free use of his studio and adjoining apartment, and he often used it to impress the young ladies of Paris; he assured them he could arrange an introduction to the artist quite easily. When he spied Viola one afternoon looking through the gallery window, he was immediately captivated and stepped quickly to the door to invite her into the studio.

Viola told him that she was studying at the Lycee Cevenol and had plans herself to become an artist. Perhaps he could show his employer her sketches? Alton recognized the opportunity this impressionable young girl presented immediately. "I would be most pleased to do so," he told Viola, taking her hand and leading her to the private salon. "Perhaps you will have a glass of wine with me?"

She had been drinking a little wine since she was perhaps twelve and agreed that a glass would be lovely. They had two, some cheeses and bread. He kissed her on both cheeks when she was ready to leave, then seeing that it had already become dark, walked her back to her school, kissing her again and making her promise to return the next afternoon, with her sketch book. In recalling the time years later, she wondered, how naïve could she have been?

She did return the next afternoon, and the one after that, but the artist himself was nowhere to be seen. "Detained," Alton explained, "by one of his patrons." On the fourth afternoon Alton took her to bed. He was tender, patient and affectionate, in a word…a crushing, disappointing bore. Viola and her classmates had talked endlessly about sex and what it would be like (or what it had been like for some of the older girls), but this was hardly the fireworks Viola was expecting. She tucked her sketchbook under her arm and left the studio that early evening, feeling as though she had just completed some chore that had to be done, and not planning to return.

Not long after her encounter in the artist's studio, Viola resolved to leave Paris and France entirely. She was tired of the endless posturing by people who claimed to be artists, when, in fact, the only real talent they had was for deception. She told her uncle on a visit home, "I don't feel that my artistic talents are being taken seriously." He smiled indulgently but privately thought perhaps she was intimidated by the arts milieu in the sophisticated city. Arthur had spent a great deal of time in France and knew just how competitive artists could be.

"Well, dear, where do you think you will flourish then?" He half expected her to say Ireland in a bid to be closer to her friend, Kathleen, but she surprised him.

"I think I should like to go to Italy, although not to Rome, perhaps Florence," Viola declared. "The light there is said to be extraordinary, and I believe the Italian people would be warmer, more welcoming."

"The Italian people may be that," Arthur admitted, "but any proper school we could find for you in Italy will be run by the nuns. I wonder if you've considered that?"

"Yes, uncle, of course, and that is why I propose we do something different about my education."

He watched her, always amazed at her precocious intelligence and wondered just where it came from. "Something different? How so?"

"I propose not to go to a school per se," Viola began.

"Not go to school! Well that is preposterous," Arthur responded immediately. "You're only fifteen years old, and young lady, you have much to learn. Any girl would be grateful to have your advantages."

"Oh, I am grateful, uncle. Don't misunderstand me." She poured a little more sherry into his glass and pulled her chair closer to his. "What I think would be best is if you were to hire a tutor for me, or perhaps more than one, and I could live with an Italian family, taking private lessons but having time to paint." With a sly look she continued, "I'm certain with all your contacts in the opera world, you could find just such a family who would be just as protective of me as you are." She did all but bat her eyelashes at him.

Arthur felt trapped. He couldn't admit that indeed he could find any number of such families, nor could he give in so easily to her outlandish request. "I will have to give this some thought, Viola, really." He came up with the spark of an idea. "And, you don't even speak Italian. How would you overcome that?"

She answered him in a torrent of passionate Italian. She had been studying and preparing to make her request. Why was he surprised? "All right. I shall make some inquiries as to an appropriate placement for you. Now, why don't you go get your sketch book and show me what you have been working on?"

Viola skipped from the studio and Arthur poured himself more sherry. He had been out-smarted by a fifteen-year-old girl...again. He set about making the appropriate arrangements and in a few short weeks, on the anniversary of her sixteenth birthday, Viola was on her way to Italy. As she would always think back to it, the countryside was spectacular but her 'placement' less so. She was in awe at the beauty of the grand stone villa outside of Florence.   Her carriage wound its way through miles of grape orchards flowing over gently rolling hills until the villa came in sight, situated on a plateau overlooking the vineyards. Her host was standing on the steps waiting to welcome her.   Viola stepped from the carriage and walked directly to him, presenting her cheek to be kissed, in the French tradition. Instead, this gaunt, tall, raven-haired man took her hands and drew her to him, gently kissing the side of her neck instead.

"Welcome to Palazzo del Lupo," he intoned in a deep baritone. "We are so pleased to have you as our...guest."

Viola answered with the appropriate pleasantries, in Italian, but wracked her mind. *Lupo*? *Lupo*? That was...wolf? Wolf! She felt very uncomfortable after his unconventional greeting, but the name of the magnificent villa sent her imagination into a tailspin, admittedly not a difficult task for a sixteen-year-old. She composed herself enough to ask, "So, are the wolves a problem here?"

He smiled very slightly. "Oh, those were different times, signorita, different times indeed."   He motioned to the carriage driver to unload her baggage, then showed her to her suite of rooms himself, keeping his hand in the small of her back or her shoulder at all times. The rooms were lovely and full of light, Viola had to admit. The bags were brought up and a young lady arrived to help her unpack. "It is our custom to dine late," her host explained, "but I will have some refreshments sent up so you may rest." He inclined his head. "I will see you tonight at nine." He backed slowly out of the room, never letting his eyes leave her.

Chapter Thirty-Three

"And when shall I meet my tutor?" Viola inquired of her host, Signor Marco Malatesta.

"Oh, I thought your uncle would have informed you," he said slowly, appraising her as he answered. "I will be tutoring you myself. It will be an education like no other."

Viola was surprised but did not want to seem ungrateful. "You know my principal interest is art," she began. He continued to look at her with his piercing black eyes.

"I assure you, my interest is the same." He leaned forward. "I can help you use art to bring beauty to canvas, to music, and to life." He stroked her wrist and she found it impossible to pull away. The serving girl entered with a silver tray bearing cheeses, seasoned flatbreads and a decanter of wine, produced in his vineyards. Viola noticed she was shaking when she set the tray down but felt the Signor had the same effect on her. The Signor motioned her away and poured the wine himself, offering a glass to Viola but running his index finger over her hand as she accepted it. "I believe tomorrow we will spend the morning in my library so that you may familiarize yourself with the works that are there. Then, we can make a list of what you must start with. You can tell me what you might already have been exposed to."

The plan sounded reasonable to Viola, but she persisted. "I look forward to that, of course, but I also need time to draw and to paint." She hesitated. "I rather hoped for a tutor in drawing and painting and not just in the...academic interests."

He smiled benignly. "When you tour my home, dear, please look at the signatures on the paintings. Many of these masterpieces were done by my own hand."

"Well, I didn't mean to imply..." Viola was embarrassed and said no more but she resolved to tour the massive villa with a more careful eye. She excused herself and returned to her rooms, happy to see the young serving girl there tidying up the suite. Viola began slowly in Italian, "Good afternoon. We haven't really been introduced, but I'm Viola McDougall, and you are?"

The girl mumbled, "Maria Fontina, at your service, miss."

"As the only two women here, I hope we will be friends," Viola started.

Maria looked surprised. "Oh, but we are not the only two. There is the Signor's wife, although..."

"Oh, I didn't realize. Is she traveling? I haven't seen her."

"No, you wouldn't." The girl gathered up the linens and made a hasty exit from Viola's room, leaving her to wonder. Where was the wife and why wouldn't she see her? The place was becoming increasingly strange indeed, but she dismissed her misgivings and looked forward to the next day.

Viola heard the rooster announce the arrival of the day and she could already tell from the light in her room that it would be glorious, a perfect day for taking her paints and easel out into the vineyards, something she had yet to do. She threw back the bed clothes and was surprised to see two long strands of red hair, clearly not her own. At first she thought it was some kind of sign from Kathleen, but she dismissed the foolishness and attributed the hairs to one of the girls who do the laundry for the villa. But the other curious thing was that the top two buttons on her nightgown were undone. Had she loosened them in her sleep? She checked herself and didn't find anything else amiss but was somehow reluctant to dismiss her suspicions. She pulled the cord next to her bed to summon Maria to help her make her toilet and dress.

When the shy serving girl entered Viola's chambers, Viola dragged her to the window. "Look at this wonderful, beautiful day! We must hurry and go out to enjoy it." Maria looked doubtful but Viola was lost in her own enthusiasm. "You come with me. We'll take a light lunch with us and spend the day. Maybe we'll be naughty and take some wine, too." Maria looked even more reluctant but Viola was not to be denied.

Within the hour the two young women were following a path leading away from the villa and out into the rolling vineyards. Viola spotted a promontory with a large oak tree and a commanding view of the valley. She immediately began walking toward it, chattering in Italian to Maria in hopes of relaxing the girl (and getting her to gossip, perhaps, about the goings-on in the villa). Maria helped Viola set up her easel, then leaned against the oak herself, enjoying the sunshine on her face. With her eyes closed, she didn't notice the approach of Signor Malatesta until he was nearly upon them.

"And am I paying you to nap beneath a tree?" he snapped at the girl, causing Viola to drop her brush in alarm. Maria was already on her feet and backing away from him.

Viola had to intervene. "Please, Signor, I asked her to accompany me. I am afraid of the wolves that are so famous around here." She looked appropriately contrite.

"I assure you, you are perfectly safe outside the villa," he told Viola, but the look in Maria's eyes said otherwise. Viola would have to get the girl alone sometime and pry the story out of her! "Please, don't let me disturb your work," he turned to Viola. Maria was nearly running back to the villa. He moved closer to Viola and began examining her painting. "This is quite nice. It does capture the light, and yet..."

Viola looked at him questioningly, still upset by his sudden appearance and the terror he obviously struck in Maria. He picked up her brush and handed it back to her. When she resumed her brush stroke, he moved behind her and took her hand, moving her fingers slightly on the brush. "Like this," he whispered in her ear, directing her brush stroke. "Relax your fingers and let the brush just flow," he continued as she added another layer of green paint to the foreground. "Just so." Viola could hardly breathe, much less relax anything, but she followed his instructions and found that indeed, the paint did seem to go on more smoothly and her hand did not feel cramped. He stayed where he was, close behind her, until the afternoon light began to fade.

That night a fierce storm blew in, rattling all the windows in the villa and forcing the vineyard workers out to tie up the vines and protect them as much as possible. Viola shivered in bed beneath her covers, not so much from the cold as from the cacophony of noises made by the old villa. The cypress trees swayed and brushed the stone walls, creating a scratching sound as if some beast were trying to get in. At some point, however, Viola slept only to awaken with more red hairs on her bed clothes. She would have to seek out the laundress and ask her to be more careful! But the red hairs were not the only thing left on her bed. There was a doll.

Chapter Thirty-Four

When at last the storm blew through, Viola ventured out of her rooms and down to the kitchen where she hoped to find Maria. She took the doll with her. When she entered the kitchen, one of the cooks who had apparently served Signor Malatesta for years spotted Viola and had a smile halfway to her mouth when she saw what Viola was carrying. The smile turned to a look of horror, and she rushed to take Viola's arm and lead her quickly to a separate pantry room. *"O, mio dio!"* She had heard Viola speaking halting Italian with the Signor, so she asked cautiously, *"Dove l'hai trovato?"* She pointed to the doll.

Viola pulled the doll to her chest. "I found it at the foot of my bed this morning."

The cook made the sign of the cross and quickly shut the pantry door. "You must not let the Signor see you with this!"

"Perche?" Viola wanted to know why the doll had to be kept such a secret. She stood blocking the doorway out of the pantry, determined to hear the answer. After a moment, the cook dusted off two large crates and motioned for Viola to take a seat on one of them while she took the other. She told Viola it was *una storia lunga*, but Viola insisted she tell her the whole tale, regardless of how long it was.

Over the next hour the cook told Viola about the early days of the villa which the Malatestas built right after their marriage. The Signor drove the workers mercilessly to complete it before the birth of their first daughter, and it was to be named Palazzo del Caterina in her honor. The baby was born and was a miniature version of her mother with beautiful blue eyes and a shocking amount of auburn-red hair. Right from the start, the cook said, the girl had a charming personality and an inquisitive mind. She was always "exploring" and making up little games to entertain herself. Her mother and father looked at her in awe of this perfect creation that had blessed their lives so completely.

The cook wiped her eyes and the tone of her voice changed completely, taking on a tone of dark resignation. "It was in Caterina's third year that the terrible tragedy befell them." Caterina was in the main hall of the palazzo and she had opened the great carved door, pretending she was a princess or some such nonsense, the cook said. While the door let the sunshine in, it also carried the little girl's scent outside. Here the cook again made the sign of the cross and Viola pressed her to continue with the story. "No one knew there was a marauding band of wolves passing through the estate," the cook explained. "The smell of precious little Catarina lured them as would an orphaned lamb." The cook said she was in the kitchen, of course, and did not see what happened, but she heard the screams.

"The wolf came right into the great hall, flanked by two others, and they pounced on the little girl, dragging her from the villa," the cook continued, wringing her hands. The Signor and Signorina were in the gallery upstairs and when they heard the screaming they raced to the balcony to see their daughter being dragged outside. The Signor ran down the stairs and out to the yard, but he was too late; the wolves had already carried their prey out to the vineyards. Their howls could be heard for hours, but those howls were nowhere near as terrible as those of the Signorina. The cook's shoulders shook as she told this part.

The Signor ordered all the men working on the estate to assemble and he armed them all, telling them to find every last wolf on the estate and bring their carcasses to the drive in front of the villa. The men found more than a dozen wolves later that day and into the night. The pile of carcasses grew until finally no more howls were heard. The Signor lit the pile on fire and stayed there nearly till dawn when at last they were all consumed by the flames.

Viola was breathless listening to the tale. "And he renamed the villa the Palazzo del Lupo?" she asked incredulously.

"No, that is what the villagers called it from that point on," the cook conceded. "At last he did accept the name and said it served as a reminder not just of his precious daughter but also of his own dominance over the wolves. There has never been another one seen around here." The cook shook her head.

Viola had been clutching the doll. "So, this was Catarina's doll?" The cook nodded. "Who would put it in my room?"

The cook stood and paced the tiny room, finally turning to Viola and staring at her solemnly. "The Signorina."

"But surely she's…" Viola didn't know how to finish the sentence.

"She never recovered from seeing her little girl being dragged out of the house." The cook sniffed. "She went quite mad, of course, but the Signor insisted that she stay in their home." Her eyes turned upward. "She has her rooms and is looked after, but only one serving girl attends her—and, of course, the Signor. He sees her."

"But still, that doesn't explain this," Viola said, holding out the doll.

The cook shrugged her shoulders but after a moment said, "Perhaps she sees you as a grown-up version of her daughter in one way and wants to remember you as a girl, so she gives you the doll and checks on you at night." That would explain the red hairs, Viola realized immediately.

"I should meet her, then," Viola said impulsively. "And thank her for looking out for me."

"No! You must not." She leaned toward Viola. "The Signor would never allow it and you must not mention it to him." She added, "I think it's best that you leave the Palazzo as soon as you can." The cook handed her a dish towel and told her to cover the doll for the journey back to her rooms. "Tell no one of this," she admonished her.

Confused and concerned, Viola retreated from the pantry and made her way quietly to her rooms, putting the doll back on the bed. Perhaps if she could remain awake that night...

Later that afternoon Maria came to her rooms to summon her to the study; the Signor wished to have a word with her. Viola tidied up her hair and descended to meet with the gentleman of the house. He had their customary tray of wine and antipasto set out in the study. He rose and assisted her into a chair. *"Buon giorno."* They exchanged greetings in a smattering of Italian but then he switched to English. "I think today we should tour the art work in the villa and I will give you my thoughts on techniques, styles and art as fashion."

She found herself looking at him, thinking of the story she'd heard earlier and wondering how he could have stayed in the villa at all. "Yes, that would be lovely," she agreed. They finished their wine and set out on a leisurely tour of the galleries in the house. He was indeed very knowledgeable about art and had collected many fine pieces, although his own works were usually given more prominent exposure. At last they came to a small anteroom and Viola spied a painting not hung on the wall but simply leaning against it. She gasped. "Why that is the most beautiful landscape I have ever seen!" The painting radiated a subtle gold and peach light and there seemed to be thousand shades of lavender and bronze, all depicting a canyon unlike anything she had ever seen.

"Well, that," the Signor said, "is the work of a casual acquaintance who toured the western part of America and became quite enamored." Viola stood holding the painting, absolutely enthralled. "I personally prefer more definite colors and scenery such as can be found in Italy, or even in France, but I suppose this has some appeal."

"Some appeal? Why it's wondrous," Viola murmured. "I should love to have such a painting."

He looked at the young woman and clearly saw her enthusiasm. "Then it is yours, my dear."

She started to protest his gift but found she simply could not. She had heard Kathleen and others aboard the ship talk about the Grand Canyon, but she never imagined a place like this could exist or that any painter could capture its magnificence.

Chapter Thirty-Five

After lying awake night after night in hopes of meeting the Signorina, Viola was forced to agree with the cook that she should indeed leave the villa. She contacted her uncle and informed him she would be moving on to France and would find her own arrangements there. She thanked Signor Malatesta profusely upon leaving and could see in his dark eyes that he had guessed the true reason behind her departure. Nevertheless, he stood by his promise to allow her to take the painting of the Grand Canyon as his parting gift to her. With that and a half-dozen trunks she departed for the countryside outside Paris. An agent had found her a small pensionne which he assured her would be perfect for an artist such as herself. When she arrived, she saw that it was indeed perfect, if small, just two rooms sublet in a home in the countryside. But the rooms had the essential feature she demanded — plenty of sunshine.

She would never live anywhere but in the sun which was as important to her as blood to her heart. She had positioned her sleeping pallet so that she would be struck by the first rays of sunshine each morning. On the rare mornings when the clouds hid the sun, she would let herself lie in bed for a few hours, thinking about her old friend, Kathleen, perhaps, and missing her aunt and uncle in London. She felt guilty about not seeing any of them in quite some time, but she simply could not tolerate the dreariness of that industrial city where smoke from the coal fires obliterated what little sunlight there might have been.

She had the soul of an artist, after all, and craved the light.

But enough reminiscing for one morning! The sun was already climbing in the sky. Viola leapt from the pallet and hastily rearranged the bedding. She used the chamber pot, then stepped to the sink to do some minimal ablutions before slipping on her shoes, stepping into a plain cotton dress and grabbing her painter's apron from its hook on the door. She could smell bread baking as she descended the stairs from her rooms to the kitchen, and as always, there was a lively conversation in progress between the landlady and one of the other boarders. Viola spoke French fluently, of course, having attended a number of private boarding schools in Paris. She chose to ignore their discussion about the proper way to age cheese, helping herself to couple of biscuits, some strawberry preserves and a thick slice of ham; she would save the ham and a biscuit for lunch later in the day, tucking them into the pocket of her apron.

"*Bon jour, madame,*" she addressed her landlady, and pointing to the food, "*merci.*" Before she could be snared into a conversation, she smiled briefly and hurried out to the coach house. Viola had designed the perfect artist's companion, a wagon about three feet long, big enough to hold her collapsible easel and a canvas, with compartments for paint, brushes and rags. One side slid down and off, and when placed on the top of the wagon served as a perfect table on which she could enjoy her lunch, or it could be a bench if she simply wanted to sit and contemplate her subject for the day. When she had first shown her sketched design to the pensionne's resident handyman, he had laughed and dismissed her, but later at the midday meal asked to have another look at her drawing. Two days later the wagon was finished. He had even taken the liberty of painting it an airy light blue and seemed quite proud of his work. Viola suspected that before long many of the women in the village would have something similar to take to the markets, but no matter that her design was being copied. She wondered if Kathleen felt the same way when she saw her exclusive dress designs being copied and displayed in shop windows.

Viola towed the little wagon out through the surrounding apple orchard to a little promontory that looked down on the village and countryside. She had sketched the gnarled apple trees and the rolling green and gold hills many times, but the whole effort was unfulfilling. Viola needed to draw and paint live people and it was difficult to persuade people who had to work for their living to sit idly for hours as she sketched them. She loved the unique Gallic appearance of the men and women who lived here, but usually it was only an old woman who would allow her the time she needed. Yes, she reflected, there was only this one thing missing from her life — people.

On the rare occasions that Viola allowed herself a few moments of self-pity, she would open her trunk and rifle through her sketch books. Although she sometimes winced at how amateurish her early sketches were, they still brought to life the natives she had seen in the port cities, the colorful sailors and their antics, and of course, the lovely Kathleen. She knew what Kathleen would advise her: "If it's people you need, then go find them." The French were fond of their time spent at the cafes, and Viola knew that's where she should go, but something held her back.

Chapter Thirty-Six

Viola avoided going to the street cafés in the village because there were just too many distractions—and most of them were men. They either tried to crudely flirt with her, or they disparaged her sitting idly at a café when she should have been home caring for her husband and her babies. She shuddered at the thought and wondered if perhaps that was something else she had learned from Kathleen: Not all women were destined to be mothers. She also did not want her undeniable talent to be recognized. Viola had carefully set up lucrative arrangements with galleries in Paris and London that she did not want jeopardized by someone recognizing her work and revealing her as a woman. It would minimize everything she had accomplished.

When Viola met with the gallery owners to show her work, she was careful always to refer to 'the artist' and never to herself. She would not reveal the artist's identity, she explained, as 'the artist' demanded absolute privacy to continue to produce such dazzling works of art. At first the gallery owners were resistant, but then they saw a way to exploit the secret identity of 'the artist'. Dinner parties in those cities often included conversations about just who 'the artist' might be, and Viola had heard of more than one occasion when someone claimed to indeed be V. McD! But demand continued and prices continued to rise.

Anyone unfamiliar with Viola's upbringing might have been surprised that an artist also possessed the mind of a businessperson. All those hours of sitting at her uncle's side while he negotiated deals with opera singers and other entertainers hadn't been wasted on the impressionable girl. And, she also recalled Kathleen's haggling with wharfside traders for beads, feathers and cloth. When Kathleen returned to the ship it was always with a satisfied smile in place. The one concession Viola did allow was to have the proceeds from her sales deposited in her uncle's account, not that she couldn't have managed them herself; it simply reassured her uncle that her financial needs were being met. Of course, this led to the amusing accusation that her uncle, in fact, was 'the artist'. Why, Arthur couldn't even draw a bowl of fruit and have anyone puzzle out what it was!

Nevertheless, Viola did occasionally tote her sketch pad and sheaf of pencils into the village in hopes of observing a particularly interesting face in the crowd. She was always careful, however, to keep a simplistic drawing of a flower cart tucked in her sketch pad that she could quickly pull out and use to cover her actual work if anyone approached her. There was one man in particular who tried to engage her in conversation whenever she visited the village square. He was polite and well-dressed, introducing himself as Beaumont Montrose, and he didn't attempt to peek at her drawing. After one such encounter, she asked her landlady if she knew the gentlemen but wasn't prepared for her response.

"Beaumont Montrose spoke to you in the village?" Viola's landlady was incredulous. "And you didn't even know who he was!"

"How would I know? You know I rarely go into the village."

"Monsieur Montrose is *tres magnifique!*" Her landlady motioned Viola to a chair in the kitchen while she herself continued kneading dough for that night's bread. "He is the richest man in the province. All of the grape vines you see for miles and miles grow on land he owns. He owns the bank in town. And the mill." Her kneading became more vigorous. "Every lady for miles around would do anything to capture even a glance from him, and here he talks to you and you act like it's an everyday occurrence."

Viola was beginning to feel a little annoyed. "If he's so wonderful, why doesn't he have a wife and a brood of children then?"

The landlady's face dropped. "Well, he had a wife. It was a tragedy." She piled the dough in a bowl and covered it with a cloth, setting it aside to rise. "She went to Paris to shop for new gowns for the season and when she came out of her hotel, she was attacked by a common thief who threw her to the ground." The landlady sniffed a little. "Sadly, she hit her head on the steps to the hotel and never opened her eyes again."

"That is sad."

"Oh, but that's not all of it. Monsieur Montrose brought her back to the manor house here and sat by her side, day and night. He wouldn't let any of the servants tend to her and did everything himself. It must have been more than a fortnight until one evening she took her last breath, never once awakening to tell him goodbye." The landlady sunk into a chair across from Viola. "And when her packages were delivered from Paris, he found that she had bought baby clothes. He went mad with grief."

"Well, I suppose he would," Viola agreed thoughtfully. She thought about telling her landlady about Kathleen's story. Now there was a sad tale.

"But I think him speaking to you may bode well," her landlady said slyly. "Perhaps this means he is no longer in mourning." She stood up and appraised Viola. "I think you do bear some resemblance to his departed Josette. Surely you could afford a decent frock, something nicer than this drab little thing," she said, plucking at Viola's sleeve. Viola could just imagine her landlady's shock if she were to learn how many dress creations by the noted stylist, Kathleen Evans, Viola had turned down! Drab indeed.

Viola left her landlady to finish her chores and returned to her own rooms. She smoothed the folds of her dress and had to admit, it was drab and had become rather shabby as well, frayed at the bottom hem. And her hair was a virtual rat's nest of unmanaged curls. What did the *tres magnifique* Monsier Montrose see in her in the first place? She had always been attractive to men—and attracted to them as well, but her artistic zeal had overtaken her passions as a woman, it appeared. Would Monsier Montrose reignite her passion? Viola couldn't believe she was even thinking about him that way on the basis of two short conversations.

Chapter Thirty-Seven

Viola retired to her room, thinking about the discussion she had endured with her landlady and wondered when such a change had occurred in herself. After a time of sitting near the window, long after the sun had gone down, she shook herself to dismiss the chill that had settled on her just thinking about the past. She always felt that Kathleen had a presence who watched over her but felt certain that presence was benign and somehow protective. Viola never had any such illusions about the presence she believed she had acquired in Italy. She pulled a shawl around her shoulders and went back down to the kitchen, asking her landlady to fill the clawfoot iron tub in her room with hot water. Perhaps it was time to do something about her appearance, and the warm water would go a long way toward driving away thoughts of her sojourn in Italy. Sometimes you learn the most from difficult experiences, she mused, but other times, well, they were just difficult experiences. While the water was being heated, Viola went out to the garden to gather eucalyptus leaves to make the water fragrant and a bit of rosemary as well. Mr. Montrose would see a new woman when she went to the village the next afternoon.

After the luxurious bath, which Viola admitted was long overdue, Viola slept well and awoke with a new appreciation of her own body and what she still might offer a man. She dressed carefully and descended the stairs to the kitchen, eagerly awaiting her landlady's reaction. No more drab, messy-haired, eccentric artist. Viola had a dark blue, form-fitting dress with a blue velvet choker at her neck and one of Kathleen's famous beaded bags over her shoulder. She looked like a lady planning an afternoon of shopping in Paris, not a simple trip to the local village square.

"*Mon dieu!*" her landlady exclaimed. "Such a change." She spun Viola around. "Let me see. I think perhaps someone has stolen our beloved Viola and left this lady in her place." Two of the other boarders smiled appreciatively and they all enjoyed a good laugh, Viola included. "I suppose you will be trying to catch the eye of a certain village gentleman?"

Viola colored and quickly responded, "I have no such thought in mind. I'm simply following your motherly advice to pay more attention to my apparel." She knew the landlady didn't believe her for a moment. She flounced out of the kitchen, flustered to have been so transparent.

She had last seen Mr. Montrose at a café overlooking the village square and found him there again. Thinking herself quite bold, she approached his table. "Monsieur, could we perhaps share this little spot in the sun?" He leapt to his feet and pulled out a chair for her with a little flourish. But, if he was impressed with her new appearance, he didn't let it show.

"So, mademoiselle, no sketching today?" Just as he had been last time he was impeccably attired in charcoal gray wool slacks, a gray and black silk vest and a topcoat of what looked like cashmere, also in black, but a lavender tie brightened up the whole ensemble, making it look less funereal. His mannerisms were reserved, however, much to Viola's disappointment. Was there any passion left in this man or did it die with his wife?

For his part, he could see that she had taken great care with her dress and her hair but found himself disappointed nonetheless. He could have his pick of the well-made-up, excessively coiffed ladies of the village, or even in Paris, for that matter. What he desired was a free spirit, something he thought he had detected in Viola when he first saw her roaming through the countryside with her little cart, completely unaware of anything but her own vision.

"I have decided to give my fingers a rest," Viola replied, stretching them out on the table in front of her. "I have been so focused on my work that perhaps I have neglected to notice some of the other...entertainments...here in the village." Emboldened as she was, she added, "And you, sir? No banking to attend to? No need to check on all of your interests?"

"My interests? I wonder what you know of them?" he said pensively.

"Only what my landlady, Mrs. LaFleur, has told me," Viola said, somewhat chastened. "She says the village is very much a better place due to all of your enterprises."

"Ah, Mrs. LaFleur. Quite the feisty one, her." He surprised Viola by laughing. "I knew her husband. He worked as a mill hand for me, a very industrious sort, but I think perhaps he drank too much wine in an effort to dull her tongue."

It was Viola's turn to laugh. "Yes, she can be quite definite about things."

"Definite. Yes, that's exactly the word for her." A waiter came by and brought them each a glass of wine, something Viola hadn't seen Mr. Montrose order. When the waiter had moved to another table he raised the glass in toast to Viola. "And you, are you definite as well?"

"Oh quite the contrary. I like to follow my passions wherever they take me." Viola blushed but seized the opportunity. "My only regret is living a somewhat cloistered life here. I enjoyed more freedom in Paris, of course, and even in Italy where I lived for a time."

Montrose brightened. Perhaps the free spirit he was seeking was only put away for the day. "You seem to move about quite freely here," he began. "It's not as if you have a chaperone watching your every move as many young ladies your age might have."

"Well, that much is true," Viola conceded. "It's just that I became used to living in a community of artists, free spirits all. Now my only companions are Mrs. LaFleur and her boarders. It's not at all the same."

"No, I suppose not." They sat companionably in the sun, watching the little activities of the village, each thinking there was perhaps more to the other than was first apparent.

Finally Monsier Montrose had to excuse himself to return to his duties at the bank, leaving Viola with another glass of wine and a promise to look for her again in the square. She finished the wine and watched the sun dip toward the horizon. As she gathered her belongings, she was surprised to see Beaumont (as he had told her to call him, or even 'Beau') hurrying toward her. "Miss Viola, you have a cable message," he said breathlessly, handing her a folded slip of yellow paper. "And also, it appears a rather large deposit has been made into your account today, also via cable."

She took the cable and read it with interest. It was from the largest gallery in Paris which had been showing her work. It seems that all of her paintings had now been sold, and they inquired, when would the artist have more? Demand was high. She looked at the deposit statement and gasped in delight. Beaumont was standing by awkwardly. Should he be her banker or her friend? Impulsively she hugged him. "Oh, this is just delightful. I am now free to pursue my dream."

"Your dream?"

"I shall tell you about it when we meet next—with champagne, however." She twirled on her heel and set off for the pensionne. On the way back she would stop and buy two fine hens for Mrs. LaFleur to prepare for dinner, or perhaps a section of prime beef with a bottle of red wine. She was giddy with all the thoughts going through her head and failed to notice the disappointment on Beaumont's face when she left him standing in the square.

Mrs. LaFleur outdid herself with dinner that night for Viola and the other boarders, cooking the prime beef to perfection. They all enjoyed the wine Viola had provided as well, and there was a lively exchange of stories as the dinner progressed, ending very satisfyingly with apple pie and a little tip of brandy for each. After the others had gone to their rooms, Viola lingered in the kitchen, not really helping but waiting for Mrs. LaFleur to complete the cleaning up. Mrs. LaFleur took an extra amount of time, enjoying watching Viola squirm with excitement. She expected that Viola wanted to talk about her afternoon with Monsier Montrose; the gossip had already reached Mrs. LaFleur, of course.

When she finally sat back down at the table, Viola burst out, "I wanted to tell you that I have been able to make certain…arrangements such that I will no longer be renting rooms from you, lovely as it has been."

Mrs. LaFleur was aghast, and not at the loss of rental income. "Why you've only known him for an afternoon! You can't possibly be thinking of..." Viola looked dumbfounded, then shocked, and lastly, amused.

"You foolish woman! This has nothing to do with Monsieur Montrose nor any other man," Viola huffed. "My financial circumstances are now such that I can plan travel to the States for a lengthy stay." She added, "I will be traveling by myself unless I can convince my dear friend, Kathleen, to join me in this grand adventure."

Mrs. LaFleur was still perseverating about the very desirable Monsieur Montrose, however. "But, won't he be terribly disappointed? You could perhaps..." She knew Viola was laughing behind her hand. "I know if I was your age I'd shock the whole village. Many think he's too prominent to take a mistress, but mark you, that's just the type who do!" Viola finally did laugh out loud and leaned across the kitchen farm table to take her landlady's hands.

"I know you just wish for my happiness, and believe me that is exactly what I will be pursuing. Now if there are dalliances along the way," she said slyly, awaiting the older lady's reaction, "well, that's just what happens."

Mrs. LaFleur flicked the dish cloth at her. "Off to your rooms you wicked, wicked girl!"

Chapter Thirty-Eight

Viola packed her belongings into two large trunks, taking special care to protect her beloved Grand Canyon painting. Even though she had been in France for less than a year, she felt sad at the thought of leaving the lush countryside and the few acquaintances she had made, especially her landlady. Viola found her sniffling on the morning she was to depart. "Oh, come now. You'll get another boarder that you can be a mother hen to," Viola tried teasing her, "one that won't be nearly as difficult as I have been."

"Oh you haven't been difficult at all," Mrs. LaFleur said. "Headstrong, yes." She dried her tears with a kitchen towel. "I still wish you would spend a little more time getting to know…"

"Yes, I know," Viola interrupted her. "You wish I would let the lovely Monsieur Montrose sweep me off my feet." She grabbed the woman and twirled her around. "You could dance at our wedding, then perhaps move into his villa to care for all our children." She could see by the look on the landlady's face that the scenario was exactly what she had been hoping for. "Instead perhaps you will get a letter from me one day saying I've fallen in love with a majestic Indian chief and am to live in teepee!" The shock on Mrs. LaFleur's face dissolved Viola into a fit of laughter.

Like many people in Europe, and France in particular, Mrs. LaFleur was fascinated by tales of the Wild West, of rampaging Indians carrying off white women, gun battles in the streets, and prospectors becoming millionaires overnight by discovering gold nuggets as big as hen's eggs. "Maybe a savage is just what you need," she said, flicking the dish towel at Viola. "I don't suppose an Indian chief would consent to your traipsing across the country just because you felt like it."

"I'm not traipsing, as you put it. I'm pursuing my dream of becoming a great artist and I must seek my inspiration." Viola realized how pompous she sounded, but there was more than a grain of truth in her statement. She had sent a cable to her uncle, asking him to meet her at his home in Ireland, and she had asked him to invite Kathleen there as well. She would endeavor to convince them both about the desire, no, actually, the *need* for her to go to the States, and particularly to the West. If Kathleen would accompany her, so much the better, but if she would not, Viola was determined to set out alone.

This determination had clearly shocked the poor Monsieur Montrose when she had informed him of her plans a few afternoons back, having met him at their usual place in the village. "Travel alone to the States! It's unseemly," he had protested. "Surely your uncle won't allow such a thing."

"It's not up to my uncle, or any other *man*," Viola said pointedly, "to *allow* me to do anything. I am quite my own person and if I choose to go to the States to pursue my art, then that is what I will do." She felt she was coming off a bit shrill and endeavored to soften it somewhat. "Of course, it would be lovely to have his blessing and to convince my greatest friend, Kathleen, to accompany me, but those decisions are theirs to make."

He sat mute for a few moments. "I regret our new friendship is coming to an end, it appears, but I have enjoyed it nonetheless. Perhaps I'll read about you in one of the New York newspapers." He grew more enthusiastic. "They seem quite keen on adventure stories and surely yours will be just that—an adventure." Viola nearly asked him to join her but she also recognized just how scandalous that would seem. And, to be honest, she wasn't all that entranced with him in the first place. He had found a profession that suited him as a banker, rather plodding and unimaginative, quite the opposite of her own tendencies. They parted with a hug and a kiss for each cheek.

Viola's trip to Ireland was uneventful as she stayed in her train compartment by herself for most of the journey and spent little time on deck for the short sailing from England to Ireland. Her uncle had made all the travel arrangements for her, so she had little to worry about. She made a few desultory sketches of her fellow travelers and toyed with one landscape of sheep dotting a green hillside, but mostly she used the time to plan. She planned her speech to her uncle and the one she would use to entreat Kathleen to join her, and she planned what supplies she would need to carry with her to America and across that great land. Adventure, indeed.

Chapter Thirty-Nine

Arthur had been spending more and more time at his country manor in Ireland and leaving the management of the London townhouse to Vivian. He was getting older, he acknowledged, and preferred the quiet of the countryside where he could conduct his business at a more leisurely pace. He was well-established enough that it wasn't necessary to attend every theater opening or operatic debut. He knew the stars and they knew him. He feared (although, in truth, looked forward to it) that his quietude would be temporarily abandoned when Viola and Kathleen arrived for the weekend. He received regular correspondence from his niece, and of course, he followed the stellar rise of Kathleen as a designer to the stars and to those who wished to emulate them. Her designs grew bolder each year yet always retained a classic underpinning that prevented them from being salacious or tawdry in any respect.

Kathleen looked forward to seeing her beloved friend, of course, and she welcomed the opportunity to thank Arthur once again for all he had done to advance her career over the years. But, she wished this impromptu request for a visit had come at a different time of the year. She was so busy! Still, she was intrigued by the request and knew how very rarely Viola ever visited Ireland, much less London. If she had gotten a letter hinting at "a matter of great importance to my future" from any other young woman she would naturally have assumed it was about a marriage proposal, but not coming from

Viola. The only man she had mentioned in her letters had been the handyman at the pensionne who had built the most ingenious cart for her, just as she directed. No, Kathleen reasoned, Viola was not coming to Ireland to tell them she was marrying the handyman.

Arthur, too, was pondering about the reason for his niece's sudden visit. Vivian had been nasty enough to suggest that Viola might be "in the family way," which had led to quite a row indeed. Arthur knew he had gone too far when he demanded of Vivian, "And what would you know about that!" Vivian burst into tears and fled the dining room where the argument had begun. It had taken Arthur several days of apologies and replenished accounts at several boutiques to soothe things between them. No, he couldn't see Viola coming to him for that issue; as independent as she was, if that were the case she surely would have dealt with it on her own. It had to be something else.

The staff had opened up two adjoining bedrooms in a wing of the manor quite distant from Arthur's as he knew the girls would stay up all night talking and giggling. He still thought of them as girls, of course, and was quite taken aback when Viola stepped from the carriage. Over the years her blonde curls had darkened to a lustrous chestnut color, although they still cascaded in an unruly tangle over her shoulders. Her body had filled out to womanhood as well. When she swept her dress out of the carriage and stood tall, one hand shading her eyes as she gazed out over the gardens, Arthur's breath was quite taken away and he could well imagine the effect she would have on younger men. They exchanged a warm embrace and the male staff scrambled for the honor of taking her bags to her room. Those who had been employed long enough to remember her as a girl were nearly rooted to their spots in seeing the change time had wrought.

Viola had no sooner finished freshening up and rejoined Arthur in the parlor than they heard the arrival of another coach, certainly Kathleen's. And with her, too, the change was remarkable. Prosperity had done much to enhance and refine Kathleen's natural beauty. Whereas before her expressions had often seemed pinched and guarded, now they were open and confident, dispelling any small lines that might have formed in her face. She was radiant even after several hours bouncing through the Irish countryside. Arthur stayed on the steps, letting the girls enjoy their greetings to each other, and he mused that where one had gotten older, the other had gotten younger. They could very nearly be sisters. Viola dragged Kathleen off to their rooms, both of them whispering and giggling the entire time, remembering Arthur just as they turned to climb the stairs. "Oh, Mr. McDougall, forgive my manners," Kathleen said, clasping his hands and kissing his cheek. "It's so grand to see you again and to be invited to your lovely home."

"The pleasure is all mine. Now I suppose you two will want to have a bit of a chat." The girls grinned at each other. "Let's meet in the library about five, shall we? We'll have a little sherry before dinner and Viola can tell us the reason for her mysterious visit." The girls ran up the stairs. Ah, youth, Arthur thought. Perhaps he'd have that sherry a bit sooner than five.

At the appointed hour the girls descended the staircase arm-in-arm, both looking radiant. Arthur wished there were two young men waiting to squire them away to a dance or some social function rather than he, an old man, but he couldn't help but feel that their youth might make him feel more lively over the next several days. "Lovely, lovely, both of you," he said with a bow, taking each of them on an arm and leading them to the library where the cook had placed trays of treats and a fine bottle of an inviting golden sherry. After the niceties had been dispensed with, Arthur decided to address the matter at hand. "Now, Viola, tell us why you have so mysteriously summoned us here."

Ever since she had been a little girl Viola had been adept at putting forth her position on any issue, and she was prepared to do so tonight as well. "As you know, I have enjoyed an educational experience that has taken me from England to France to Italy and back once again to France. It has been quite extraordinary." She paused for effect. "But now I intend to extend my education, if you will, to distant shores." Both Kathleen and Arthur looked uncomprehending. "I propose to leave within the fortnight for America." No one said anything for the moment so she continued. "Kathleen, dear friend, I would love for you to go with me. We would spend perhaps half a year touring the various States and certainly return to the West about which you've spoken so eloquently in the past."

"A year in America? Well, I can't possibly…"

"Not to worry about a thing," Viola said, grasping Kathleen's hand. "I shall arrange everything."

Arthur finally came to his senses. "I have no intention on financing your frivolous — and quite possibly dangerous — jaunt through the West."

"I have no intention of asking you to finance anything, uncle," Viola answered defiantly. "As you monitor my funds yourself, you see that I am in no need of financial support." That was true, he had to admit to himself; she had done quite well already from the sales of her paintings. "I shall pay my way — and Kathleen's — out of my own money."

Arthur and Kathleen exchanged stricken looks. "But you're just a young girl," Arthur said, knowing that not to be the case any longer. "It's unseemly."

"Unseemly. Well, that's just what Mr. Montrose said," Viola answered. "And little import did he have in the matter!"

Kathleen felt compelled to defend Arthur and couldn't understand what Viola was proposing. "But your uncle is right, you are an inexperienced young girl, and to go off on your own to such a place..."

Viola was wounded that her friend would support her uncle over herself. "I am not inexperienced. I speak four languages and have studied in a half-dozen schools. I've made money on my own. I've, well, I've had lovers, too!"

'Damn Frenchmen,' thought Arthur.

Viola was steaming. "Didn't you go across the country on your own?" she accused Kathleen. "You survived the experience at a younger age than I am now."

"I survived, Viola, on the kindness and protection of others, and I certainly did not set off to do it on my own. My da died before the journey could even begin, and if it hadn't been for Padraig helping me, well, I don't know where I would have ended up." Kathleen became teary at the thought. "Well, I do know where I would have ended up. The only other person willing to help me was a madam. I would have ended up a whore! That's what!" Kathleen then began to feel indignant. "And furthermore, I have a business to run now. The spring season is coming. I have commitments to three theater companies and dresses to design for a dozen women. I can't simply drop everything because some impetuous girl wants to drag me off on an adventure!"

Arthur knew he needed to intervene before things went too far between the young ladies. "Let's all take a breath. I believe I see the cook signaling us that dinner is ready. We can talk some more tomorrow about this."

Viola was still defiant. "There is nothing more to talk about it. I'm going to America." Dinner was subdued with an unusual amount of conversation about an ordinary roast of beef.

Chapter Forty

Arthur hadn't spent his career dealing with demanding divas of both sexes to be undone by a headstrong twenty-year-old woman who happened to be his niece (and who had, in fact, been manipulating him most of her life). A compromise was reached. Viola would pursue her education further in New York City, at least until the fall. If Kathleen were commissioned for costume design for the opening of the Metropolitan Opera in New York in the fall, she would at least go visit Viola and see if she was still of a mind to go further West—on her own.

So it was that Viola found herself sitting in an airless studio in New York City with a half-dozen other students, all staring at a nude female model. There was the usual amount of tittering when the model dropped her robe, all of which Viola took in stride; she had lived in France, after all, where such things were nowhere near as shocking. The class was supposedly on portraiture, all the rage now in America, so Viola wondered if the model's nudity was simply to satisfy the instructor's obvious lust. "Narrow your vision!" he constantly reminded the class. Viola noted how, indeed, his eyes did narrow when the model, male or female, ascended to the platform in the center of the studio. "See those lines by her mouth. Note how the curve of her arm compresses her breast." Viola had to stifle a yawn.

The other students were far more enthusiastic, particularly as the class was designed to make them portraitists in the 'grand tradition' of John Sargent. Well, Viola had met the great John Sargent in Paris and was far less impressed. He had implored Viola to model for him, or at least that was his approach, telling her she was the very epitome of a French country girl. "Well, Mister Sargent, so much for your powers of observation," she had told him one spring day. "I am not French, in fact, nor am I a country girl. I am an artist like yourself."

"Like myself! I very much doubt that," he had sputtered and then peevishly declined to look at her work. "I look forward to the day when your work hangs next to mine."

"I look forward to the day it hangs above yours, sir."

Viola stifled a giggle just thinking about that encounter, but one of her fellow students noticed her smile. "So are you spending your commission check on a new dress?" Viola looked startled. "I saw you smiling and thought that was what you were imagining," a young man to her left asked.

"Oh, no, not at all," Viola said, meeting his eye. "I was just recalling an amusing conversation I had with another artist."

"I'm Thomas, by the way," he said, extending his paintbrush as if it were a goblet.

"'By the way,' what an odd surname," Viola teased him. "Is it Irish?"

"So you mock me already, without even getting to know me. Truly, I am grievously wounded," he laughed.

"I think your pride will recover from its wounds," Viola sparred with him.

"Oh, only with some gentle ministering, I'm afraid." He put down his brush and wiped off his hand. "I am Thomas Whitfield, from Boston, English through and through." Viola shook hands with him.

"And you fancy yourself becoming a portrait artist?" she inquired.

"If I could get a fat commission, I would paint a portrait of a gentleman's cat, if need be." He made a purring sound and Viola had to laugh.

"Careful what you wish for," she chided him. "Cats can be pretty tricky after all. Best that you hope for a commission to paint his pretty mistress."

"Ah, but there's the rub. If I were to do such a thing, the world would never see my prodigious talent as surely the gentleman couldn't display my work. Ah, more's the pity."

"Prodigious talent. Well, I suppose I shall have to look over your shoulder more often," Viola sighed dramatically, looking over his shoulder to see the instructor glowering at them. "Our esteemed instructor looks about to lecture us. We'd best apply ourselves."

They went back to work sketching the model, but after class Thomas waited for Viola to clean her brushes and pack up her supplies. "Would you join me for an early supper, perhaps?" he asked.

Viola looked truly pained to decline. "I'm afraid I cannot. I am a prisoner, or that is to say, a resident, of Miss Marshall's Guest House for Proper Ladies and we must be present and accounted for by four each afternoon." Viola had come to think of the rooming house as Arthur's revenge, as naturally he had selected it after making some inquiries. Apparently there were no openings in the local prison, Viola thought angrily. The formidable Miss Marshall ruled with an iron fist and all the other young ladies were quite cowed by her. This was not the Bohemian lifestyle Viola had enjoyed in France. The inhabitants, or inmates, as Viola referred to them, were expected to be in the house by four each afternoon except on Sundays when they were to be home an hour earlier. They were required to attend church, Methodist preferably, although Lutheran was marginally acceptable; Catholic Church was out of the question. And, each evening the young ladies were expected to engage in no less than one hour of polite conversation. That was the part that rankled Viola the most.

"Did you see what those scoundrels at City Hall are up to now?" she asked one night. "They're stealing properties from their owners just to build a bigger monument to themselves. It's an outrage."

"Now dear," Miss Marshall had begun. "Proper young ladies certainly do not discuss political matters."

Apparently they also didn't discuss art, theater, dance, music or much of anything else other than finding husbands and then how to care for them properly. Viola seethed every evening and managed to make only the most perfunctory comments before excusing herself at the earliest opportunity. She would stay at the rooming house until the fall, but that would be the end of her obligation to her uncle's compromise. By Christmas she expected to be on a train heading west.

Chapter Forty-One

As spring gave way to summer, the art studio became even more stifling, both temperature-wise and intellectually. Over and over the master repeated, "Narrow your vision. Intensify your focus! What are you missing?"

Viola took a long look at the nude model draped in what she supposed was a languorous pose on a chaise situated in the center of the podium. She began to sketch in earnest until her friend Thomas interrupted her. "And just what is that which you are attempting to capture in such exquisite detail?"

"She has a pimple on her arse," Viola replied. "I'm narrowing my focus, you see."

Thomas had to turn away so the instructor wouldn't see him laugh. "Yes, quite so, and you've brought it out so brilliantly!"

Viola tore up the sketch and threw it on the floor. "Let's be truly wicked, shall we? Let's leave right now and go out on the streets, find something truly interesting to draw!"

Thomas knew he was looking at something truly interesting already. He hesitated. "You know, I'm here on scholarship so it might not do for me to upset the instructor." Viola looked so disappointed, however, that he relented. "But, yes, let's." They both packed up their pads and pencils and made a quick break for the door while the instructor's back was turned. Thomas thought tomorrow he would tell the instructor he had been struck with a sudden bout of indigestion, or perhaps even food poisoning, and thought it best to leave immediately before an embarrassing event might have taken place. Surely the instructor would understand. Viola was obviously much more talented than anyone in the class, so she wouldn't have to rely on any excuse.

Once out on the street Viola linked her arm through Thomas'. "I'm so happy we're doing this! Look at what a beautiful day it's become and we're out in it." They came to a small park that seemed to be a dividing line between Chinatown and Little Italy, yet both groups could be seen on the benches lining the gravel walkways. Viola found a spot where they could see the entire park and immediately plopped down on the grass. Thomas took his jacket off and spread it out for her, but when she declined he sat on it himself; no sense making a mess of his trousers, too.

Viola lay back looking at the clouds. "I don't want to narrow my vision—I want to expand it," she declared, thinking of her precious Grand Canyon painting stored safely in the bottom of her trunk. "When I think of the beauty we could capture, I think of all of this," she said, throwing her arm out, "not just the curve of an elbow or the swell of a breast."

At the mention of a breast, Thomas blushed, as it was exactly what he had been thinking about! "When I close my eyes and think of beauty, I see you, Viola."

She heard the tenderness in his voice but thought it best to ignore.

"Oh, poor boy. I doubt I shall be commissioning you to do my portrait any time soon." When Viola closed her eyes there was only one face she ever saw. She supposed he would be an old man by now but aging might have made him even more compelling.

Thomas interrupted her thoughts. "Viola, I do think about you all the time. You're a lovely girl and your personality is so...enchanting. You've cast quite a spell on me, I'm afraid."

"I have done no such thing, Thomas." She didn't want to spoil their time together but she couldn't lead him on either. "You know it is my plan to leave here in the fall for the West."

"That's months off. You don't suppose in the meantime you might come to love me, just a little bit?"

Viola took his hand. "You deserve more than someone who loves you just a little bit." He started to protest. "I do care for you, as a friend."

Thomas was crestfallen but recovered his dignity. "Very well then. I shall apply my prodigious talent— I did mention that it was prodigious didn't I—to doing your portrait when you at last become engaged to some lucky dog." He winked at her. "I will make you look as virginal as the falling snow."

"If you're able to do that, then your talent surely is prodigious," Viola shocked him. It was closing in on four o'clock, so Viola began to gather up her things then sat back. "I doubt as I shall ever marry. I fear I am too consumed with seeing the world and everyone in it to focus on one man alone."

"Oh, Viola, don't say such things. You truly make me sad at times." He took her hand. "You have so much to offer that any man would be honored."

Viola tossed back her hair. "Let's not end our adventure on a dark note, Thomas. "I think we should find a way to do this every week."

"Small chance of that, I'm afraid."

"No, I think I will propose it to the instructor. You know, I believe he quite fancies me," Viola teased him. "If I say we should go to the park or the train station or anywhere, I believe he'll be only too happy to oblige." She started to laugh. "Of course, we'd have to leave the nude model behind."

"Well, let me think about the trade-off there then," Thomas laughed heartily.

Viola did propose to the instructor the next day that they go out into the world to capture real people in real life, and while he was skeptical at first, all she had to do was toss her curls back and smile shyly at him. Every Friday hence the class set out on an expedition to "find humanity," as the instructor described it. And fresh air, Viola, thought.

On one such outing they came near an exposition hall recently constructed in the city to host all manner of meetings and shows. Madison Square Garden covered nearly all of Madison Park and replaced an earlier structure that had been open to the air and therefore quite inappropriate for New York City winter events. The new building had the largest meeting hall in the world as well as a grand theater. Viola reminded herself to tell Arthur about in the next cable she sent him. None of the students had ever been inside. What captivated their attention on this day more than the building itself was what was outside in the park. There were horses of all colors, cattle with long curling horns, and even a few buffalo, something only Viola had seen before. The animals were penned separately and watched over by cowboys who prevented any passersby from coming too close. Another group of men worked to hoist a colorful banner on the outside of the Garden. "Ranger Rowdy's Wild West Show and Emporium" would be appearing that night and for ten nights to come.

Viola clapped her hands in delight. "Oh, we must go!"

"But what about your curfew at Miss Marshalls?" Thomas asked.

"Dash that! Everything I saw in my trip across the West was so colorful and fascinating, and now here it is, right in front of us. We'd be fools *not* to go!"

Thomas had heard about Viola's train trip as a child and thought it best to indulge her. "Perhaps you could get enough tickets for all the young ladies and Miss Marshall herself to attend in a tight little flock, as it were."

"That's a splendid idea! I will do just that." She headed for the box office with Thomas trailing behind. "And I will get you a ticket in our same section, so it will be like we're enjoying it together." She was giggling with excitement, a mood Thomas had never seen her display (or anyone else, he thought).

Chapter Forty-Two

Viola's enthusiasm was almost uncontrollable during the Wild West performance. She couldn't take her eyes off the longhorn cattle, tossing their horns back and forth as the rodeo clowns taunted them. And the buffalo—so stately, she thought. The other young ladies from Miss Marshall's had eyes only for the cowboys, of course, although Viola did see one of them shyly stealing glances at Thomas, whom Viola had arranged to sit directly in front of her. Thomas was oblivious to the woman, turning his head so that he could make comments under his breath to Viola throughout the performance.

One act nearly stole the show, however. When the announcer stepped into the ring to introduce, "The fastest gun-slinger the West has ever seen," the crowd expected a tall Texan with a black cowboy hat and silver spurs. They were totally unprepared for the young woman who rode into the ring standing on her saddle, reins in one hand, silver six-shooter in the other! "Let's give a big hand to Rosie the Red Rider!" The crowd jumped to its feet, no one sooner than Viola.

Rosie the Red Rider was quite simply spectacular in her white leather fringed chaps and vest embroidered with red and black roses the size of a man's palm at her thighs, tapering to rosettes at the bottom of the chaps; the vest was similarly embroidered and fringed. Underneath she wore a red silk blouse with black piping and roses embroidered around the wrists. Black pants underneath the chaps perfectly matched the saddle, making her appear one with the horse. Her white straw cowboy hat sported red and black feathers, not from any bird Viola had ever seen. Her red hair tumbled in waves down her back nearly to her waist. At one point she put her six-shooter in its holster and did a handstand on the horse, still circling the arena at a full gallop. Viola's thoughts probably matched those of every man in the arena. "I have to meet her!" although, Viola's interest in doing so was probably not the same as the men. She wanted to draw a strong woman for a change instead of the half-asleep-looking models from her art classes. Rosie dismounted and showed her trick-shooting abilities with all sorts of targets. Some spectators wondered if it was all a carnival trick, but their neighbors assured them it was legitimate shooting, even if by a woman barely over five feet tall.

When the next act came into the arena, Viola dismissed all thoughts of Rosie. There would be a reenactment, the announcer told them, of the "bloodiest, most hard-fought Indian battle in our history." He even went so far as to warn the audience. "Any delicate women in our audience might want to cover their eyes." A few of Viola's guests from Miss Marshall's pretended to for a moment, but curiosity won out. Teepees were hastily assembled in the center of the arena to set the stage and a group of Indians in full regalia—feathers and war paint—carrying shields and bows with quivers of arrows on their back, took the stage. In moments a thundering could be heard. It was the cavalry galloping into the arena. Gunfire erupted and arrows flew through the air. With the dust from the horses and the smoke from the rifles, it was almost impossible to follow the frenetic action, but when it came to an end, the Indians all lay dead while one soldier circled the ring holding the American flag high. The crowd once again jumped to their feet in wild applause, but Viola remained seated, stunned into tears at the mock slaughter. Thomas glanced back at her but, of course, was powerless to comfort her. The next time he looked back, she was gone.

She walked back to the rooming house in a haze of tears. How could the Indian actors be forced to endure this indignity night after night, in city after city? She had thought to attend every performance, but now she knew she could not. But, she did make plans to return to the arena the next day. When the ladies returned to the boarding house that night the one who had been eyeing Thomas approached Viola. "Did you notice that handsome young man seated directly in front of you?"

"I don't think I was paying any attention to the audience," Viola answered stiffly.

"Oh, it seemed like you knew each other." She sighed. "If you did..."

"No, we don't." Viola turned away and went to her room to be spared the breathless giggling of the other boarders that was sure to go on for hours as they talked about which cowboy rode better or which had broader shoulders. Viola felt she had been given a sign tonight and she needed the quiet to think about what it meant.

One early difficulty that Viola had dealt with on first coming to New York was finding a place and a time to paint. Doing it at the boarding house was out of the question. Because her paintings had sold rather well, Viola was fortunate in having money of her own (and wise enough not to put all of it under her uncle's control). She sought out a small studio and was able to find one on the top floor of a building with offices below. The tall windows let in the strong morning light and no one paid any attention to her, the perfect combination. It was to her studio that Viola went early the next morning after a sleepless night thinking about the performance. Her landlady thought she left every morning for other classes, so no explanation was needed for her disappearance.

Viola struggled through the morning to get something on the canvas, even starting with a rough sketch of Rosie the Red Rider done from memory, but nothing would distract her from the previous night's performance. The only way she knew how to confront a problem was head-on. Even Uncle Arthur would tell Vivian, "You'd sooner use your breath to cool your porridge than to try to change Viola's mind once it's set." Viola simply had to go back to the arena and talk with the show's manager, not to convince him to change the show because she knew that wouldn't happen, especially given the crowd's enthusiastic enjoyment of it, but to ask how true any of it was. She washed up her brushes and returned to Miss Marshall's where she freshened up and put on her best dress. She would not be going to art class this afternoon.

When she arrived at the arena the scene was relatively quiet. Workers were spreading out the truck loads of dirt that had been hauled in to fill the arena floor, while others cleaned up between the rows of seats. She approached one man who looked to be a foreman. "I should like to speak to the director of the show, if you can direct me to him." He looked her up and down.

"He ain't hiring no girls for the show," he leered, "although you'd look fine as a saloon girl."

Viola thought about slapping him for his insolence but squared her shoulders and in her best imitation of his poor diction said, "Well, I ain't lookin' to be no show girl." He was surprised. "I would like to speak to him about another matter. Now if you would please tell me where I might find him, and also what his name is."

He had no choice but to comply and was much more courteous about it, directing her to one of the tents in the adjacent park. She found it and as she approached heard men arguing rather heatedly. In a moment, the tent flap was thrust open and one of the show's cowboy's strode out, red-faced and clearly on the losing end of the argument. She waited a moment to let tensions abate, then ducked into the tent. "Mr.

Archibald, sir? Do you have a moment?" The short, balding man had his shirt sleeves rolled up and was busy macerating an unlit cigar.

"I'm busy here. We're not hiring."

"I'm not applying. I would only like to discuss a matter with you in just a few minutes of your time."

He took note of her English accent and her fine dress. Perhaps she was a member of the foreign press here to do a story on the show? He would love to raise the money to take it to England where people were said to be enthralled over cowboys and Indians. "Well, please, miss, take a seat." He pointed to a chair. "I'm afraid I don't have any refreshments to offer you."

"That's quite all right." She paused and considered how to continue. "I'm here about the Indians."

"Indians?"

"Not necessarily the ones in your show. I'm sure you treat them very well," she said, very much doubting that. "Indians in general. In the West." He waited for her to continue and couldn't imagine the direction the discussion would take. "You see, I plan to journey to the West very soon and I wonder if you could enlighten me as to the true situation there. I recall as a child traveling through the Great Plains and beyond, and the Indians were a frightful menace." At least one was. "Tell me, are they still?"

He couldn't stop himself from laughing out loud. "Miss, the Indians here in the show—that's all an act, you see."

She colored with embarrassment. "I'm quite aware of that, sir, but I'm sure you have actually been to the West, have you not?"

"Oh, that I have, recruiting these cowboys and whatnot for the show." He realized how serious she was. "I have to say the Indians are no menace to anyone. There's hardly a one of them left free." He leaned back in his creaky chair. "I'd say the only menace is us." He stepped to the door of the tent and yelled at a passing actor. "Bring us some drinks, would you?" They spent the rest of the afternoon talking until the dimming light heralded the time for the start of the show when he had to excuse himself. Once again, Viola left the arena in tears.

Chapter Forty-Three

Viola was back at Archibald's tent the next day with more questions. He knew he shouldn't have wasted the time with the young English woman, but truth was, he was flattered that a woman such as herself would ask his opinion and be interested in his stories. He should have been attending to cowboys too drunk to shoot straight, horses coming up lame, longhorns threatening to gore one of the cowboys, and a hundred other details, but it was quite pleasant to pass a spring afternoon talking to a lovely young lady like Viola.

"But why didn't they just say no?" Viola asked at several junctures.

Archibald sighed every time she asked the question. He fashioned himself somewhat of an expert on the Indians, having had some personal exposure to them and also having read up quite a bit. When his wife left him, he had nothing but time to read about things. It was ironic, he thought, since he had never thought much about reading in school; now he positively lived for it. He also found it interesting that the European visitors who attended his shows often left their newspapers behind and those papers quite often featured news about American Indians that the local papers never carried.

"I think it all started with the railroad," he tried to explain to Viola. "When the railroad expanded across the country, it opened up lots of land that was real attractive to speculators and, heck, to the passengers on the train." Viola nodded her agreement, having been one of those passengers herself. "And then there was the other thing—the buffalo." He invited her to walk outside and led her to where the buffalo were corralled. "Those railroad builders had to eat and they paid top dollar for buffalo. There were men who made fortunes slaughtering 'em. They shot 'em or ran 'em off cliffs, anyway they could kill 'em, they did." He paused. "And guess who depended on them buffalo? The Indians did, that's who."

Viola remembered seeing the vast herds of buffalo when they crossed the Great Plains, and that was less than twenty years ago. As they were standing there looking at the mangy, shaggy-haired buffalo, one of the Indian actors from the show wandered up to stand with them. "Mr. Archibald has been telling me that the Indians have had a very hard time of it recently. Is that true?"

"Yes, miss, it's true. It's not a good time to be an Indian." He spoke so quietly she had to move closer to him to hear his next words. "Not so good to be a buffalo either, dragged around the country and put on display for white people."

Viola caught his meaning at once and was quickly offended. "So the Indians are no longer the menace they once were to innocent travelers?"

Archibald sought to avoid a confrontation between the high-spirited English girl and the Indian. "No one is completely innocent, I'd say. The government has been trying to help them." At this, the Indian spat in the dirt and walked away, shaking his head.

Viola had more questions. "How are they being helped then?"

"Well, the politicians decided they were going to do what was best for the Indians, so they rounded them all up and told them exactly where they could live. Some of them they marched to death, just getting them where they wanted them on these reservations they created, on worthless patches of ground no one else wanted."

"But then they all got their own homes? Isn't that what all you Americans are after?" Viola asked innocently.

"That's not how Indians are made up, miss." Archibald lit a cigar while he thought. "They're more communal people and more free than any of us have ever thought of being. You can't take a hunter and turn him into a farmer, 'specially when you give him land that can't grow nothin' but tumbleweeds anyhow." He took a few puffs. "A lot of them starved to death in the first few years in those so-called safe havens."

Viola was silent, for once, and unaccountably, Archibald began to laugh. "There was one thing that shook the politicians up pretty good though." They sought shade on a bench beneath a spreading oak by one of the tents. "There was this Paiute—that's an Indian out in Nevada, one of the tribes. His name was Wovoka, although the people he worked for gave him a Christian name, too. Anyway, Wovoka came up with this Ghost Dance." Viola's eyes widened. "It weren't no more than a round dance, like you saw in the show, but the Indians did it for hours, even days, and Wovoka said he got this vision that if all the Indians everywhere did this Ghost Dance and lived right, they would be reunited with all their ancestors, and more than that, all the whites would just pick up and leave, and take all the disease and violence and troubles they brought with them." His laugh turned rueful. "The whole thing caught on pretty good until the soldiers watching one of these dances got spooked and killed a prominent chief. Well, that was the end of that." He pulled out his pocket watch. "Okay, enough Indians for the day. I got to get the show on the road, as they say."

Viola was left with no other questions to ask for the moment, but she thanked Archibald for his time and left the park. She was so deep in thought that she almost didn't notice Thomas standing by the entrance to the park. "I thought I'd find you here," he said shyly. "Everyone at class is asking about you."

"Oh, I just..." Viola tried to compose herself while taking Thomas' arm. "I just was so moved by the performance the other night that I had to learn more about it." Thomas seemed to accept her answer and was just grateful to have her arm on his. "I've been to the West, as I know I've told you, and I couldn't believe the Indians have come to such a sad ending."

"Well, that's what happens when war is waged," he offered gently.

"But it wasn't war. It was outright thievery!" Viola sought to say more, but realized she would be talking to the wrong person. Instead, she grabbed his arm a little tighter. "Come with me. There's something I want to show you."

He would have followed her anywhere, of course, but was surprised to end up in front of an office building where most of the tenants had already gone for the day. Viola took a key out to open the door to the stairway and led him up to third floor where another key opened the door to an artist's studio. "Who's is this?" he inquired, moving toward the windows. When he turned back again, Viola was standing near one of the easels clearly displaying her own work. "You have your own studio?" He was clearly shocked but then began to look more closely at the paintings standing against the wall. "How did, and I mean, how do…"

Viola came up behind him and slipped his coat off his shoulders, which were broader than she had ever noticed. "Don't ask me questions now, please." She loosened his tie and at the same time dropped her cloak on the floor and stepped out of her shoes. It made it more difficult to reach the top button on his shirt, but she pressed up against him and was able to undo it. He was nearly paralyzed with shock and desire but finally turned around to embrace her. It made it that much easier for her to undress him further as he fumbled with the hooks and eyes and other intricacies of her dress while she drew him to the small bed in the corner of the room. Soon, they stood naked before each other. "But I don't have a…" Thomas stammered, wondering how he could explain that he was unprepared for such an encounter, when, in fact, he was unprepared entirely. Viola kissed him and drew him down to the bed. She could tell it was his first time, but it wasn't hers and she sought to reassure him with kisses and moans of delight. While she lost herself in the lovemaking, Thomas realized she was only unleashing emotions she didn't know how to deal with otherwise. It was their first time together, and he knew, very likely their last.

It was dark when they finally left the studio and at the bottom of the stairs, she pressed something into his hand. It was the key to the studio. "The rent is paid through the end of the year. I want you to use it." He looked questioningly at her. "I won't be here. Your talent is truly too good to be confined in that school. Come here and let your imagination guide your brush." She wouldn't even consent to let him walk her to Miss Marshall's.

Chapter Forty-Four

Viola returned to the rooming house to find all the girls huddled around the New York Times, only the society page, of course. "Oh, it's so dreamy! Can you imagine?" The girls were fairly swooning over something and when they noticed Viola come in the door, they immediately began peppering her with questions. "Don't you know Kathleen Evans? Will you be going to the wedding? Will she make your dress?"

Viola was bewildered by their questions. "Whose wedding?"

They made room for her on the settee and one of the more loquacious girls began to tell the story. "The heir to the throne of England, Prince Wellington, is going to marry Princess Sophia of Spain. Well, the Queen Mother is beside herself, of course, that he's not marrying an English girl, but of course, they're all so dowdy." Viola started to protest. "Well, not you Viola, but you know. Anyway, in order to marry her, he is going to give up the Church of England to become Catholic! It's positively scandalous."

The girls looked to Viola to comment. "You ninnies. What in the world do you care about that for?" They were used to Viola's rudeness but this was even more biting than her usual comments. "There are so many more important things in this world that you know nothing about!"

"Oh, and I'm sure you'll be only too happy to enlighten us," one of the girls said under her breath.

"And what does Kathleen Evans have to do with this?" Viola asked, recalling the earlier thread of conversation.

"She has been chosen to make the wedding dress." The girls shoved the newspaper toward Viola. "The sketch is right here." Viola looked it over and indeed it did look like something Kathleen would design. "It says the dress will have a train fifty feet long made of handmade Spanish lace in a pattern to be used only for the Princess." The girls sighed almost in unison. "And the bodice will have a thousand crystals sewn in with more crystals seeming to cascade toward the floor."

Viola couldn't help herself when she found herself drawn into the conversation. "And when is this grand event to take place?"

"Oh, not for a year. Kathleen is quoted as saying it will take her at least that long to make the dress, although she's starting on it immediately." The girl pointed to a paragraph in the story. "It says she will have to give up her designing for the theater for the time being as she will be traveling between Paris and Barcelona to arrange for the fabrics and meet with the Princess."

Viola looked suddenly sad. Obviously, Kathleen wouldn't be coming to the States to accompany her on any journey west. "Well, good for her," she told the girls and excused herself immediately before they could ask any more questions about Kathleen. She couldn't wait another year for Kathleen to perhaps be available. After talking to Archibald, she knew the time was now if there were any chance at all of her painting the Indians in their true natural state, something she was determined to do.

She stayed away from art class the next day and once again sought out Archibald at the Wild West show encampment. The show's last performance would be that evening and Archibald had put up new posters promising something "so exciting that even previous patrons will want to return." Viola hoped it would be a show of the Indians fighting back and winning, but she highly doubted that's what Archibald had in store. She caught him rushing into the arena. "Mr. Archibald, just a moment, please." He looked annoyed but stopped nevertheless. "I wonder if you would give me your thoughts on where I might go to see some Indians still living in their traditional way, free to roam."

He cocked his head at her. What an interesting young woman she was. "It wasn't five days ago you was asking me if the Indians were still a, what did you call them, a menace? Now you're wanting to go chasing after them? I swear."

Viola was caught up short. "I think it would be important for my understanding of the West to see them, is all."

"Let me think on it. Come help me with these flyers," he said, thrusting a handful at her. "Put them on the carriages and whatever else you can find, doorsteps, what have you." She looked around and set off to do what he suggested. When she ran out of the leaflets she came back to find him smoking a cigar outside his tent.

"You planning on coming back tonight for the show?"

"I hadn't thought about it, no." Viola thought of all the things she had to do to get ready for the trip she was determined to make.

"I shouldn't tell you, but I will," Archibald winked. "There's going to be fireworks at the end of the show, right inside the arena."

"Fireworks inside? Won't that be dangerous?"

"Oh, the Chinaman that sold 'em to me said they'd be perfectly fine." Archibald puffed away. "I'm a little worried about scaring the horses, but we'll get them out of the arena first." He yelled at one of the passing workers. "Tell Hansen I need to talk to him about the horses before the show."

"So, have you thought about where I might find some likely Indians?" Viola persisted.

"I don't know how likely they'll be, but there's a group up above Cheyenne in the Wind River Range that's still said to be roamin' around, though I don't know as you could find them on your own."

Viola thought back to their train stop in Cheyenne years ago. Maybe they would still come to the train station to sell their trinkets? "Hmm, well Cheyenne it is then." She reached out to shake Archibald's hand. "You've been so very kind to me this week, to tell me all you know about Indians."

"Oh, I ain't told you all I know," he laughed good-naturedly. "I probably just told you enough to get you in trouble." Viola's expression darkened. "But I surely hope not and that you get to find what you're looking for out there." Viola made no move to leave. "You know, young lady, those plains are lonely places. Even an experienced scout could get lost and never be seen again. Wouldn't want that to happen to you."

"I shall have to take my chances, Mr. Archibald. That's what life is all about, taking chances, isn't it?" He had told her as much when she asked him about starting the Wild West show. On impulse, she hugged him. "I'll do everything a prudent person could do. But I'll find my Indians."

Chapter Forty-Five

Before Viola could launch her expedition west, she had a few loose ends to tie up. She regretted impulsively giving Thomas the key to her studio but felt she could convince the landlord that she had lost her key so he might let her in. When she reached the studio, however, it turned out she needn't have worried about it as the door stood open. She walked toward it cautiously, "Hello?" She heard a chair being pushed back. "Who's there?"

Thomas stepped into the doorway. "I'm sorry if I'm intruding," he began. "I didn't expect..."

"No, I'm the one who is intruding. After all, I gave you the key and expected you to use the studio," Viola stammered. "It's just that I forgot to pack up my work, and since I'm going to be leaving as soon as possible, I really need to just do that and I'll be out of your way." Viola had money in her account but knew if she were to be gone any great length of time, it would be wise to send her completed canvasses off to the gallery in Paris where her previous works had sold so quickly. She moved toward the easel on which her latest portrait rested, but Thomas intercepted her.

"Please, Viola, hear me out." He knew the approach he was about to take was wrong but couldn't stop himself. "Don't you think you could postpone your trip for a while to give us time to, well, get to know each other better and perhaps..."

"There is no time to postpone anything, Thomas." She took his hand in hers. "You simply don't understand how important this journey is to me. It's like a part of my soul will not let it go."

"Then let me go with you!" Thomas could scarcely believe he had made the suggestion and he could tell by the look on Viola's face that his plea would surely fail.

"Oh, Thomas, let's not make this any harder. You're a very nice man and you'll make a wonderful husband and father when you're ready, but I have a completely different path in mind."

"We could marry and I would go with you, support you in everything you desire." Thomas moved to pull her closer but she stood her ground and dropped his hand. After taking a deep breath, he squared his shoulders. "Well, then, that's settled. I'll leave you to it, the packing and all, and I won't come back here for a few days unless you send word for me."

Viola knew he was grievously wounded by her steadfast refusal to let him further into her life, but she also felt the kindest approach was to let him leave on his terms. "Yes, that's best. I shall leave the key with the landlord in the office on the first floor. You'll have the studio to yourself by the end of the week." She gave him a weak smile. "Really, try to do the great work here that I know you're capable of." Hugging him would have been his undoing, she knew, so she simply turned back to the easel and let him leave.

Viola stayed in the studio until early evening placing her trademark "V McD" signature on the completed paintings. She would arrange for a packing service to crate them the following day for shipment. She looked at all of the dozens of brushes and tubes of paint and wished she still had the little cart she had designed in France, but ultimately decided to leave them all for Thomas. She took only a small set of pastels and any unused sketch books.

That night when she returned to Miss Marshall's, the mood was decidedly different from the night before when the girls were giddy over the wedding details. Tonight they were somber and met her eyes hesitantly until Miss Marshall herself stepped forward holding a cablegram. "This came for you earlier, dear. I went to the school but the master there said you hadn't attended in more than a week." She looked disapproving but nevertheless put her arm around Viola's shoulders. "Come into the parlor and sit. Patsy, you go make some tea for us, would you?" Viola couldn't imagine what would warrant such treatment from the normally stern landlady. Viola unfolded the cable and read its contents, something the landlady had clearly already done.

"Dear Viola. It is with great sadness that I inform you your aunt Vivian passed this morning. It was peaceful and without precipitating illness. Funeral mass will be Friday with burial at Holy Cross. She left a small bequest in your name which our solicitor will convey to you as soon as can be arranged. Fondly, your devoted uncle, Arthur."

"Hmmph." Patsy stood in front of Viola with a teapot, which Viola ignored. She refolded the cable and made to leave the parlor.

"We're all so sorry, Viola, for your loss," Miss Marshall stated. "Please sit with us, won't you, and tell us a little bit about her, that is, if you feel up to it."

Viola felt a wry smile spread across her face. "I certainly realize it's not nice to speak ill of the dead, but honestly, she was a heartless shrew who never showed anyone a glimmer of affection or kindness her entire life!" Miss Marshall and the other girls were shocked, Patsy nearly dropping the teapot. "I expect she is ordering the devil around already." She started to laugh. "I'll wager that the 'small bequest' is probably her old bloomers that I'll be expected to mend." She walked to the fireplace where she dropped the cable onto the logs. "Miss Marshall, I expect to be vacating my room by the end of the week, so you may begin to seek another boarder." With that pronouncement, Viola drew up her skirts and headed for the stairs.

In the privacy of her room, Viola recalled various incidents with Vivian, particularly her being so scared by the Indians, and soon she was laughing until tears rolled down her face. She realized she did, after all, feel some genuine affection for the woman who had been so stern and unfeeling toward her over the years, but who had at least let her go to pursue her dreams. Viola realized her life could have been so much worse if Vivian had sought to keep her under her thumb. Instead, Vivian had let her go away to schools. While Viola thought it was selfishness on Vivian's part in not wanting to take care of Viola herself, perhaps it was in small part Vivian's desire to see Viola be fulfilled as an artist and a woman, something Vivian never achieved.

Viola also began to reflect on Vivian's passing and how it would affect her uncle. It was true that there had always seemed to be very little affection between them, more that Arthur suffered her ministrations with a forbearance only a saint could have managed. Still, Vivian did manage the mundane details of his life so that he, too, could pursue his desires. What would he do now, Viola wondered? Would he at last take a wife or a mistress? Viola immediately thought of his obvious regard for Kathleen. True, there was a significant age difference, but now that Kathleen would be spending more time in France, she might see how many younger women there took older men as their lovers and benefactors. Viola lay back on her bed and tried to imagine it, ultimately failing.

Chapter Forty-Six

Viola had corresponded with Samuel Clemens, whom she met in San Francisco as a young girl, but hadn't seen him since then. His letters in return to hers were always filled with witty observations about the people in San Francisco and the various other locales he found himself. Viola's correspondence was undoubtedly more mundane, since, of course, she was no writer. Still, she told him about the artistic challenges she was facing and often included little sketches, particularly from her time in the Italian countryside and from the streets of Paris, which seemed to interest him greatly. When she at last came to New York she found it far less interesting and her correspondence decreased accordingly. When the Wild West show departed, she thought to write him again but then was overwhelmed with all it was going to take to launch her own Wild West expedition. She was surprised therefore at the depth of feeling she experienced when she chanced to see a snippet in the society column—the girls in Miss Marshall's, where she still remained, were obsessed with it and there was always a copy lying about. She surreptitiously read the column for any further mention of the royal wedding, but never would have admitted her interest in the affair.

"The bon vivant of Hartford are desolate at the imminent departure of the lovely Livy Clemens and her husband Samuel, better known to readers of popular works as Mark Twain. The couple is in the process of closing their grand home here in preparation for their decampment to Europe for what they say will be an extended stay. The home, as

loyal readers know, was many years in the building and furnishing, and Mr. Clemens has been quoted many times as saying the house embodied the true meaning of a home. We wish them well in their new adventures and save a place in our hearts for them on what we can only hope will be their speedy return.

Viola wondered if there would be time to get a letter off to her old friend, but then impulsively decided a visit would be better. As it was, her trip west might be better put off since fall was already upon the country and winter not far behind. She went to the train station that afternoon and secured round-trip passage to Hartford, Connecticut, less than a day's journey. She also appealed to her landlady. "Miss Marshall, I know I told you that you could let my room, but I wonder, could you allow me to stay for another few months, at least until spring?"

The landlady was grateful for the change in Viola's plans as she had found little interest in the room as she had advertised it, being totally unaware of the reputation it had gained in the city as a virtual garrison for young women. She also saw a business opportunity, knowing of Viola's recent inheritance. "You know I have spent quite a few dollars in advertising which I will have no way of recouping," she began.

Viola immediately guessed her intent. "Of course, Miss Marshall, and I would certainly pay you for those costs and perhaps another ten dollars a week for my room." Viola put on her most contrite expression. "You know how impulsive we girls can be and we must look to women like yourself for guidance. I think the extra rent will be a good penance for me."

"I think that's quite right, Viola," Miss Marshall said stiffly, although she was nearly giddy at the increase in rent and the extra fees coming her way.

"Oh, I also need to tell you I am leaving as soon as I can get a train ticket for Hartford, Connecticut, to visit my dear friends, Mr. and Mrs. Clemens, before they leave for Europe. I wonder if you could recommend a guest house there for a night or two?"

Miss Marshall wasn't used to the girls telling her what they were going to do; it was usually the other way around. "I have only been to Hartford once myself," she said slowly, "but I think you could inquire at the local Women's Christian Association. I know there's one there. They might let out a room for a night or two or know of a safe hotel for a young woman traveling alone." The emphasis she placed on the last two words conveyed her disapproval of Viola's plans.

"That's an excellent idea. Thank you very much." Viola shocked her landlady by giving her a quick hug. "I'm off to the train station then." She walked the few blocks to Grand Central and found that she could get a compartment the following morning and would arrive in Hartford in the early afternoon. She had no way of warning her friend of her imminent arrival but expected that he would welcome her anyway.

Miss Marshall insisted on accompanying her to the train station the following morning, which was a help because Viola was struggling with a valise and her shoulder bag containing her ever-present sketch book. The train chugged into the bustling station on time and Viola was directed to her compartment by one of the porters. She had a fondness for trains that she suspected had roots in her journey to San Francisco some fifteen or so years ago. Every time a conductor or train master passed her window, she expected it to be Mr. Nulty.

When the train arrived in Hartford, she inquired of the station master where she could find the Clemens home and whether it was walking distance. He assured her that any coachman would know the home and it was too far from the station to walk. He suggested what the fare might be to save her the embarrassment of asking. Within a quarter of an hour she found herself pulling up in front of a three-story home equally as grand as the Crocker Mansion in San Francisco. En route the coachman had told her it was nearly twelve thousand square feet with twenty-five rooms including seven bathrooms that had hot and cold running water and flush toilets. At night, he said, the house was truly elegant, lit by gaslight as it was.

The door was answered by a servant. Viola introduced herself and allowed that she was not expected but would certainly be seen by Mr. Clemens if he was in residence. The servant disappeared down a long hallway without a word, leaving Viola to stand awkwardly. While the house was ostentatious from the outside, the rooms she could see were plainly furnished but comfortable. She could hear a fire crackling in a nearby room. "Viola McDougall!" boomed down the hallway. "In my very own home! Well, I'll be." Samuel appeared, with his cane in hand but without his trademark white suit jacket, rather in shirt sleeves rolled up, a lit pipe in his other hand. "Let me have a look at you." Standing before him was a poised young woman, not the shy ten-year-old of San Francisco. He wasn't certain whether hugging her was appropriate, but she solved the dilemma by throwing both arms around him.

"Come, come, let's go in the parlor." He motioned her toward the room where she had heard the fire. There were two fine wingback chairs arranged in front of the hearth with a small table in between. He set his pipe in the ashtray there and continued to appraise her. "I don't suppose chocolate milk would be appropriate," he laughed. "Let's have some sherry in honor of your uncle. The man did enjoy his sherry." Viola laughed, agreeing with his observation. "So what brings you here? You'll stay the night won't you?" The servant returned with sherry and some crackers. "Livy will be so pleased to see you. How is your uncle?"

The questions overwhelmed her. "My uncle is thriving, I believe. My aunt, however, passed on. I believe you met her once, Vivian?"

"Oh, indeed I did. She would have been an excellent character for the stage—provided the stage was leaving in an hour!" He laughed at his own trite joke. "Still, I'm sorry to hear that. Your uncle must be lost."

"I expect he will do just fine. There are probably a number of ladies only too eager to help him." She sipped her sherry. "When I read of your imminent departure, I felt I had to come."

That provoked another loud burst of laughter. "My imminent departure? Only from this house, my dear, not from this earth, as far as I know anyway." They discussed his and Livy's plans for Europe and Clemens confided that the trip was the result of some 'reverses of finance.' Viola could only imagine, looking at the size of the house and its out-buildings. "Perhaps I shall look up your uncle if we are in London for any time."

"He would love that! I'm sure he would love to escort a celebrity such as yourself to the theater and the parties afterward," Viola said, partly teasing him.

Gradually the conversation drifted toward Viola's other reason for visiting. "It is my intention, when the weather allows, to travel to the West in hopes of painting any Indians who are fortunate enough to remain living in their native status."

Clemens put down his pipe. "Indians? First it was your obsession with the Irish and now the Indians. Two lower classes of individuals would be hard to imagine."

Viola was shocked, but Clemens had much, much more to say on the subject. "You and so many other readers have been drawn in by the foolish romanticism that Fennimore Cooper puts out about the 'noble savage.' Well, he got half of it right." He lit his pipe again. "That fop probably never met an Indian, and he certainly never saw them staggering drunk down the street, intent on going back to beat their wives and get into all manner of mischief."

"That's not my recollection at all," Viola countered. "I felt they possessed a quiet dignity in the face of their inevitable oppression."

"Inevitable oppression! Let me say this, young lady. All history and honest observation will show that the Red Man is a skulking coward and a windy braggart who strikes without warning." He cited several reported massacres to Viola who listened with increasing disappointment. "He kills helpless woman and little children, and massacres the men in their beds; and then brags about it as long as he lives, and his son and his grandson and great-grandson after him glorify it among the 'heroic deeds of their ancestors'." Clemens spat into the fireplace.

"I believe if those accounts were true, they must have been forced into it," Viola said weakly.

"I said there was nothing so convincing to an Indian as a general massacre. If he could not approve of the massacre, I said the next surest thing for an Indian was soap and education." Clemens tapped his cane on the floor. "Soap and education are not as sudden as a massacre, but they are more deadly in the long run; because a half-massacred Indian may recover, but if you educate him and wash him, it is bound to finish him some time or other."

Viola would have reason over the years to recall that comment, but she was too stunned in the moment to reply. Livy rescued her by returning home and exclaiming her delight in having her company for the evening, but Viola declined. She was accustomed to her old friend's acerbic wit, but he had become bitter and rather hateful, she discovered. Whereas his biting criticism that made his columns so popular was meant to be humorous, his assessment of the Indians was cynical, if not hateful, and Viola could listen to it no longer. She thanked the couple for their hospitality and wished them well in their journey, but she could not stay under the same roof and left even more determined to pursue her dream.

Chapter Forty-Seven

When winter settled on the city, it found Viola with a certain ennui. She had given up her studio to Thomas and dropped out of the art class so really had little to occupy her days short of fantasizing about her trip West planned for the spring. It snowed, the snow melted, it snowed again, and soon the Christmas holidays occupied everyone's time, everyone but Viola, it seemed. She stayed on at Miss Marshall's, and when the other girls found out about her ability to pay what they considered an exorbitant rent, they resented her even more. One afternoon she found them in their usual positions, draped around the parlor.

"Can you believe he said no?" one of the girls asked the group, pointing to an item in the society column. "To the royal family? Honestly, he must really be full of himself."

Viola thought she should force herself to be a little social. "Who said no to what?"

At first the girls ignored her, but the opportunity to gossip and get her perspective as an English girl was too good to pass up. "Philip Evans, the pianist, has refused Princess Sophia's request to play at the wedding. It's scandalous." She waved the newspaper in Viola's direction. "Saying no to the royals, really!"

Viola caught sight of a photograph and snatched the newspaper from the girl's hand. A shiver of recognition ran through her. Where could she have seen this man with his very light complexion and flowing blonde hair? His penetrating gaze seemed to come right off the page. And his name, Philip Evans. Could this be Kathleen's former husband? She told Viola once that her husband had played the piano beautifully. Most people who knew Viola as an artist expected that she would also love music, but she had never paid any attention to it, even when her uncle had taken her to countless performances of the most important performers of the day. Subconsciously she also associated music with her parents' deaths, something she couldn't overcome. She quickly read through the article noting Philip's willingness to play for an evening soiree but nothing in the church and nothing during the day. How odd.

"Do you remember the drawing of the dress we saw months ago?" the girl asked the others, taking the newspaper back from Viola. "Apparently that's the last we'll see of it as the princess has forbidden anyone to even discuss it until the wedding." The girls nodded knowingly. "Apparently Kathleen, the designer, has virtually been forced into hiding to complete it." The girls hadn't made the connection between Kathleen and Philip at all, it seemed, and Viola was not about to enlighten them. She didn't like the thought of her friend being hounded by the press, but if anyone could handle it, that would be Kathleen with her Irish temper.

"Can't you write to your friend and ask her to send you even a swatch of the material?" one of the girls entreated Viola. "You never did tell us—are you going to the wedding?"

"No, certainly not. After all, I am not a friend of Princess Sophia," Viola replied stiffly, dashing their dreams. "Kathleen is nothing more than a hired hand, really, like the person who will make the canapes or the one who will shovel up after the horses." She realized how mean she sounded and was at a loss to understand why. Even the girls who were well used to her rude comments looked away and returned to ignoring her. Later, in her room, Viola forced herself to admit that she was angry with Kathleen for not being there for the trip, although in all honesty, there was no good reason for her to go as Viola had told her repeatedly over the years that she was independent and self-reliant and needed no one's guidance or support.

Meanwhile in a smoky lounge in San Francisco the Philip Evans in question was sulky and petulant with his mentor, some might say creator, Vicente. "You fool! You think you could have just waltzed into a church, a church of all places, and flipped out your tuxedo tails at the piano bench?" Vicente was beside himself. "I suppose bursting into flames would have provided quite the added attraction at the wedding, rather upstaged the bride's gown, don't you think?" The sarcasm wasn't entirely lost on Philip, but he refused to acknowledge it.

"But it would have been my chance to see her!" he moaned. "Surely Kathleen will be there, making last-minute adjustments and so forth." Philip hung his head. "I could have just spied her from the wings as I used to do at the opera house when she was just the wardrobe mistress." Philip looked truly bereft and it did spur a certain amount of guilt in Vicente who was, after all, completely responsible for Philip's 'transition.' "I still don't see why I couldn't go in the evening to the reception, just play a few tunes toward the end and everyone would be happy."

Vicente took a deep breath. As much as he loved Philip and felt responsible for him, the young man tried his patience. "And you don't suppose when Kathleen sees you—and she would, you know—your presence would be overpowering to her—that she wouldn't notice how stone cold your lips are when she springs into your arms? Or how cold your touch?" Vicente knew he was being cruel, but it had to be done. "Leave off with this fantasy right now, I warn you. Nothing good can come of it." Philip moaned in anguish but said nothing.

Kathleen, in a small garret in the south of France, had come to the same conclusion. Nothing good could come of Philip coming to Paris to play for the royal wedding. "You made your decision when you left him that letter in San Francisco," she told herself. "He was your husband then, but he is no longer." She returned to sewing the seed pearls on the voluminous gown but kept returning to the vision of Philip sitting at the bench of a gleaming white piano brought specially into the church. The photographs she had seen of him looked as if he was still a young man in his twenties; he seemed the same yet somehow different. Perhaps if she saw him for just a minute she would know if the passion they had once shared was still there. "Stop it! You're no longer a foolish girl mooning after him with a pile of costumes in your arms!" she chided herself. There had been a few men over the years who had taken her to the theater or to dances and dinners, but none had awakened any sort of passion in her. She felt that had died, along with Padraig in the mines and with his baby (she still didn't think of it as hers). Leaving Philip was painful but she had to remind herself almost daily, "It was for the best." Look how their careers had soared! Yes, it was for the best and it would be best to let sleeping dogs lie.

Arthur, relaxing at his country home in Ireland, read the society columns faithfully as part of his job, and, of course, he made the Evans connection immediately. "I wonder if it wouldn't do to have a little reception, perhaps a few nights before the wedding, and invite Kathleen and Philip, each without the other's knowing?" He swirled the sherry around in his glass. "Ah, what business do I have as a match-maker?" He had kept in touch with Kathleen over the years and sent many a client her way, at least in the early days. Now her career needed no such boost. "She has so much to offer," he mused, "and evidently no one to offer it to. She seems truly a woman without a passion other than work." He was alone in the house and hoped he hadn't been talking out loud, one of the pitfalls of aging. "I'd best stay out of it," he resolved finally. He knew the life entertainers lived and recognized that if Philip wanted a woman, he'd have one. And Kathleen, well, Kathleen was beautiful and could have any man she wanted, if only she did. Young people these days. Arthur stopped his train of thought, knowing it would only lead to his worrying about his niece, Viola, another woman whose passions seemed yet to be discovered.

Chapter Forty-Eight

They found him with his sherry glass still in his hand although the amber liquid had drained down onto the carpet. The fire had gone out in the fireplace and the lights had not been lit. The houseman noted, however, that he seemed quite peaceful in his final repose. Arthur had indeed died thinking of the two lovely women in his life he had been fortunate to know, and he liked to think, to help. Kathleen was well-established, but Viola still concerned him, although he knew that her determination would carry her far — or be her utter undoing. He was laughing to himself when he died, remembering her joy at walking through strange neighborhoods in San Francisco or her brazen attempts at conversations with complete strangers aboard ship. He just hoped she was happy in her own way.

Of course, Viola's happiness was shattered when she received yet another telegram at Miss Marshall's, this one informing her of her uncle's death. Miss Marshall had read the contents when it arrived, but recalling how little Viola reacted to the death of her aunt, she was unprepared for the great gasping sobs Viola emitted when she herself read the message. Viola threw herself into Miss Marshall's arms and it was some time before she could disengage herself. She didn't think she had ever seen anyone so bereft as Viola was now. When Viola calmed down, however, she began giving orders.

"Go to the terminal and book passage for me on the fastest steam ship leaving for London—even if it leaves tonight or tomorrow," she told one of the girls who had come to the parlor to see what all the commotion was. "And, get my packing trunk out of the attic." Viola hesitated. "No, not my trunk, just my larger valise." To Miss Marshall, she directed the following: "Send a cable in reply, saying the funeral should be scheduled a week hence, in London. The staff who sent this cable will know the church we always attend, or attended." She paused. "Tell them to put a notice in all the papers, London, Paris, Dublin, Barcelona, Vienna, wherever else my uncle had clients." The wave of grief seemed to have passed over her in favor of her efforts to organize her uncle's funeral and her own departure for London. But Miss Marshall heard the grief return later that evening when she took a small dinner tray to Viola's room. Viola lay sobbing on her bed, her valise open and clothes strewn about the room. She was clutching her old velvet bag, something she said Kathleen had made for her long ago.

The next morning Viola was the picture of efficiency as she checked her steamer tickets and prepared to leave for the wharf. She had received confirmation orders from her uncle's attorney that all the appropriate notices had been sent out and the church officiates notified. Her ship would take her to London the day before the funeral. Her uncle's body would arrive the day before that from Ireland. Viola wished to spend no more time than necessary in London and informed the attorney that any bequests or instructions from her uncle should be read out on the day after his burial. She spent the next four days on the ship locked in her cabin, not sketching, barely eating, but also no longer crying. Her uncle's death was yet another signal, she perceived, that she was to go on with her life and not be tethered to any place or any person. When she arrived in London she was touched to see that Kathleen waited for her at the wharf, waving a handkerchief overhead — as if anyone could miss her flaming red hair. They hugged and cried and hugged some more while Viola awaited her baggage.

"I suppose you'll be staying on in London, then," Kathleen began. "Your uncle's estate will take some handling, no doubt, and now you'll have those lovely homes."

"Actually I've already booked my return passage for a week from today. The bequests are to be read out on the day after the funeral and all will be settled then I suppose."

Kathleen was shocked. "But what will you do? Where will you go?" The porter arrived with the bags and Kathleen directed him to the waiting carriage. She turned to find Viola looking off at the skyline. "I know you don't fancy this as your home, but still..."

"You know I don't fancy anywhere home and never have since my parents died." Viola saw the anguish on her friend's face. "But it doesn't mean I haven't been happy wherever I've landed." She smiled. "I seem to remember an old friend telling me to bloom where I'm planted."

At last Kathleen laughed. "Well, you certainly have bloomed." She spun Viola around. "Let me look at you. I suppose you didn't turn out badly after all, and if you had some decent dresses..."

"I think where I'm headed, trousers might be more appropriate." This remark even caught the attention of the coachman who had been waiting for the young women to climb aboard.

"Whatever are you talking about?" The realization then came to Kathleen. "You're going out West, aren't you? Even alone?"

"I most assuredly am, so don't put aside your work on the famous royal dress to make anything for me." It pained her to think about Kathleen foregoing their adventure for a mere dress, but, being honest with herself, she realized it wasn't a mere dress by any means. It was the centerpiece of Kathleen's career and the recognition she had always desired. "I would ask you to make me some trousers, but I know how enamored you are of velvet and brocade. I think any creation you might come up with would scare the horses!" The tense few moments dissolved in gales of laughter.

The next day that shared laughter allowed them to attend Arthur's funeral with dry eyes. Hundreds of mourners packed the chapel and came to the old-fashioned Irish wake Kathleen had organized afterwards at the house. While everyone expressed their sympathies, many were just as eager to meet Kathleen and to get a glimpse of Viola, a single young woman rumored to be very attractive and now very wealthy. Both young women had to call on their best manners to fend off the requests that came their way that day.

The following day proved to be more challenging, however, as Arthur's will and instructions were read. Kathleen attended, at Viola's insistence, along with members of the household and the various agents Arthur had worked with over the years. Arthur, it turned out, had a few surprises planned. The attorney read the usual preamble to the will and then began. "To my dear friend Kathleen Evans, I leave my home in Ireland and all the contents therein." Kathleen gasped. "And I leave with her also a letter stating my intentions." The attorney produced the letter and handed it to the disbelieving Kathleen. She tore open the letter and immediately began sobbing.

My dearest Kathleen: You've been an inspiration to me, and I know to Viola, over the years with your courage to pursue your dreams. I have so enjoyed seeing your tremendous talent emerge, and it is I who has been honored to refer clients to you; they tell me they are forever grateful. You should have a proper home in your own country. I hope you will enjoy it as I did, as a place of peace, although if you marry and fill it with children one day, that's fine, too. The attorney will inform you about the account set up to maintain the house and grounds for many years to come, many years of enjoyment for you, I hope. Your friend, Arthur McDougall.

A few lesser bequests were made to friends, including Arthur's vast library which was to go to a newly-established school for the children of artists. When these requests were finished being read out, Viola assumed that was the end of his instructions. However, the attorney once again consulted his notes. "Mr. McDougall also wishes to convey this home to his loyal staff to be their own to live in as long as they desire." The houseman looked as if he might faint as did several of the maids. "He makes a further comment."

Loyal friends, and yes, that is how I regard you, as my friends and not simply my employees: I realize you have dedicated a large portion of your lives to making mine more comfortable. So now the opportunity has come for me to return your kindness. Many of you have put aside having families of your own, but now you have a home quite commodious that should allow several of you to live together comfortably, and I hope, happily. Arthur McDougall."

All eyes turned to Viola. No mention of her had been made, and the attorney was already putting away his papers. Kathleen finally broke the silence. "Surely, Arthur wouldn't have excluded his niece from his estate?"

"Quite right, I'm sorry to have overlooked this." The attorney fumbled in his case. "This letter is addressed to you, Viola McDougall." He snapped the case shut and left the room. The housekeepers quickly left also, leaving Kathleen alone with Viola who just stared at the envelope. Finally Kathleen took it from her and read aloud.

Cherished and treasured Viola: Certainly I hope you don't think your old uncle forgot about you! Not at all, dear. You've been the most precious gift I ever received, but what I'm giving you is the most precious gift of all and one I think you, above anyone else, can appreciate. I am giving you your freedom. You will not be encumbered by any house or the people required to maintain it. Nor will you have to sift through my belongings in order to find proper homes for them. So, I am leaving you nothing material (all right, a bit of money) so that you may wander freely and find your true passion in life, whatever that may be. When you leave this house, and my guess is that it will be soon despite Kathleen's protests, you need never look back. Look forward, Viola. Look forward to life.

Chapter Forty-Nine

Viola barely alighted off the ship in the New York harbor before she hired a carriage to take her to the train station. Her uncle had left her more than "a bit" of money, so she had no need to budget her money or sell more paintings for the moment. "I would like a first-class ticket, private compartment, to Cheyenne, Wyoming, leaving tomorrow if possible." The ticket agent consulted the schedules and said her request was indeed possible, that the train would leave promptly at nine the following morning and arrive in Cheyenne at two in the afternoon three days later. He also advised her to buy a meal ticket, which she did.

"What's a little lady like you going to do out in Cheyenne? Got a teaching job lined up or a husband waiting for you?" Viola was ready to be insulted but realized he was just making conversation while he wrote out her tickets.

"If you must know, I'm going out there to paint Indians, or pictures of Indians, I should say." She knew it sounded ridiculous. "You know, their whole way of life is disappearing and I wish to see them before it goes away entirely."

"Why Cheyenne? Aren't there Indians a little closer than that?"

"I expect that there are, but the last time I saw one was in Cheyenne, so I'm going back to my source, so to speak." The ticket agent laughed and handed her the sheaf of tickets. Viola thanked him and he wished her well, but she could see how dubious he was of her plan. The carriage had been kept waiting, and Viola now directed it to Miss Marshall's boarding house.

"Oh, you're back so soon!" Miss Marshall looked quite surprised when Viola entered the parlor. "I thought you'd be months organizing your uncle's affairs, and I, well, I, rented your room out."

"That's perfectly fine. I'm not staying." Viola thought she should have tormented the woman a little, or at the very least asked for her rent payment to be returned, but she had no time for foolishness. "I just want to pick up some of my things and I'll be on my way."

"One of the girls boxed them up for you. I'll get her to unpack them for you." Miss Marshall left the parlor and came back with Victoria in tow. "Show Viola where her things are and help her unpack them." Victoria was the most industrious of the girls, and Viola was certain she wouldn't have missed anything in her packing duties.

"I really only want my Bible, the one my aunt gave to me. It's bound in white leather. And, most important, I had a painting which was protected in several layers of cloth." Victoria produced both items quickly, to Viola's relief.

"But what about your clothes?"

"Oh, just divide them up among the girls, whatever. I won't be needing them."

This made no sense to Victoria, but then nothing Viola had ever done had made any sense to her. She refrained from saying it aloud but thought privately that Viola's clothes were so shabby, most of them paint-spattered, that none of the girls would want them anyway. She'd leave them packed up and take them to the poor house after Viola left.

Viola walked out the door without a backward glance down to the waiting carriage. She would spend her last night in New York in a hotel near the train station. She briefly considered going by her old studio but then thought she had probably pained Thomas enough already without putting him through another goodbye.

The next morning the train was right on time. Viola smiled to herself thinking of Conductor Nulty telling her years ago why that was so important. A porter took her two small bags and led her to a compartment furnished with a couch and a fold-down bed plus a little wardrobe. He explained that he would turn down her bed and make it up while she was in the dining car for the evening meal, and if she needed anything else she had only to ask. She tipped him generously, something her uncle had always done for her, she realized.

Viola spent the day in her compartment reading and writing letters to Arthur's friends who had been unable to attend his funeral. When the sun started to set she realized she was famished and quickly made her way to the dining car where her porter seated her and inquired if she would perhaps like a glass of sherry before dinner. It seemed like Uncle Arthur was somehow blessing her journey and she gratefully accepted the aperitif. While waiting for the main course she chanced to look at the dinnerware, noting the lariat design on the plates and cups. The silverware was made to look like fence posts, all very western. When Viola lived at Miss Marshalls she remembered afternoons when the girls there did nothing but talk about china patterns, what they hoped for when they married, and on, and on. Now she had to wonder, "Why don't I have any interest in such things?" Maybe it was being raised without a mother who would have stressed their importance, although Viola grudgingly had to admit that Aunt Vivian had always insisted on a properly set table when Arthur entertained his guests. "I'm just a different kind of woman," she concluded and accepted a second glass of sherry.

The trip passed uneventfully. Viola recalled her earlier train trip as a girl and thought then that the country had seemed so vast. She didn't expect to feel the same way now as an adult, but she was surprised that she did. The train huffed on for miles and miles without a single settlement in sight, and mountain peaks that seemed an hour away weren't reached in the length of a day. She began to feel a little trepidation about being out in this windswept landscape by herself.

Chapter Fifty

When the train pulled into Cheyenne (right on time) Viola was surprised to see that an actual town had grown up in the intervening twenty or so years since she had last seen it. It was still windy and dusty and she had to watch her step as she crossed the main street lest she put her foot into a clump of horse manure, but she could see several hotels, at least two mercantile stores and other small businesses, plus several blocks of houses. The smell from the stockyards wafted down the street still, so some things hadn't changed. The one thing she didn't see, however, was an Indian. She looked around for any sign of the Indian market that had been set up by the train station when she passed through as a child but saw no evidence of it.

"Pardon me, sir," she asked a passerby. "Could you direct me to the Indians, please?" With her striking good looks and her English accent that persisted despite all her years of living in the United States, Viola had clearly startled the gentleman.

"Indians? Here in town?"

"Yes, I recall they had a thriving little market set up to sell goods to the train passengers."

"Here?"

"Perhaps I should ask someone else. You're clearly not familiar with Cheyenne," Viola said rather imperiously.

The man laughed and tipped back his hat. "Not familiar with Cheyenne? Why, I'm the mayor of this town and have been for the past eight years. Probably will be for the next eight, too, miss."

"Well, I beg your pardon then, but my recollection is quite clear." Viola actually grimaced when she thought of the Indian tearing up her sketch of him and stomping it into the dust.

"No, your recollectin's good enough, but things have changed around here." He took Viola's arm and turned her to face the main street. "We got families livin' here now, so we can't have no Indians riding up and down the street. They've all been run off." He looked quite satisfied when he made the statement.

"But they can't be run off, as you say — I've come here expressly to paint them!"

"I 'spect you'll have to rely on your imagination, or, as you put it, your recollections, to do that. There's probably about one band of Indians left in this territory, and I don't think they'll be coming to town to pose for no pictures." The mayor laughed heartily. "Maybe you can paint one of me that I can hang up in my office."

While the mayor continued laughing and greeting other passersby, the realization struck Viola that perhaps her trip had been for nothing. "But there are still Indians?"

"Well, of course there's still Indians, although they killed off a lot of 'em and pretty much penned up the rest of 'em." He could see Viola was upset and became more serious. "You know the governments been trying to help them, get them settled down so's they can farm and build settlements just like the rest of us."

"But Indians aren't like that," Viola began, "they're more nomadic. I don't think they will become farmers." She was growing more exasperated with the mayor and with the situation. "You say there is a band of Indians somewhere nearby though?"

"Well, like you say, they move around a good bit, but sometimes one of the soldiers will see them camped out, getting ready for a hunt, I guess."

"Soldiers?"

"Yep. We've got 'em here to see that the Indians don't go raiding the settlers' farms and such."

"I suppose they would go raiding given how all the buffalo they depended on have been killed," Viola said indignantly.

The mayor laughed again. "Well, miss, I don't know where you got your information, but there's still thousands of buffalo out there, especially higher up on the plains. They don't come to town neither."

Viola was starting to get a kernel of an idea. "I do thank you for your time, Mr. Mayor, but I really must be going now." She bent to pick up her bag, but he beat her to it.

"I'll just walk you to your hotel, then," he said, taking her arm. "Get you settled for the night so you can catch the train back east tomorrow."

Viola didn't answer him but thought to herself, "I won't be getting on any train heading east any time soon." He took her to what he assured her was the finest hotel in town, tipped his hat to her and left her in the lobby. After she was sure he was back out on the street she inquired of the hotel desk clerk, "Where might I find some soldiers?"

He looked shocked and snatched back the hotel ledger. "We do not allow that kind of behavior in our establishment!"

"Behavior? I simply meant to talk to…" Viola finally realized what her request had implied. "I assure you I am a most proper young woman who has no intention of carrying on with any men, here or elsewhere! Now, if you will rent me a room, for at least a week but probably longer, please do so."

He still looked suspicious but also let his gaze wander over her. "It's cash in advance." He slid the ledger back toward her while she fumbled in her bag for a handful of bills.

"I hope this is sufficient," Viola said, pushing forty dollars toward him. "Now summon a porter to take my bags to my room."

"We don't have any..." the clerk started to say, but instead came around from the desk and picked up her bags himself. "Right this way, miss." He showed her to the largest room in the hotel, a corner suite. "I hope you'll be most comfortable during your stay with us."

When he left, Viola threw herself down on the bed and wept out of sadness and frustration. This was her dream and it was appearing to slip away on a cloud of dust. After a while she dried her eyes, however, and washed as much as she could in the basin in her room. The hotel may have been grand for Cheyenne but it was no Palace in San Francisco. If she wanted a relaxing bath, she would have to sign up for one at the bathroom down the hall. Perhaps her view of the West was too romantic, as her friend Samuel had suggested. Before she could begin to cry again, she looked at herself in the tiny mirror. "There are buffaloes. There are Indians. Now just get out there and find them!"

Chapter Fifty-One

Viola left her hotel room only briefly that night to take a light supper. She was the only guest in the dining room and drew attention from the staff who were certainly unaccustomed to seeing women traveling alone. One waitress finally spoke to her. "You know, miss, if you'll be staying on a bit you can arrange to have your meals in your room, might be more comfortable for you." Viola thanked her for the offer but thought perhaps the smarter course of action might be to find a restaurant with more diners and the chance for polite conversation.

She slept well and awoke with fresh resolve, the first chore being to find dresses that weren't the black she had been wearing since the funeral and were insufferably hot and attracted every bit of dust in the air. Surely the local mercantile would have something ready-made. She made her way down the main street and entered the first such store. It carried an amazing array of ranching and farming implements, food stuffs, guns and ammunition, but the millinery department was sadly lacking. She finally caught the attention of a female clerk. "Can you help me, please? I need at least three new dresses and the appropriate undergarments." The clerk looked her up and down, taking in the expensive lace detailing on Viola's current frock and the velvet trim on her bag and shoes.

"We don't have no call for fancy dresses, I'm afraid," the clerk apologized. "There's seamstresses here could make you one but I don't know where you'd be wearing it."

"I don't need something fancy. I need something simple and proper that will keep the sun off me and be cool enough to wear in this heat." Viola tried to sound as patient as possible, but it was a struggle. "Just show me what you have, if you will."

The clerk reluctantly led Viola to the back of the store where a rack held about a dozen drab shifts with blouses to wear underneath. They were as ugly as anything Viola had been forced to wear in boarding school. She picked out three, one brown, one tan and one another shade of brown, plus three plain blouses and a pair of shoes that more resembled boots a soldier might wear. The clerk had one camisole that might be small enough for Viola, and she took that as well. "Now if you would package it up and send it all over to the Cheyenne City Hotel, I would be most appreciative." Viola gave the clerk her name and paid for her purchases, the total being less than she might have spent on a pair of gloves in Paris. That done, she had one more request. "I wonder if you might also direct me to the mayor's office?" The clerk gave her an odd look and explained the mayor didn't have an office per se but he could always be found on the street or in the Longhorn Saloon, some four doors down.

Sure enough, the mayor was holding forth at a round table in the center of the saloon, but he and the other men there jumped to their feet the minute Viola pushed the door open. "Miss your train, did you?" he inquired, while pulling back a chair for her at the table. "Gents, this is our guest, uh..."

"Viola McDougall, thank you," she said, accepting the seat but being careful not to put her purse on the sticky table.

"Anyway, Miss McDougall here traveled all the way to our town with the hopes of painting some Indians." Everyone at the table laughed, except Viola. "Turns out, we're fresh out of Indians and she didn't think I was handsome enough to be a substitute." Even though it was only midmorning, the men were already drinking so this provoked even more laughter. "So I guess you'll be leaving us soon as you can?"

"No, quite the contrary," she began carefully. "Actually I've come looking for you so that you might recommend a guide for me, someone to accompany me out into the countryside so that I may paint such scenery as might interest me." One of the men offered to hook up a buggy and run her out to the hills that very morning, but his base intentions were clear so Viola ignored him and the other men. "I'm sure you'll agree it might not be safe for me to go alone, although I have a mind to if a suitable guide cannot be found."

The mayor picked up his cigar and after a long puff directed his comments to his friends, "I'm thinking of Billy Johnson, you know, Abe Johnson's son?" They all nodded. "Billy's not the brightest apple in the basket, but he darn sure knows this countryside." He added, "Plus, you'd be safe with him, no nonsense. If his daddy found out he'd disrespected a woman, there'd be hell to pay for sure."

"And how do I find this gentleman?"

"If you'll allow me, Miss McDougall, I'll escort you to him myself." The mayor stood, a little unsteadily, and picked up his hat, offering his arm to Viola. The two made their way down the main thoroughfare with numerous interruptions from the mayor's constituents. They arrived at a stable bustling with activity. "A cattle run just finished up so they've got to get the horses re-shoed and all," the mayor said by way of explaining the commotion. He yelled over the din of blacksmiths' hammering and horses neighing. "Say, is Billy here?" One of the blacksmiths pointed to the back of the stable. Viola gingerly picked her way through the horse droppings and thought about the new 'practical' shoes waiting back at her hotel. When they entered a small tool shed a young man poked his head up from a work table where he was repairing a bridle. "Hey, Billy, come out here for a minute," the mayor called, "want you to meet someone."

Billy put down the leather awl and stepped of the shed, squinting at the bright sunshine. He couldn't help staring when he saw Viola. Surely the boys were playing another of their jokes on him if he thought for a minute this woman wanted to meet him. But Viola surprised him. "Viola McDougall," she said, offering her gloved hand, which he shook ever so lightly. "The mayor here tells me you know the countryside quite well, and I am in need of a guide to show me the sights."

Billy stood gaping at her. "Well, yes, ma'am, I do know the countryside, ain't a part of it I ain't been over in a hundred miles any direction."

The heat and animal smells seemed to be affecting the mayor who quickly announced. "I'll be leaving you to it then. Good day, Miss McDougall, Billy." He half-staggered back to the street leaving Billy to his staring.

Viola took charge. "I am an artist, a painter mostly, although I do sketches and sometimes work in pastels." She could tell Billy wasn't listening to a word she said. He was perhaps a couple of years older than she but clearly mentally deficient in some regard. "What I am trying to tell you is that I wish you to take me out to some of the more scenic, picturesque areas of the countryside so that I may paint or draw them." She left out the part about trying to find Indians for the moment. "Do you see what I'm after?"

Billy had taken off his hat but quickly put it back on, pulling the brim low. "I believe I do, yes, ma'am, I believe I do." He hesitated. "I work here for my father, but he pays me and so…"

"Well, I certainly plan on paying you for your time," Viola assured him. "I would think, oh, about, ten dollars a day, perhaps?" She had no idea what a living wage might be, having only made money from the sale of her paintings.

Billy was grateful for the hat's low brim so she couldn't see his eyes dancing in delight. Ten dollars a day was a fortune in these parts. His father paid him thirty-five cents an hour. "Well, I suppose my father could spare me for a few days, you know, here and there, after we get these here horses back to the trail."

"I'm anxious to get started as soon as we can, but I do understand your prior commitment," Viola replied, regretting what some would call her 'high-falutin' English. "That will give me time to get some painting supplies in order, so, all's the better." She started to walk out, but turned back to see Billy smiling. "And one other thing. I'll need to rent a horse. Perhaps you have one here?"

Billy seemed to ponder the question. "Well, we got one. I'll go get 'em for you." He left for a corral out behind the shed, leaving Viola to fan away the flies. The horse he came back with looked like a mistake. Its legs were too long, its neck too short, and one ear levered off at an unusual angle. It was mostly a dark brown, but black in splotches and white in others. "This here's Rufus," Billy said, holding tightly to the reins. "He's a solid old boy."

Viola moved to pet the horse which immediately lunged toward her, getting a good bit of her hair in his mouth. "Ow!" She twisted to get away as Billy kneed the horse in its stomach so that it opened its mouth. Viola retrieved most of her hair although it was coated in a thick slobber. She would be signing up for a bath tonight for certain.

"He must've thought your hair was fresh straw. I've never seen him do that before." Billy seemed embarrassed but Viola sought to reassure him.

"Well, horses have their personalities, don't they?"

"Yes, ma'am, they do that." He hesitated. "You want I should saddle him and you can take him around the corral a few times?" He eyed her dress and hoped she would decline.

"Why don't you? We'll see how we get along, won't we, Rufus?" Viola had been forced to take equestrianism classes at nearly every boarding school she had attended, but it was hardly one of her favorite activities. When Billy came back with a blanket and Western saddle, she looked dubious. In school the girls had always ridden the fussy side saddles because of their dresses. She had always resented having to be lifted onto the horse by someone else, in fact. Billy cinched the saddle up, once again kneeing Rufus in the stomach so he would expel any extra air and the saddle could be snugged in place. He held the reins and looked expectantly at Viola. "Yes, well, here we go," she said while trying to reach up to the saddle horn and maneuver her foot high enough to catch the stirrup, all the while holding up her skirts. Finally, Billy pulled the horse over to the fence so Viola could use one of the rungs to stand on and gain the height needed to reach the stirrup. She dragged herself up onto the horse who stood placidly. Billy handed her the reins and opened the corral gate. Rufus walked out without any encouragement from Viola, then promptly dropped to his knees and sat down on his haunches, clearly intending to roll over with Viola in the saddle! Billy scooped her up before Rufus could crush her. Viola was shaking and determined not to cry. "Perhaps a buggy might be easier." Billy sighed with relief and bit back his laughter. That had been his plan all along.

Chapter Fifty-Two

Billy's father had always taught him to be a God-fearing man. They said prayers every night before the evening meal and again when they went to bed. There was a time, however, when the Good Lord decided to take Billy's mother when she was giving birth to his sister, that Billy stopped believing. Now, however, his faith was restored. Even though he knew it was blasphemous to think this way, there must be a God if he was going to get ten dollars a day to drive a pretty girl around the countryside. He worked like a dervish in the stables repairing bridles and saddles, shoeing horses and doing anything else his father asked, as long as it would get him out of the stable faster and back into the company of Viola. He found himself walking around saying her name in his head and remembering her coppery blonde hair. He knew he could easily put both hands around her tiny waist; she probably didn't weigh as much as a newborn foal. He counted the hours until Friday morning when he was to collect her from the hotel.

At the same time Viola wasn't feeling attractive in the least as she tried on her new dresses. If the girls at Miss Marshall's had thought she was drab then, they should see her now. She finally looked in the mirror and laughed imagining what the British press would say about their "glamorous young heiress" now. But, she had to admit, the dresses were practical with pockets on the sides and a comfortable, loose-fitting style. They hung straight from her waist so wouldn't require all the starchy slips she was used to wearing.

Friday morning finally arrived and Billy pulled the buggy up to the hotel to find Viola already standing outside waiting. He jumped down from the seat and took the satchel and a box she was carrying, stowing them in back, then helped her climb up onto the buggy's only seat. He could smell her hair with its light lavender scent. Her dress was not nearly as nice as the one she had worn to the stables, but he supposed it was all she could find in Cheyenne, and he could still make out her fine figure even through its sack-like shape.

"I reckon we'll head up to the bluffs, give you a view of the whole valley," he said, flicking the reins on the horse. "Cooler up there, too." He had put a few little bells on the harness and they made a musical sound as the horse picked up speed. Billy delighted in seeing the other men on the street turn their heads to see him heading out of town with such a beautiful woman. Pride was a sin, he knew, but still.

"Cooler most assuredly sounds good. I'll leave our ultimate destination to your discretion." As soon as the words left her mouth Viola felt like apologizing for being so pompous. "I mean, wherever you think."

Billy said nothing, hoping she would keep talking. He would have been happy to listen to her accent all day. But they rode out of town in companionable silence, dust rolling up behind them and the heat causing shimmering waves in the distance. The flat plains gradually gave way to grassy foothills with interesting rock outcroppings, and the higher they climbed the more pleasant the day became. Viola had arranged for the hotel to put a lunch together for them and at what seemed like midday, she finally asked Billy to pull the wagon over near a grove of pine trees. "Let's have something to eat and let the horse rest, shall we?"

He could have eaten the leather reins by this time and was relieved to see the contents of the box she'd brought, a cooked chicken, some bread, a few apples and a big jug of water. He spread out a blanket and Viola arranged their lunch on it. When they'd eaten she leaned back against one of the pines and looked back toward Cheyenne. "Well, you certainly never would see a view like this in England." She drew her sketch book out of its satchel and made a few preliminary strokes.

"I've been there, you know," Billy said hesitantly.

"England? My, and how did that come about?"

"There was this Wild West type of show and they come through town on the train, like you did, looking for 'gen-u-wine characters' and somebody who could tend horses." He smiled. "I wasn't no character but I could keep the horses in good shape, so off I went. My father liked to have a fit."

"And how did you find it?"

"Well, I didn't have to find it. Someone else was driving the ship," Billy replied, wondering why she would ask such a stupid question.

"I meant, how did you enjoy your experience?" Viola answered slowly, wondering just how stupid he was.

"Well, horses are horses just about anywhere you take 'em, and they worked us pretty hard so we didn't get out to see much." He appeared to be thinking. "I thought it was pretty gray and cold. I don't think we ever did see the sun. But that weather was probably good for business, you know."

"The weather can be dreary, you're correct."

"But I think it made people grateful for any little entertainment they could find, like the show." He took a long drink out of the jug. "I think we're all looking for something different in our lives and lots of people never get the chance I had, so it was all right, I guess."

Viola sensed he was rather more thoughtful than she first suspected. "And why did you leave the show?"

"Oh, things just happened in life." He didn't say more and she didn't press the subject, returning to her drawing. He stretched out on the blanket and was sleep in an instant.

Viola spent the afternoon filling in the sketch using only a pencil but shading in the canyons and paying careful attention to the shrubbery and rocks. She could use the sketch later as the basis for a painting, or perhaps Billy would take her someplace with an even greater vista. She shook his shoulder lightly when the sun started to dip behind the mountain. "Do you think we should start back to town?"

He was disoriented for a moment looking up at the face of an angel but then came to his senses. "I reckon that horse is well-rested by now." He blushed. "And the driver, too." They gathered up the lunch box and the blanket, Billy helping her climb into the wagon for the ride back to the dust and heat of Cheyenne. He wanted to see her drawing but was too embarrassed to ask.

Over the next two weeks they made several more forays into the countryside, and conversation became easier. On a lunch break Viola asked Billy, "So why are you so knowledgeable about all this land?"

"My father and I, before he took over the stables, we were trappers and hunters for the railroad." She looked quizzical. "You know, all the workers had to be fed, so my dad contracted with them to supply deer, buffalo, whatever we could shoot. I was just a boy so I couldn't shoot, but I could look at the land and recollect just where we had gotten every animal, where the best hunting spots were, you know."

When he mentioned buffalo, Viola thought it might be the conversational opening she needed to inquire about Indians, so she took the chance. "And, when you were out hunting, did you come across Indians?"

"At first we did, but then less and less."

"Because?"

"For one thing, the soldiers were pretty much chasing 'em away, and the game was getting pretty thin." He added hurriedly, "It wasn't just me and my father out doing the hunting, there were dozens of hunters."

"So you don't see the Indians any longer?"

"There's a few of 'em around, but they stay away from town. We stay away from them. Sort of works, I guess."

Viola tried not to let her disappointment show.

Chapter Fifty-Three

Billy and Viola fell into an easy pattern. He brought the buggy around on Tuesdays and Fridays and worked at the stables the rest of the week. Viola rented the hotel room adjacent to hers and turned it into an art studio of sorts. The Cheyenne Mercantile was able to order the paints and canvases she needed from Chicago. She took the sketches she made on their outings and used them as the inspiration for her paintings. A gallery in Chicago and two in New York told her they would buy every one she could produce. There was a great deal of interest in everything Western, it seemed.

When the chambermaid came to clean Viola's rooms she gasped in delight. "Why that's the most beautiful picture I've ever seen of Black Mountain!" She had never spoken to Viola and was immediately embarrassed.

"Thank you, of course. You know the area?"

"My pa used to take me and my brothers up there sometimes when he'd go hunting." She busied herself dusting the bureau. "I never thought it was so beautiful though until I seen it just now the way you done it up."

"It's quite an interesting countryside, all right," Viola said distractedly.

"You should take it down to the lobby and let them hang it up there for everyone to see." Viola continued to rifle through her sketch pad. "You know, everyone's curious about what you do up here and all."

"I'm sure now you can tell them," Viola said, a little more sharply than she intended.

"Sorry, miss, I just meant...."

"No, I'm sorry. Perhaps the next painting. This one is already sold." She knew the chambermaid was embarrassed. "I think I'll go for a stroll and let you finish your job here." Viola picked up her satchel and left the room.

Billy was being questioned at the stables, too. "So what do you and that gal do all day?" his father asked. "She even talk to you?"

"We talk a bit. Mostly she draws and I just watch out for things." He adjusted the strap on a bridle he'd repaired. "She's from England, you know?"

"Oh, well then I suppose you two have high tea together then," Billy's father laughed, "you having become so well acquainted with England." He shook his head at how Billy blushed, but it wasn't in his heart to tease him any further. The other cowboys coming into the stable more than made up for it. They were all hoping Billy would give them any little detail about Viola that might allow them to approach her for a date, but Billy was tight-lipped on the subject.

The wait from Tuesday to Friday seemed interminable but finally the day arrived. "Good morning. Looks to be a really nice day, no wind or nothin'."

"Yes, Billy, I believe you're right." Viola put her satchel in the back of the buggy while the hotel clerk loaded in the box with their lunch. She noticed something different. "What's wrapped up there in back?"

"Oh, that's nothing to concern you," Billy answered quickly and helped her into the buggy. "With the days long now I think we have enough daylight to go further up the canyon today, if you like."

"You're the guide, Billy, whatever you think best," Viola replied, still puzzled about what why he didn't answer her question. They said little for the rest of the ride until they entered a canyon barely wide enough for the buggy. "This is spectacular!"

"Oh, you ain't seen the best of it yet," Billy said with a grin. When the canyon opened up there was a meadow filled with wildflowers, bisected by a quickly-flowing stream. He heard Viola's musical laughter.

"You are full of surprises, aren't you?" she teased him, lightly pinching his arm. "It's just wonderful."

Billy let the horse out of the harness and tied him to a tree with plenty of slack line then helped Viola spread out a blanket far enough away from the horse. He reached in the bag of the wagon to retrieve the secret package, revealing it to contain a fishing rod. "I believe we may have us some trout for lunch today," he said, heading off to the stream.

Viola didn't know what to sketch first, the flowers, the narrow mouth of the canyon, or the rock features that seemed to have faces in them. They both were lost in their endeavors in no time, but eventually Billy came back with a string of fish and proceeded to build a small fire to cook them over. She had learned on their outings just how resourceful he was and how confident in the wild outdoors. Viola realized she was used to men who had other men do everything for them. Billy's self-reliance was very attractive, but she knew better than to encourage him.

After they had devoured the trout Viola expected Billy to take his customary nap, but instead as she returned to her drawing she discovered him staring at her intently. "Whatever are you looking at?"

"You. I'm looking at you."

"Why?"

"I thought that's what I was supposed to do, you know, watch you."

"You are supposed to watch *over* me, not just stare at me," Viola said with a laugh.

Billy pretended to raise his gaze over her head. "That better? Now I'm watching over you."

"All right you. If that's how you want to be, come over here and sit on that rock, and take your hat off, or at least push it back so I can see your eyes." Billy hesitated but did as he was told. She had never noticed how doe-like his brown eyes were. "Now, sit still." She reached for her sketchpad as he started to protest. "Sit still and no talking!" For the next hour Viola drew his face and shoulders, gradually working down to his hands which were folded over one knee. Billy stayed remarkably still, a skill he had probably learned through hunting, and he said nothing until she closed the pad.

"What, I don't get to see what you've made of me?"

"Not today, sir." She left him sitting there while she looked for another vantage point to see the canyon mouth. When she returned, there was a bouquet of flowers on the blanket. She wanted to think of him as a sweet, simple boy, but realized he was, in fact, older than her and a complex man in his own right. She inhaled the bouquet's fragrances while Billy pretended not to notice.

The sun was starting to dip below the canyon walls. "We best think about getting back to town," Billy said, harnessing the horse to the buggy and packing up the lunch box and blanket. "Going down the canyon in the dark might not be wise." Viola agreed although perhaps for different reasons.

When they once again exited the slot canyon Viola noticed that the grass had been trampled down in a wide swath, and Billy noticed it too, reaching behind the seat for the rifle he always kept there. He stopped the buggy and jumped down.

"What is it?" Viola asked with some alarm.

"It's a band of Indians, but they're long gone by now, probably passed through while we were eating."

"How do you know?" Viola was fascinated.

"Come down here," Billy said, taking her hand. "See them long straight ruts?" She nodded that she did. "Those are from dragging their teepee poles. So it's not just a hunting party out scavenging, more like a small village on the move."

"Are we safe?" Viola said, moving closer to the wagon.

"Oh, I expect so. If they'd a wanted to harm us they woulda done so." He looked thoughtful. "I imagine it's Silver Wolf and his clan. Ain't seen him in a while." He helped Viola back into the buggy. "We're not likely to see him at all unless he wants to be seen." Viola was pensive on the ride home, and the rocks that had looked like faces had become suddenly eerie.

Chapter Fifty-Four

Viola's excitement was palpable on the following Tuesday when Billy arrived at the hotel. On the ride out to the hills, she talked more, talked faster, asked endless questions and made more observations about everything. Billy's excitement rose with hers though he truly had no idea of the source. She suggested they head toward the slot canyon they had visited last week, but when the buggy neared the entrance to the canyon, she made another suggestion.

"Let's go the way the Indians did, why don't we?"

"I'm not sure that's the best idea, especially if they're out hunting," Billy said uncertainly.

"We won't disturb then. We can just ride on a ways and see where they went." Viola tugged on his shirt sleeve. "Please?"

Of course, he couldn't say no, and clucked the reins. At the same time, however, he reached behind the seat and picked up the rifle he always carried, settling it across his knees. Viola continued her chatter, asking about birds and plants that she previously had evinced no interest in, but Billy said little, relentlessly scanning the tree line. Finally, he slowed the wagon and pointed off toward the horizon. "See that? See those plumes of smoke? That's probably their camp."

Viola was beside herself. "Can we get close enough to see it?"

"Not unless you want to get your hair lifted!" Billy was astounded at her naiveté.

"Oh, I think they'd see we're just out for a pleasant ride and mean them no harm," she persisted. "Let's ride up a little further."

He was reluctant but let the horses follow the trampled-down path the Indians had made. He spotted the Indian scouts watching them but said nothing to Viola for the moment. She would probably stand up and wave her hankie at them! The buggy gradually crested a small hill, revealing the camp below them. It was much larger than Billy expected, probably forty teepees in all, with well over a hundred horses penned up in a makeshift ramada. Billy jumped out of the wagon and tied up the team to a nearby tree, but he never let loose of his rifle. When he saw that the scouts were staying put, he lifted Viola down from her perch and helped her set out the blanket. He could just imagine what his father would be saying now.

Viola immediately pulled out her sketchpad but made no move to pick up a pencil. She sat raptly staring down into the valley while Billy stood guard near the horses. He often brought along an axe to chop up firewood to take home or did a little hunting, but there would be none of that today. Finally she began roughing in a sketch of the camp itself but curiously left out any of the people milling around in it. Billy asked her why. "Oh, I'll have to wait until I'm much closer to do that." All he could do was shake his head. The scouts stayed where they were and Billy stayed where he was for the remainder of the afternoon in an uneasy truce.

"When we came across their tracks a few days ago you mentioned it might be Silver Wolf's band," Viola began tentatively. "Do you still think so?"

"Oh, it's Silver Wolf all right." He moved closer to Viola. "See that teepee in the center with the drawings around the top?" She nodded. "That's his sign there."

Viola was thoughtful but added a few details of the teepee to her rough sketch. "How did he get that name?"

"Normally, I think the Indians get sort of a vision, or an inspiration, when a baby is born and they sort of pick the name based on that," Billy began. "His story was a bit different." He relaxed his stance a bit but kept his eyes trained on the Indians. "When he was just a little boy a silver wolf wandered into camp, bold as can be, and went right up to him." Viola shuddered thinking about the wolves in Italy. "Anyways, it followed him around like a dog, never nipping at him or nothing, but nobody could get near him unless that wolf allowed it."

"So his parents changed his name because of that?"

"No, the story goes that his old man got angry at that wolf one day—I guess it bit one of the wives. Anyway, he told the boy he had to get rid of it." Billy paused in the telling. "Well, he couldn't run it off or nothin' so he finally had to kill it."

Viola gasped. "But that's horrible. It was his pet by then!"

"Yes, I reckon they were pretty close," Billy agreed. "But there was no going against the chief, so he done what he was told." He debated about telling Viola the rest of the story. He took a deep breath. "But then he took it one more step. He cut the heart out of that wolf and ate it right in front of his father." Viola was wide-eyed. "So, in that way he took on the spirit of that wolf and he renamed himself in that wolf's honor." Viola was in tears. "If you saw him close-up you'd see he still wears that wolf's pelt, or most of it anyway. The Indians seem respectful that way, I think." Billy walked back toward the horses, leaving Viola to her thoughts.

Billy knew the story had upset Viola, but he justified it to himself. That girl has to learn that the West is a hard place and real Indians are not like those in the travelling shows. He was torn, however, between the desire to protect her and his reluctance to deprive her of an experience she clearly craved. For a bit he wondered about asking his father to ride out with him one afternoon to talk to Silver Wolf. Maybe he would agree to let the young woman come to his camp? But what if he and his pa did get to the camp and the Indians scalped them? Then who would take care of Viola? It was a bothersome thing for sure.

With the daylight waning, Billy finally approached Viola again and said it was time they loaded up. She had been so enthralled by the appearance of the camp that they hadn't even had lunch. Billy put the lunch box between them on the seat in hopes that she would offer him something on the ride back to town, but she was mute until the hotel came into sight. "Could we go out again tomorrow?" she finally asked. "To the same place."

"I'd have to see what pa's got in store at the stables," Billy said, not surprised by her request. "I guess I could come by in the morning and let you know." She beamed at him, but he knew, this was going to be a problem.

Chapter Fifty-Five

They edged closer to the camp each day. The sentry scouts stayed where they were, never taking their eyes off Billy and Viola. Billy never took his eyes off them. Viola watched every aspect of the Indians' camp life, even physically leaning toward the camp as she sketched. Billy prayed each night that Silver Wolf would simply break camp and disappear. Problem solved. But, it didn't happen and now there were times when Silver Wolf sat astride his horse for long periods of time, just watching them, it seemed. What would Billy do if the Indian leader rode out to meet them? He agonized about it all day and never put down his rifle. After a week of them encroaching even further on the camp, Billy tried another tack with Viola. "My pa says there's a big herd coming in tomorrow, so I guess I won't be able to take you out here for a week or so."

"Pardon me?" Viola hadn't heard a word he'd said.

"I said, I can't come out with you for a week or so. I've got to help pa at the stables."

"Well, all right. As long as the buggy's available I don't suppose that will be a problem," she said distractedly.

"What will you do with the buggy?"

"Silly, you don't expect me to ride Rufus out here do you?" Viola laughed for the first time in days.

"You'd come out here on your own!" Billy was incredulous and furious at the same time. "That's not safe and I won't let you do it."

"We've been perfectly safe," Viola countered, and then in a haughty tone only the English could master, added, "and it's not up to you to *let* me do anything." Billy felt like shaking her. "I will come to the stables and pick up the buggy in the morning." She went back to her drawing while Billy, rebuked, still seethed. Why did they ever find the Indians in the first place! But, the next morning he was outside the hotel with the buggy and his rifle but bearing a sullen look which Viola ignored. His stomach was paining him something awful. They rode in silence out to the camp site, which Billy was dismayed to see still in place. As soon as the buggy stopped, Viola jumped down on her own, grabbed her satchel and set off for the perimeter of the camp. Billy had no choice but to follow her, grabbing the rifle and the blanket while hastily tying up the horses. She picked a place not fifty feet from the camp and imperiously motioned for Billy to set out the blanket. He felt exposed, which, of course, he was, and angry but sad as well. He missed the little talks they used to have as he told her about the countryside. He was surprised therefore when she directed a question at him.

"Do they speak English?"

"Uh, oh, some do, more than they like to let on," he began. "Not so much the women or children, but some of the braves for sure." She nodded and went back to her drawing. He waited for a few minutes. "Some of them have been to town a good bit, trading and all, even talking with the soldiers, so..." She was no longer paying any attention to him, he realized.

The afternoon dragged on and Billy was finally forced to sit on the edge of the blanket. They were so close to camp now that some of the children even dashed out to quickly touch the blanket, then scamper off. Viola wasn't listening, but he told her anyway. "They're counting coup. Warriors do it. They get close enough to touch their enemy without the enemy even knowing." He tried to sneak a glance at Viola's drawings and noticed she still had not included any faces. Otherwise the drawings were quite detailed and showed the lively camp life in a very agreeable way.

When Billy finished feeding the horses and putting the buggy away that night, his father called him aside. He could tell something was bothering his son. "You ain't said much about that English gal lately. She still paying you and all?"

"She pays me every other week, just fine." Billy was a little ashamed that he hadn't given more money to his father but would rectify that. "She just don't pay me no mind." He sighed and leaned heavily against the top rail of the fence. He was reluctant to tell his father where they had been every day but finally told him the whole story.

"You been spending every day within shot's distance of Silver Wolf? No wonder your stomach's botherin' you." His father was having a hard time picturing the whole situation. "I think maybe you best tell her you can't go no more."

"I tried that and she just said she'd go on her own. And she would, too!" Billy looked ill. "And then what would happen?" His father put his arm around Billy's shoulder, recognizing the boy was half in love, maybe without knowing it himself. He'd pray on it that night. It was going to take something major to bring the boy and that foolish girl to their senses, that much was certain. Maybe Silver Wolf would gather up and leave. He sure hoped so.

The next morning found Billy once again in front of the hotel where Viola was already waiting impatiently. They went to the same spot as before just a few dozen yards from the camp perimeter. Viola made a few desultory comments about the weather to Billy on the way but said little else. Billy noticed the sentries still in place, and the day went on just as the days before. As they were preparing to leave, however, Billy noticed Viola place a small parcel where the blanket had been. "You forgettin' something?"

"No, I am not." She saw how morose he had become and softened her reply. "It's just a little gift. After all we've been their guests," she said, gesturing toward the camp. "And, I think I'm taking something from them, too."

"You're lucky they're not taking our scalps as gifts," Billy said in a huff, not bothering to help Viola up into the buggy.

They were back again the next morning and Billy noticed the parcel was gone. "Well, I guess they enjoyed your gift, as you put it." He was curious to know what she had left but damned if he'd ask her. When they left later in the afternoon, she carefully left another parcel, but this time she told him what it contained — spools of colorful ribbons.

Viola surprised Billy when they reached the hotel. "I won't need to go back out for a few days." He was relieved and disappointed. "I need to paint, something I've been neglecting, and my agents in Chicago are clamoring for more work." She laughed in a self-deprecating way, something he hadn't heard in days. "Oh, to be an independent woman." He'd heard rumors from the train stationmaster that she'd crated up a half-dozen paintings a month or so ago, and the stationmaster heard from the banker that they fetched a pretty penny indeed.

As he drove back to the stables Billy thought, "Maybe she's had enough Indians to last her for a while. Maybe they'll leave while we take a few days off. Maybe it will go back to the way it was with us before." He somehow doubted it and his stomach clenched in pain.

Chapter Fifty-Six

Billy smelled the campfires before they actually saw the plumes. It had been nearly a week, but clearly Silver Wolf was still there. Before they got any closer, the sentries revealed themselves and virtually escorted them to the camp. Billy noticed that Viola's satchel was fuller than usual, even after she took out her sketchpad and pencils. More gifts, he supposed. He sat in the shade of the buggy watching the sunlight play off Viola's curls. He noticed that she curled her upper lip under her teeth when she was sketching and that she could look at an object without blinking for minutes at a time. She had told him once that she tried to memorize every small detail so that she could add them back into her paintings later. He tried it himself, memorizing every small detail about her, then closing his eyes for a minute. No matter how many times he tried, he'd still open his eyes and realize he forgot the button at the edge of her shift, or the way she had tied her scarf around her shoulders. Viola was so absorbed in watching the camp activities that she didn't notice Billy at all, he realized. He'd grown a mustache in the week they were apart, but she had never commented on it.

They did take a break for lunch that day, and for a change Viola served him, setting out the food and filling a plate for him before she filled her own. "So, I'm wondering," he said tentatively, "why you never fill in their faces," gesturing toward the camp, "when we're sure as heck close enough to see them now."

"It's a matter of respect," Viola answered. "The Indians, well maybe not all of them, but the one I had an encounter with, feel that you're taking their soul, maybe even their life, by drawing in such an...intimate way."

"Well, you drew my face that time? Does that mean you took my soul?" Billy looked genuinely worried, which made Viola laugh uproariously.

"Unless you have become an Indian in the time I've known you, I don't think that's likely!" He was embarrassed but loved to hear her laugh again. She had been so serious and so quiet ever since they found the Indian camp.

"Well, that's good then. I sure ain't no Indian. And glad of it." Viola said nothing in response.

At the end of the day, he began to gather up their belongings when she turned to him. "Go on back to Cheyenne without me, Billy. I mean to stay here." He couldn't believe he'd heard her correctly, but she turned on her heel and walked directly to the camp. He'd already untied the horse and didn't dare turn loose of it to chase after her. He had feared just this moment and stood by helplessly.

Viola walked directly to Silver Wolf's teepee. The Indians who had not already gone to their own teepees watched her approach but did nothing to stop her. She pulled the flap aside and bent at the waist to enter his teepee. His wives were attending him, one feeding him from a bowl of stew while the other lifted the heavy shell plate that covered his chest. Another younger girl stoked the fire in the center of the tent. Silver Wolf looked at Viola intently across the flames, then with a flick of his wrist motioned his wives to leave them. She made to approach him, but he signaled her to stay where she was. He could see the flames dancing in her violet eyes and making her chestnut hair seem ablaze. Finally, he beckoned her to him. She approached slowly and sat somewhat beside and behind him. She began to slowly undo the long braid that hung down his back. As she did, she took a silver hairbrush from her satchel and began to comb out his silky black hair as each twist of the braid was undone. Where the braid had looked heavy, his hair now felt light and silky in her hands. She arrayed it across his bare back then gently massaged his scalp, then his neck, letting her hands slide around to his chest. He grabbed one of her hands and held it to him, gradually drawing her around him. With a look it was agreed — they would be together.

The lovers Viola had taken in the past had been men with skin as soft and perfumed as her own. The only hands that had ever touched her roughly had been those of a sculptor whose advances she rebuffed, although she bore the bruises of that encounter for days afterward. Silver Wolf was clearly a man. His hands were like leather from holding the reins of his horse, fingertips like flint from pulling back on a bow. She kissed the rough spots on his chest where the protective shell plate had chafed. His arms and legs were sinewy with muscle that rippled when he moved over her. Silver Wolf knew plenty of English but spoke none of it that night. As they stretched out on a buffalo rug, Viola wondered if the heat came from the fire or from this incredible man, a man she never could have imagined even though many times she'd tried.

Billy, meanwhile, had driven the buggy back up onto the bluff overlooking the camp. He sat watching Silver Wolf's teepee for a long time, his heart slowly breaking. Night after night he came back to repeat the lonely vigil but never did find Viola waiting for him.

Over the days that followed Viola was rarely away from Silver Wolf's side. As wildly passionate as the nights were, the days were peacefully idyllic. They bathed together in the river, and he easily swept her up onto his horse for rides high up into the mountains. He did speak to her in short bursts about plants or animals they saw, but he asked nothing of her. She was content to feel him next to her, naked in the river or riding behind him up an aspen-lined canyon. Her artist's eye never strayed from him, barely even seeing the scenery they rode through. She could tell he was troubled, however.

Chapter Fifty-Seven

Viola enticed Silver Wolf to make love as often as she could in hopes of lifting his spirits which seemed to grow darker by the day. She had been obsessed with him ever since she and Billy first approached the camp. Thinking about Billy made her feel both sad and ashamed. She knew he still rode out to the bluff hoping for a glimpse of her, or more likely, hoping she would return to Cheyenne with him. Viola knew her obsession with Silver Wolf would be impossible for anyone to understand. If she were honest with herself, it was probably an attempt to bury the memory of the only man who had ever rejected her—the Indian at the train station years ago who had stomped her drawing into the dirt and scared her so badly. Silver Wolf never questioned why she had come to him after her weeks of watching. Women had always offered themselves to him, and Viola being white was only mildly curious to him.

The other Indians in the camp, even the women, seemed to accept her. She learned to cook over the campfire and to do some of the embroidery work on the deer hides after they had been properly dried and stretched. They had seen other white women, of course, and over the years a few had even been kidnapped by the band, but their stays were usually short-lived. If Silver Wolf accepted her into his tent, then that was that. If there were jealousies, they were well-hidden.

Nearly every day there was a meeting of most of the band, excepting those who were out hunting or keeping watch as sentries. Viola imagined that she could understand some of the Indian words, but regardless she understood their intent and the emotion behind them. Silver Wolf explained to her, "Our scouts ride far each day but they see no other camps. Our brothers have been rounded up like cattle and marched to the white men's prisons. We fear we are next." And then he confessed something else to her. "When you first entered my teepee and I saw your violet eyes I thought you were a witch/spirit come to distract me, but now I know the truth of it." Silver Wolf ran his hands over her shoulders. "It is you who are bewitched, I believe." Viola could only mutely agree.

In Cheyenne Billy was distracted from his misery at least temporarily by the arrival of a large cavalry troop whose horses needed shoeing desperately after having marched through the Badlands. Billy never left the stable from sunup until well past sundown, and on the second afternoon the troop was in town he chanced to overhear the commander talking with his father. "We mean to ride up into that canyon and take the Indian camp that's up there, soon as the horses are fit to ride." Billy's father could see Billy listening intently. "They're about the last bunch of 'em out there, and we're determined to take 'em in, one way or the other."

Billy coughed loudly to draw their attention. "There's something you should know about that band," he began. "It's Silver Wolf's group and there's about a hundred of 'em or more."

"Yes, that's what the scouts reported."

"But there's something else." He looked at his father. "There's a white woman with them."

"Kidnapped her, did they?" The commander swore under his breath. "Nothing but savages is all they are."

"Well, not exactly," Billy looked imploringly at his father. "She kind of just joined up with them."

Both men looked at him with confusion written on their faces. "Joined up with them?" his father asked. "How could you have let her go off with them!"

"It's not like I *let* her do anything," Billy sighed. "She's a headstrong one. She just got it in her head, I guess, that she wanted to be with them." He thought of Viola entering Silver Wolf's teepee and not emerging until morning. "So, she's with Silver Wolf and if you go in there, maybe you could watch out for her."

His father looked disgusted. "Like you did, son?" Billy hung his head with shame and walked slowly back out to the corral.

Silver Wolf knew the cavalry had come to Cheyenne and would soon be approaching their camp. He also knew they were outnumbered and would be out-gunned by the cavalry. He posed the question to the braves. "Do we fight to the death and uphold our dignity, or do we surrender to protect our families and live to fight another day?" Silence hung heavy around the campfire and, at least that night, no one answered. The following morning the question became moot as Silver Wolf and the others awakened to an unnaturally quiet dawn. The cavalry had come in the night and surrounded the camp entirely. All that could be heard was the rippling of the American flag carried by the lead rider. A bugle rang out and the commander rode forward toward Silver Hawk's teepee. Silver Hawk stepped outside the teepee and could see that his own sentries were already tied up and had been unable to warn them of the cavalry's approach.

"By the order of the President of the United States, I hereby order you to surrender to my command and to follow me to a reservation that has been designated as yours."

Some of the braves were reaching for their bows and arrows, and those that had them, their rifles, but Silver Wolf stopped them with a gesture. "We will not fight you today, but we will never surrender, as you say." Viola emerged from the teepee, shocked to hear his words.

The commander alerted one of the soldiers to Viola's presence. "Go get that girl!"

Viola clung to Silver Wolf's arm. "Please, you can't let them take me. I belong with you." She was sobbing as the soldier approached her. "Tell them I will stay with you."

He turned her toward him. "Your place in life is with your people, just as my place is to lead my people to safety." She still clung to him, but he continued, "In your paintings, show them, show the world, what we were and what they have taken away from us forever."

"But I could do that with you," Viola protested.

"No, because you will not see us again as the free people we were, the people who protected and cherished this land. We tried to guard it from the greed and stupidity of the white man, but they are too many now for us." He grabbed her hand and held it to his chest. "My heart will always remember." He then held his hand to her chest. "Yours will go on." He handed her over to the waiting soldier who had to half-carry her to a wagon.

The Indians were told to break camp and ready for a march of some hundred miles. Viola was returned to the hotel in Cheyenne and dumped rather unceremoniously at the steps. Word of her having willingly gone with an Indian band had already spread through the frontier town, and she was met with icy stares and backs turned. Not even Billy dared come to see her.

Chapter Fifty-Eight

Viola was oblivious to the fact that the town was shunning her. She was in a fog of misery that nothing penetrated. After four days of leaving her alone, the chambermaid finally ventured into her room, Viola having ignored, or not even heard, the knocks on the door. She found Viola prostrate on her bed surrounded by dozens and dozens of sketches of the Indian encampment. The sketches were tear-stained and crumpled, but even the chambermaid could appreciate the artistic talent they represented. She began gradually gathering them into a stack. "Now look how lovely that is. I can see why you wanted to ride all the way out there every day," the maid began. "Dusty as it is here, you forget there's pretty areas out there, too." Viola didn't stir.

The chambermaid picked up the room as much as she could, but since the hotel was nearly empty she decided to stay on for a while with the grief-stricken young woman. "Aren't men just the worst? I remember when I was just crazy in love with Bob Perkins, worked on the railroad." She sat on the edge of the bed and began stroking Viola's hair. "Oh, gosh, I couldn't wait for the train to come. When I found out he had a wife and a family in St. Louis, it didn't mean a thing to me. I just wanted him, you know?" The memory of it nearly provoked the maid to tears. "It made me just do crazy things to spend any time at all with him." She put Viola's hair in a loose braid. "And you know what, he didn't care at all. The little scraps of attention I got from him were what I lived on, but for him, it was just like a cigar after a big meal." Now the maid did cry. "And plenty of other men here in town would have had me, but after the way they saw I acted with Bob, well, that was that." She let out a long sigh and walked to the window. "He's still in St. Louis with his family and I'm alone, working as a maid. I don't know what keeps me here but the sound of that train whistle."

Viola had pushed herself up on one elbow. "I don't know if I'll ever be able to look at these mountains again." She began crying. "I really just *gave* myself to him with everything I have in me."

The chambermaid crossed to her and began patting her back, both of them crying. "Well, ain't that just the way it is? You give them everything, they'll take it all, but if it don't work, it don't hold them back none."

Viola started to protest. "Oh, he wasn't like that. He was…"

"Honey, they're all like that, trust me." She wet a cloth from the basin and handed it to Viola then got one for herself. "Look at us, two smart women cryin' the day away over men that have already put us out of their minds, such minds as they've got." She laughed and even Viola brightened a little. "There you go. I'm going to put you on the top of the list for a bath later. That'll do wonders." Viola doubted it but agreed anyway. She also accepted a meal that was sent up to her room and was amazed at how ravenous she was.

The next day when the chambermaid knocked, Viola answered the door, fully dressed but with a work apron over her dress, her hair done, and what could pass for a smile on her face. "I'm just going next door to paint for a while, so you've got the room to yourself." The chambermaid had fresh towels over her arm and a bucket of soapy water and set about cleaning up the room, opening the windows to let the air, albeit dusty, into the room. She realized that Viola had no awareness of being holed up there for nearly a week.

Viola sat down at her easel and the hours flew by. When it was nearly dusk the maid came back to light the lanterns and admire Viola's work. "Would you look at the colors in that sky?" she said, standing behind Viola who set her paintbrush down.

"Yes, that's exactly the color I wanted to achieve," she admitted. The sunrise in the painting was a peach and lavender hue set as the backdrop for the silver-gray smoke curling up from the teepees, the mountains still a deep blue-green in the background.

The chambermaid seemed to be in no hurry to leave and watched as Viola cleaned her brushes. Finally, she blurted out the questions she'd been turning over in her mind for days. "What was it like? How'd you know they wouldn't scalp you? Why him? How'd you know…"

Viola looked at the painting. "It was just like that sunrise, all so promising and clear." The maid didn't know what to make of her answer. "We would watch each other over the meadow and I felt he saw something deep in me."

"Well, sure more than a fat old railroad man saw in me, I guess." She smiled sadly. "And a lot more romantic, too."

"It was more than romance like you read about in books," Viola countered, although she realized the young woman might not be able to read at all. "I think it was also about respect and understanding." She thought about how little Silver Wolf had actually talked to her. "There was something from the first moment that allowed us to just be ourselves and be completely open with one another." It was her turn to smile sadly. "I don't expect to ever find it again."

"Well, you won't find it in Cheyenne, that's for sure. I wish I'd left just as soon as old Bob was done with me." The train whistled in the background. "I could have gotten on that train and just moved on down the line to a place where I could have been anyone I wanted to be."

Viola thought about her comments for the rest of the evening as she enjoyed her dinner in her room away from the contemptuous glances of the other hotel patrons and staff. There was one unfinished piece of business to attend to in Cheyenne, however. She pulled out her sketchpad and put a few final touches on one of the pages, detaching it gently from the book when she was finished.

The next morning she walked to the stables, it being early enough that she expected to find only Billy working. Instead, his father stopped her at the doorway. "Don't you be coming around here. Billy won't be taking you around the countryside or nothing else," the old man threatened. "You've hurt him enough already and put his life in danger, too." He spit in the dirt. "It's time you best leave, miss."

She wouldn't let him see her cry, but she gave him a rolled up piece of parchment. "Let him know that's how I saw him, soul and all." Billy could hear the whole exchange from his position in the shed, but he couldn't disobey his father and couldn't make himself go to Viola. He knew that if he told her he'd forgive her, her reply would be that there was nothing to forgive; she was never his in the first place.

Viola walked back to the hotel, ignoring people on the street who made comments under their breath. There was no place to go for her but further west.

Chapter Fifty-Nine

Before she prepared to leave Cheyenne, Viola virtually closeted herself in the second room she had rented to use as an art studio. She laid all her sketches out in a circle on the floor and instructed the maid, whom she now knew as Christine, not to move them, even to clean. All day and well into the night she painted, and when she was completely satisfied with a canvas she applied her flourishing "V McD" signature.

This time when she painted Silver Wolf's camp, she did paint in the faces. The children were happy and mischievous, playing with the many camp dogs or acting like brave hunters with miniature bows and arrows. The women were strong and stoic although Viola also depicted their faces with an underlying sense of humor. The young men were shown posturing as wiser than their years, hypervigilant but not aggressive. The few old men smoked pipes together or played games, all the time casting a watchful eye over the camp. It was only Silver Wolf whose face Viola never revealed. She painted him in profile or from behind, his shoulders flexing as he swung up onto his horse. The memory of his face was hers alone. She could see the creases by his mouth and the early crow's feet beginning to narrow his eyes. The sensuous lips she had enjoyed so many times were as vivid to her as if he were sitting in the room with her — how she wished!

When she became weepy, she picked up her paintbrush. She painted and painted, barely taking time for the meals Christine brought up to her room. She kept her sense of humor, she believed, even wondering if the tears imbued a certain depth to a paint color as she applied it. Did the sunset and the glow of the campfire coals seem deeper in her painting because of the tears she shed thinking of how she and Silver Wolf never seemed to need the fire to keep them warm? One painting showed a bare brown arm opening the teepee flap as the sun rose. Silver Wolf had done that, but then, seeing the day would be fine, returned to her in the teepee and it was hours before he emerged again.

Finally, when she could cry no more and paint no more, Viola knew it was time to leave Cheyenne for good, but to go where? She had grown used to the dry, dusty summer and fall in Cheyenne and couldn't face a rainy, wet fall reminiscent of England. The thought of being snowed in anywhere filled her with dread. As always, she would be drawn to a place with light. Perhaps the stationmaster could help with her decision. Viola checked her appearance in the room's small mirror and did what she could to restrain her hair. She supposed by now the townspeople had stopped talking about her, although truly she hadn't ventured out of her rooms other than to the bank and the train station to ship her paintings and collect art supplies. The paintings she had shipped out before her time with Silver Wolf were selling exceedingly well, and the new ones she thought of as post-Silver-Wolf would undoubtedly set a new standard for western art.

She entered the station and saw that an artist (a term she might not have used for him given his crude work) was painting a mural on one wall of the station showing the railroad's new routes. Each of the cities served had a representation of the city itself, Virginia City with its silver mills, Reno with the Sierras in the background, and so forth. She had never ventured south of the original transcontinental route and was intrigued by the depiction of a Spanish mission at a town called Albuquerque. She approached the stationmaster's window, clearing her throat to gain his attention. "Hello again, Mr. Schultz. I'm wondering if you might help me with something."

Mr. Schultz was a deacon at church and hated to even be seen talking to the strumpet who had run off with the Indians, but his job forced him to accommodate her (and she had tipped him rather generously for crating up her paintings). "Yes, Miss McDougall. What is it today? More works of art to thrill the New Yorkers?"

She detected a certain snide tone but chose to ignore it. "Actually, no. I think I've sent out as much as the market can bear." He didn't respond to her attempt at a joke, so she continued. "I wonder if you might know anything about the town of Albuquerque." She pointed to the new map on the wall.

"I know that we serve them, but that's the extent of my knowledge or my interest," he condescended. "Now, if there's nothing else..." He began to close the drape on his window.

Viola was frustrated but simply asked, "Perhaps you'll give me a copy of the schedule to Albuquerque before you go off to your well-earned lunch." He slid the schedule out to her and quickly closed the ticket window.

"My wife has kin out there," someone said behind her. "They like it real well."

She turned to see one of the porters who worked at the mercantile and therefore spent a lot of time in the train station awaiting shipments for the store. "Pardon me?"

"I heard you asking old Schultz about Albuquerque." He took off his cowboy hat. "Sorry for listenin' in, but not much else goin' on around here," he said, pointing to the empty station. "I said my wife has a sister who lives in Albuquerque with her husband, and my sister says she likes it, her sister likes it, that is." He added. "I ain't never been but my wife says when her sister has a baby we'll be goin' down there for sure."

"What is it that she likes about it?"

"She writes these letters that describe it as being real quiet, but there's a river runs through town and there's mountains kind of like here, but red." He thought for a minute. "I think the river's red, too."

"How peculiar? Why do you think that?"

He ran his hand through his hair. "Well, it's call the Rio Grande, and I don't know, I musta heard somethin' somewhere." He laughed. "I think it's on account of the mud that it carries along, all the way to Mexico, red mud from those red mountains."

"Well, it doesn't sound very picturesque at all."

"I'm probably not tellin' it right is all," the cowboy said, lowering his head. "If I could talk better or was smarter I wouldn't be sittin' in this station waiting for a box to come in on the train. I'd be the one standin' behind the counter waitin' to sell that box to someone else." He scuffed his heel on the floor. "We're probably never goin' to Albuquerque 'cause I'll never get enough money put by."

Viola could see how morose he had become. "You have a wife who loves you enough to stay here, so things are not so poor as you think." She almost started to cry thinking of how alone she was. "You could make some extra money, if you'd like, helping me pack up all my belongings in the next day or so, maybe after you finish up at the store?"

"Yes, ma'am, I'd be pleased to." He stood and awkwardly shook her hand. "You just ask for John at the store and tell them you're ready for his help."

Viola took a bill out of her purse. "Here's to seal the deal—isn't that what the land speculators say?" The speculators were notorious for meeting unsuspecting passengers at the train stops to sell them land they had no title to. She pressed the bill into his hand. She looked at the train schedule and saw the next departure for Albuquerque was three days hence. "John, I will expect to see you on Tuesday." He gasped when he saw the denomination but nodded his head vigorously. Viola rang the bell at the stationmaster's window, eliciting a grumpy response. "One ticket to Albuquerque for Wednesday, please."

Viola returned to the hotel feeling more energized than she had in weeks. As she climbed the stairs to her room, a plan began to crystallize in her mind so that when Christine brought her dinner tray in, Viola was ready with her proposal. "Good evening. Thank you so much. I'm afraid I'm getting frightfully spoiled by you waiting on me all the time."

"Oh, it's nothing. Gives me a chance to talk to someone besides those rough old men downstairs."

"Yes, it is lovely to have another woman to talk to," Viola conceded. "And we do seem to have a bit in common."

Christine looked doubtful at that. "I guess you mean our poor taste in men."

"I wouldn't call it poor taste as much as poor luck," Viola said, a little wounded by the comment. "I want to tell you what I did today and what I think should happen." Christine set the dinner tray down but left the lid on. "I bought a ticket to Albuquerque for this coming Wednesday, and I want you to go with me."

"Go with you? To Albuquerque?"

"Yes. You could be my helper, do what you do now for me, and I'd pay you, probably more than you make here." Viola was increasingly excited. "We'd find a nice little house and we would have our own rooms and you could just tidy up and cook. You can cook, can't you?"

"I can cook all right, but..."

"And if you wanted to get another job outside, you could, or not. Say you will!"

Christine had slumped into a chair when Viola began her proposal but now she walked to the windows and pulled back the curtain, looking wistfully out to the train station. "That sounds grand and all, but I think I best stay here. I think they'd be mighty unhappy if I up and quit in just two days and all."

Viola followed her glance and knew just what Christine was thinking. "You know if he comes back it'll just be long enough for the train to go on to its next stop and come back. Is that really wall you want for your life?"

Christine sighed. "No, but I expect it's all I can get and I'll have to find a way for it to make me happy." Viola crossed the room to hug her and they both ended up in tears, thinking of what might have been but never would.

Chapter Sixty

John came to Viola's hotel the minute the mercantile closed on Tuesday. The clerk showed him to Viola's rooms, but only after observing that it was "highly suspicious, a woman accepting a man up to her room." John was beet-red with embarrassment when Viola opened the door, but she dismissed the clerk without a glance even though he clearly had his hand out. "I plan to carry a valise with me in my compartment on the train, but the rest of this," she said, indicating the art supplies, "must be packaged up to go as cargo."

"Yes, ma'am." He stood there holding his hat.

"Tonight?"

"Oh, yes. I've got some tools down in the wagon and I can build you up a crate just fine." He turned to leave. "Can I work up here or do you want I should take everything down there and crate it up?"

"I suppose I would prefer that you work up here rather than have all my belongings on display in the street," Viola agreed. "I'll stay out of your way in my other room." He cocked his head. "I rented two rooms, this one as a studio, but I only have clothes in the other, which I can attend to." She opened the door for him to leave and then followed him out of the room, stopping at the door to her other room. "Thank you for helping me, John. Not many people in town would, it seems."

He blushed again. "I expect you're right, ma'am." In less than two hours he had built a crate with hinges that allowed it to be opened rather than just nailed shut. He carefully stowed all of Viola's art supplies in it, then knocked on her door to invite her to inspect it. "You see, you can open and close it so when you get to where you're headed, you could use it as storage or what not."

"It's perfect, John!" Viola was reminded of the clever cart she had designed for herself in France. "Too bad you've packed all the paint—we could have decorated it." John looked stricken. "I'm joking. Traveling in cognito suits me just fine right now." She had tucked a few bills into the pocket of her dress and handed them to John. "Thank you for helping me. I don't know how I would have handled it otherwise."

He looked at the money. It was more than she had promised him, certainly, but he understood her gesture. "I hope you'll do real well in Albuquerque." He hesitated before adding, "Sometimes it's good to make a fresh start."

"That it is, John, that it is," Viola impetuously hugged him, which just made him blush furiously. She turned away from him as she opened the door. A fresh batch of tears was welling up. If only she could have convinced Christine of the very same thing. Viola had made a lot of fresh starts already in her life and expected she'd make more before it was over.

Viola was waiting at the train station the next morning, John having delivered the crate the night before. There were only two other passengers waiting to board for Albuquerque. She stayed outside the station somehow hoping she'd see Christine coming down the street, but when the whistle blew, she climbed on board and found her compartment. She drew the curtains, certain her heart would break at seeing the mountains she and Silver Wolf had ridden through fading into the distance. She could still feel the muscles of his back rippling as he fought to control the pony when they reached a gallop, flying down a canyon, and the way his thighs would tense before the horse jumped over a fallen log. She fell asleep smiling and was surprised when the porter knocked on the door to her compartment indicating dinner was about to be served. She thought about staying alone in her cabin but then forced herself to freshen up and head for the dining car, the first step in her fresh start.

Dinner was a pot roast with potatoes and carrots, and Viola was surprised to realize how famished she was, even requesting a second helping, much to the amusement of the porter. She also drank two glasses of wine and was contemplating a third when the gentleman seated across the aisle from her pointed to her glass. "Don't drink alone, darlin'." He was dressed in a western-style suit with a narrow bolo tie and looked like the shifty land speculators that preyed on passengers disembarking the trains.

"I'm not 'drinking', as you put it. I'm simply having wine with my dinner," Viola said, hoping her sharp comment would dissuade him from talking to her any further.

"Ah, but now your dinner's gone and you're wanting that glass of wine, or maybe a port?" He chuckled. "If you'll allow me to join you, we can have that wine and perhaps pass the time as the night isn't offering up much in the way of scenery."

He was well-spoken. Viola hesitated. "All right." She picked up her satchel off the chair across from her. He slid into it easily, bringing a bottle with him and requesting another glass from the porter.

"Monty Jacobs, pleased to make your acquaintance." He held out his hand which Viola shook with a firm grip as her dear uncle had taught her—no shrinking violet would she ever be!

"Viola McDougall, pleased as well."

She watched him as he poured a glass of the amber liquid for her. His hands were immaculate with long, tapered fingers and his shirt cuffs were spotless with heavy gold cufflinks. He topped off his own glass then raised it in a toast. "To the West."

"To the West." The liquid was the smoothest brandy Viola had ever tasted. "Oh, that is lovely." He had been watching her reaction and seemed to be enjoying it.

"I have it shipped over from France, a case at a time. Costs a pretty penny, but I'd say it's worth it."

"I quite agree. I don't recall ever drinking anything quite this good in Paris."

He had detected her English accent but was surprised. "Oh, you've been to Paris, have you?"

"Many times." A frown crossed her face as she thought of Kathleen. "I also lived in the French countryside for a time." She didn't know why, but she felt it necessary to add, "I also lived in Italy for some months, at a villa."

"Hmmm, well those travels ought to serve you well as a school teacher." He poured more brandy for both of them.

"School teacher? Why would you think I'm a school teacher?"

He pointed to her satchel. "Just thought you were going to Albuquerque to teach in that new school, bringing some books with you."

"It so happens that I am an artist and those are my sketch books." Viola laughed. "I can't imagine teaching children anything."

He laughed also. "Well, some children you can't teach anything, so there you have it."

"And what about you, sir? What takes you to the city on the Rio Grande?"

He seemed to consider the question. "I own a bit of property here and there, houses and businesses." He slid his hand into his pocket, coming out with an engraved card. "I rent them out, make a fair amount of money, but mostly I just like to travel, and I'm a pretty fair hand at poker."

"Oooh, a rambling gambling man," Viola laughed. "Do you have any houses for rent in Albuquerque then?"

"I believe I could find a place for you, miss. You just come see me when you're ready." He was already imagining just how he could set Viola up in Albuquerque.

"Tell me about the new school you mentioned."

"Of all things, it's for Indians." She looked shocked. "I know, seems crazy to try to teach those heathens anything, but I guess that's what they aim to do." He went on to tell her about how the children were being rounded up from the various reservations and brought to the school, to board there full-time. Viola had stopped listening at the word 'Indians' and suddenly pushed her chair back from the table.

"Thank you for the brandy, Mr. Jacobs, but I must retire now. Perhaps I'll see you again before we reach your city." She was gone before he could get out of his chair.

Chapter Sixty-One

Albuquerque was a surprise. When Viola alighted from the train the porter told her she would have to take the new electric street railway into the "New Town" part of the city where the finer hotels were located. For some reason the train station was actually about three miles out of town, although time would fill in that distance. She could see the Sandia Mountains in the distance, although they were nowhere near as inspiring as what she had seen outside of Cheyenne. She had avoided Mr. Jacobs for the rest of the train trip but had managed to talk to other passengers familiar with Albuquerque who told her about the mountains. Sandia, it seemed, was the Spanish word for 'watermelon' and the mountains, at sunset at least, were said to resemble one. An ore, granodiorite, turned the mountains pink at sunset while the green from the forest provided the rind color, she was told.

Even though New Mexico wasn't a state yet, it already had the University of New Mexico, and the Albuquerque Indian School had been established some twenty years before Viola's arrival in 1902. Still, as Viola discovered when she entered the New Town area, it was as dusty a cow town as Cheyenne had been and it wasn't long before she was questioning her decision to come to the high-desert outpost.

The conductor had told her there were a handful of rooming houses for single ladies such as herself, but the thought of another Miss Marshall's was enough to make Viola rule that option out entirely. He told her it was rather irregular for a hotel to rent to a single woman, but if that's what she preferred, the newly-opened Hotel Alvarado was her best bet. It had become something of an artistic and cultural hub as local Indians displayed their pottery and jewelry in the lobby. Viola was delighted with the Hotel Alvarado's outer appearance with its pebbledash stucco exterior and Spanish-style arches. She was equally delighted to find out, upon registering, that the hotel had been designed by a woman, Mary Jane Colter.

After being shown to a spacious corner suite with a timbered ceiling and foot-thick whitewashed walls, Viola hurriedly washed off some of the grime of the trip then immediately returned to the lobby to see the Indian crafts. A dazzling display awaited her of silver bracelets and necklaces with heavy chunks of turquoise plus several different kinds of woven baskets. "It's hard to decide which one you like the best isn't it?" a voice behind her asked.

She turned to find Monty Jacobs leaning against one of the pillars in the lobby, a satisfied smile on his face. "How did you know I'd be here?"

"I figured the conductor probably tried to steer you to one of the boarding houses his aunt runs, but you didn't seem the boarding house type."

"No, I've had quite enough boarding house experience in my life already," Viola admitted. "This hotel is quite lovely and has already made me look forward to my stay in your city."

"Well now that you're a mite happier to be here, will you do me the pleasure of joining me for lunch? I know the chef here and he'll do just about anything you'd like."

Viola was tempted by the offer. She had never been so hungry as she was on this trip! "I will, with the proviso that you allow me to pay my own check."

"I don't know as I've ever had a woman offer to do such a thing, but if that's what it takes to enjoy your company, I guess I'll have to accept." He held his arm out to her. "Shall we?" When they entered the spacious restaurant he asked for a table in the back, away from the windows. No sense having his wife stroll by and see them. There'd be no end of explaining and probably a new piece of jewelry involved.

The chef's special consisted of a large piece of puff pastry topped by a mixture of beef and beans, tomatoes and green onions. Viola began eating it with great gusto, much to the amusement of Mr. Jacobs. "This is heavenly! What is it?"

"It's something the Indians make a lot of, sort of a cross between a Mexican taco and a doughnut. We call them Indian tacos." Viola sighed with delight. "A lot of folks won't eat them. They consider them low-class on account of the Indian part of the name."

"Well those people don't know Indians and they don't know food," Viola pronounced, already halfway through eating hers, washing it down with the sangria Jacobs had ordered. "Is there really that much hostility toward the Indians here?"

"I don't know as I'd say it's hostility," Jacobs answered, pushing his half-eaten meal aside and lighting a cigar. "I think folks are just wary of them. They hear about uprisings in other parts of the country and wonder if it could happen here."

"And could it?"

"I suppose it could. There's a good deal of resentment about having been forced off their land and into these government settlements, but for the most part they don't seem like a violent bunch to me." He puffed on the cigar. "Sneaky, maybe. You best mind your purse when you're around them."

"Well, that advice could be given in any major city in America or Europe, for that matter." Viola was actually eyeing his half-eaten taco but would never ask to finish it. "My own parents were murdered on the streets of New York City."

He reached for her hand. "I'm very sorry to hear that, Miss McDougall. It must have been terribly hard on you."

"It's been a long time ago now, but yes, it was in the beginning." Over several more glasses of the refreshing sangria, Viola poured out her story, leaving out the part about Silver Wolf. The afternoon slipped by and soon the staff came around to light the candles for the evening dinner. Viola was embarrassed at having talked so much to a virtual stranger. "I'm so sorry if I've taken your entire afternoon. You must think I'm terribly selfish." She reached for her purse to pay her check, but Jacobs once again covered her hand with his.

"The pleasure was all mine and one I hope we have again very soon." He paid both checks and then drew her chair back for her, lightly kissing her neck as he did so. "Keep in mind my offer to find you suitable housing for your stay here."

"Oh, I don't know that I will be staying," Viola confessed. "It doesn't appear very interesting to me." She hastened to add, "I mean, as an artist, the vistas leave much to be desired."

He concealed his smirk by bending to kiss her hand. "Oh, I think you'll find it interesting enough."

Chapter Sixty-Two

Viola forgot about Monty Jacobs as soon as he left the hotel lobby. She went to her room to lie down for a while before dinner but was alternately too warm or too cold and slightly nauseous, although the sangria could have contributed to that. The thought crossed her mind for a fleeting instant that she could be pregnant, but she recalled the pungent tea that Silver Wolf made her drink after every time they were intimate. The wives in the camp had indicated to her that it was very effective in preventing pregnancy and all she could do was trust them. She finally fell into a deep sleep, awakening as the sun was coming up. She was still fully dressed and was grateful for her own private bath. The cool water would surely revive her. As she lay in the tub, she thought about the intense hunger she had been experiencing and finally realized, it was just longing. She was longing for Silver Wolf. She not only longed for him physically, but also for the excitement he represented, escaping from everything proper. "Well, and look where that got you," she told herself. "You've escaped from everything and ended up here."

After a voluminous breakfast in the hotel, Viola set out to see the town, such as it was. The mercantile was slightly larger than that in Cheyenne so she was able to buy a few additions to her wardrobe. As she stood waiting for the clerk to total up her purchases, she looked out to the street and saw a group of about thirty young boys in military-style uniforms marching past the store. "Good heavens. Who are they?"

The clerk glanced up. "They're from the Indian boarding school. They march them around half the day, trying to march the Indian right out of them." She laughed.

"But they're mere boys, to be dressed as soldiers. What can they be thinking?"

"I doubt anyone knows what the Indians are thinking, miss." The clerk began wrapping Viola's purchases in brown paper.

"I meant, what are the administrators at the school thinking. Treating them like little soldiers will only make them more aggressive, not more peaceful, which I believe is their goal." Viola was clearly distressed.

The clerk hurried to finish her task and get this peculiar customer on her way. "I wouldn't know about that. The school has its ways, I guess." She handed Viola her package and turned to another customer.

By the time Viola reached the street the little marching troop was gone, but the sight of them had ruined her morning and she returned to the hotel in a foul mood. It was doubtful even an Indian taco would improve it. "Miss McDougall, please, you have mail," the hotel desk clerk called out to her as she pushed through the hotel doors.

"Mail? How on earth..."

"It just came in on the train and apparently Mr. Jacobs was there and knew you had come to the Alvarado." The clerk held out a small packet of letters.

She had intended to go directly to lunch but clutched the mail and hurried to her room. She had seen from the postmark that the letter on top of the bunch was from Kathleen. She made herself comfortable in the window seat of her room before tearing open the envelope.

Dearest Viola,

I hope this letter finds you well and happy in your Great Adventure to the West.

I don't know how much exposure you have to the society pages, so perhaps you haven't read much about the Royal Wedding and my small part in it, so let me tell you. It was simply fabulous. The bride was glowing and even the thousands of crystals we so laboriously sewed into the gown couldn't have matched the radiance of her smile – or that of the prince when he saw her at the altar. It was like the fairy tales I heard as a child and there were times when I thought my mum would pinch me awake. Truly. The wedding dinner was unmatched in history in its extravagance. I wouldn't be surprised to learn that there wasn't a bottle of champagne left in all of Europe, nor any kind of animal one would eat. And flowers! Your artist's eye would have been entranced by the beauty of it all.

I was surprised to receive an invitation to the event, being, after all, only a laborer like many others on the nuptials, but I did receive one and was determined to go. I think of your uncle every day, but on that occasion especially as for once I wasn't pinching pennies and could just design a dress for myself and damn the travel expenses. The princess acknowledged me warmly during her remarks at the dinner and even hugged me afterwards, telling me much of the romance of the day was due to the gown I had created for her. I'm sure I blushed at the comment, and I know you'll think it's terribly prideful of me to say it, but I believe she was right.

The dancing went on well into the night, and nearly at midnight, a surprise! My former husband, Philip, stepped onto the stage and began to play the most captivating waltz for the royal couple. I myself shrank into the background, not knowing if I wanted him to see me, but I feel that he did anyway. He played for well over an hour, then closed the grand piano and left to thunderous applause. We spoke not a word to each other but I feel secure in saying that I feel he was comforted by knowing I was safe. What I felt about him I still cannot say. Philip was never cool or detached, but the man on the stage was. He seemed almost other-worldly, a silly thing to say, I know, but if you had seen him I feel you would say the same.

The exposure I received from designing the royal gown has opened up even more doors, and now I am going to begin designing for the "common" woman. As if there is such a person! A company has asked me to design a half-dozen dresses that any woman could buy and wear to church, to lunch or wherever. After so many years of designing one-of-a-kind creations for the well-heeled, this feels like just the challenge I've been looking for.

And what challenges are you facing, aside from controlling those curls of yours and trying to stay clean in the Wild West? Do you have a half-dozen cowboys mooning about? Or perhaps a rich railroad baron? Knowing how independent you were even as a girl, I know you're giving them a run for their money! I did chance upon two of your paintings in a Paris gallery and was breathless in viewing them. The West I remember from my wagon train journey many years ago was certainly nowhere near as beautiful. I feel certain you could be teaching your old teachers with the skill and refinement you have attained.

I do so hope to see you again although I know great distance and time divides us. Stay strong and never lose your dreams, Viola. We'll always be alike in that, won't we?

Love,

Kathleen

How curious. This was the second time in as many days that someone suggested she could be a teacher, a profession she had never considered even at a time when all little girls did. Viola spent the rest of the afternoon daydreaming, perched in the window seat, and therefore didn't notice Monty looking up at her from a seat in the saloon across the street.

Chapter Sixty-Three

Viola emerged from the hotel the next morning with a definite plan. She would visit the Indian boarding school on the outskirts of town. The walk and fresh air would do her good, besides. She was unprepared for Monty standing out in the street next to an enclosed carriage. "Good morning, Miss McDougall," he said, slightly doffing his hat. "Lovely morning for a ride. I do believe you're missing the many charms of our city which I will endeavor to show you if you'll be so kind?"

She couldn't help scowling. This wasn't at all what she had in mind. In seconds, however, her mind raced to her buggy rides with Billy out into the hills around Cheyenne and her scowl turned to a wistful smile. Those trips had turned out rather well in one respect at least even though she'd left behind a 'mooning cowboy', as Kathleen had phrased it. Monty was watching her mercurial mood shifts but simply opened the carriage door and stood waiting. Viola evidently made up her mind and with a smile accepted his assistance into the carriage. "And what charms do you have in mind, Mr. Jacobs? Do show me."

"I thought we would ride up to one of the Indian pueblos," he said, noting Viola's immediate excitement. As a gambler, he was well-versed in looking for people's "tells," the little signs that gave them away when they drew the perfect hole card or busted out when they needed one more face card.

He'd seen how excited Viola was by the Indian crafts in the hotels, and, of course, men will talk. He'd already heard from the stationmaster about her outrageous escapade with a band of Indians.

The driver put the horses up to a fast pace and before long they'd left Albuquerque behind and were climbing up into scrubby pinon and then more towering pine forests. It was noticeably cooler and the skies were bluer than any Viola had ever seen. She was sitting on the edge of her seat in excitement while Monty lounged in his, smoking his ubiquitous cigar. They finally reached a clearing where the driver stopped the carriage then jumped down to open the door. Monty climbed down first, offering his hand to Viola but not releasing it when she was fully out of the coach. Viola looked around but saw nothing but trees, the disappointment evident on her face.

Monty reached back into the coach for a small sack. "It's a bit of a walk up to the pueblo itself. When we get there we'll have to have a little talk with the guards and see if we can get an invite." He held up the sack. "And we brought gifts, but I guess you'd know something about that."

Viola was so excited she missed his inference entirely as she set off at a brisk walk up the trail. She reached the entrance to the pueblo seconds before Monty, completely surprising the two Indians who were evidently sentries. Silver Wolf would never have allowed such laxity, she thought. When Monty approached the two men, he said a few words in an Indian language, holding the sack out at the same time. After conferring between themselves, the Indians pulled aside a small fence and beckoned them to enter. From the outset Viola felt it was a very spiritual place. Dwellings were made of mud brick, or adobe, as Monty told her it was called, in circular shapes. The whole pueblo was a large circle, in fact. Their guard/escorts walked with them, pointing out kilns where pottery was being fired and other areas for gardening and livestock. Viola couldn't discern if there was an actual chief. Everyone seemed to be working equally at one task or another. When they passed one of the dwellings a woman stepped out to offer them warm cornbread which Viola gratefully accepted.

She grabbed Monty's arm. "Oh, thank you so much for bringing me here. It's just a magical place." Her eyes were shining.

"Didn't I promise to show you the local charms?" he winked. Viola wanted to sit and sketch the pueblo but Monty told her that wouldn't be wise. Before they left she turned slowly, willing herself to memorize every inch. She was quiet as they rode back down the hill. "Penny for your thoughts?"

Viola had been thinking about the Indian boys in faux military uniforms being forced to march through the streets of Albuquerque. "Why can't they just leave them alone!"

"Leave who alone?" Monty asked, genuinely baffled.

"Why can't the white man just leave the Indians alone? Look at what we saw today, a perfectly peaceful community where the people had everything they needed. And your government wants to tear it all apart." She looked on the verge of tears as he put his arm around her shoulder, drawing her closer. Her hair smelled like lavender. Should he pretend to agree with her or just let her talk it out? It was a roll of the dice either way, he figured.

"What you saw today was special," he began.

"That's what I'm saying!"

"No, I mean they may not all be like that." She didn't reply but also didn't pull away. "Maybe the men who are in charge of these sorts of things know better. Maybe they've seen the Indians in a pretty rough way and are just trying to help them."

"Help them?" A bitter tone crept into her voice. "Help them by killing them and taking away their land and their whole way of life." She shook her head and looked out the window as the town of Albuquerque came back into view. She thought of the boarding school and of her old friend's comments about soap and education being the ultimate death of the Indian. Maybe there was a way to make the transition less painful. "Before we go back to the Alvarado, would you please also show me the boarding school?"

Monty nodded and shouted up instructions to the driver. In minutes they pulled up outside a Spanish-style building somewhat similar to the Hotel Alvarado with its arches and red-tiled roof. However, that's where the similarity ended as the Alvarado was not surrounded by a fence and guards. Viola's mood darkened even more. "They're little boys and they're treated like prisoners!"

"Oh, there's girls, too," Monty said lightly.

"I've seen enough for one day," Viola said, turning away from him. "Let's go back to the hotel, please." Monty knocked on the side of the coach. They were back at the hotel when Viola turned to him. "I haven't been very good company, I'm afraid, but I do appreciate your taking me up to the pueblo." He tried to pull her closer but as soon as the carriage came to a stop, she was out the door and striding briskly into the hotel.

So, today was a push, he thought. Tomorrow might bring better cards. Thinking of it, he climbed out of the coach and headed for the saloon. There might be a game to be had if the train brought a few new visitors to town.

Chapter Sixty-Four

The next morning Viola was determined not to let Monty Jacobs or any other obstacle prevent her from visiting the Indian boarding school. She left the hotel earlier than usual and walked to another hotel around the corner to have breakfast. When the waitress seated her and took her order, she hesitated for a minute before going off to the kitchen. "Are you here to teach at the new university or the boarding school?"

"No, I'm just visiting, although I am thinking of paying a visit at the Indian school this morning," Viola told the waitress.

"None of my business, ma'am, but we keep hearing how they'll be a bunch of new teachers coming to town, so naturally..." she indicated Viola's bag with her sketchbook.

'Yes, I've heard that as well, although I doubt I'll be one of them," Viola replied with some finality, causing the waitress to go place her order. When the food came, she ate ravenously again and wondered if the demand for teachers was so high everywhere in the West, although she had scarcely heard it mentioned in Cheyenne. Fortified by the hearty breakfast, Viola set off on foot for the school. The high altitude and rising temperatures made the walk a bit strenuous and Viola was happy to see a bench set beneath a group of pine trees just outside the school compound. She sat and leaned back against one of the trees, taking in the clean pine scent. She could just see some of the students marching back and forth in the school yard but heard no laughter. She pulled out her sketchbook and began to rough in the details of the timbered fence with its pointed spires, the red tiles of the roof and the blindingly white walls of the school buildings. The students wore drab gray uniforms and all had the same haircut; distinguishing one from the other must be nearly impossible for the teachers, Viola thought.

She became so engrossed in her sketching that she didn't notice the man who walked up behind her until he cleared his throat. "I dare say you'll get the job if you show them a drawing such as that," sounded a distinctly English accent." Viola jumped off the bench. "So sorry to startle you, miss." She turned to see a man perhaps her uncle's age dressed in a light tan suit and a small porkpie hat like those favored by many men in England. "Charles Burnham, English teacher therein," he said, offering Viola his hand and gesturing toward the school.

Viola took a moment to get over her surprise at being disturbed and also at finding an Englishman in Albuquerque, a teacher at the school no less. "Viola McDougall," she said, shaking his hand and making a slight curtsey, "and yes, you did startle me." They stood for a moment in the shade then both started to speak at the same time. He deferred to Viola since it was clear they both had the same question in mind. "How is that you are in Albuquerque?"

"Oh, I was caught up in the romance of the West," he laughed, sweeping out his hands, then in a lower tone of voice, "and I'd been let go from four schools in London, a clear message it was time to move on. And you?"

"Actually, the same. I was caught up in the romance of the West, although I've never done anything naughty enough to be let go." She patted his shoulder. "I'm just having a little fun with you. I'm sure it was nothing naughty."

"Nothing more so than perhaps enjoying strong spirits a bit too much for a man set out to be an example to his students." He didn't laugh when he said it.

Viola was helpless to think of a reply and sought to change the subject and the mood. "Well, sir, perhaps you can be my entrée to the school, although I fear it will disabuse me of yet another romantic notion about the West."

"I would be more than happy to, my dear." He extended his arm and the two walked through the imposing gates and the quiet schoolyard. Inside the hallways were broad and cool, and as they passed classrooms Viola could see students, boys in separate classrooms from girls, hunched over their desks. "I happen not to have a class for another few moments, so let me show you what passes for our art department." They reached a room at the end of the hall that was empty of students but contained a dozen desks and an elevated table in the center on which rested a vase with a wilted arrangement of flowers. There were no pictures on the walls and no evidence of any drawings done by the students.

"As I feared," Viola said, "a lifeless space in which to inspire students about the beauty around them."

Her companion laughed out loud. "Inspire students! What an idea. We do nothing of the sort here." His rueful tone conveyed his own disappointment. "We simply try to eradicate any vestige of them being Indians." He picked up a piece of pastel chalk. "We grind them down until their lives and their imaginations are as dry as this, and then we congratulate ourselves on having made them better citizens."

"But how can you..." Viola's question was interrupted by the arrival of a stern-looking woman. Mr. Burnham turned to face her.

"And this is our administrator, although I suppose in England you would have referred to her as the head mistress, Mrs. Jacobs."

Viola flinched at the name but put out her hand to the woman. "I am Viola..."

"I know perfectly well who you are, Miss McDougall. I believe you've made the acquaintance of my husband, a Mr. Monty Jacobs." Viola blushed and Mr. Burnham used the awkward moment to look at his watch and announce that he had to leave for his classroom.

"Your husband has been very gracious to me," Viola began uncertainly.

"Oh, I'm sure he has, showing you the sights and all." Her tone was imperious but not threatening. "And did he offer to find you just the perfect little house? That's usually how he reels his little darlings in."

Viola was instantly affronted. "I am no one's little darling, ma'am. He said he had a number of rental properties, but I told him I had very little desire to stay in Albuquerque and that there appeared to be nothing here of interest to me." Viola was satisfied with her answer, but the woman gave nothing away.

"Well, of course, you've only been off the train a few days." Mrs. Jacobs' mind was racing. She admired Viola's grit but wondered if her presence would be too much of a temptation for her husband whose conquests were widely known in town and a source of constant humiliation to her. "I'm sure he will find other opportunities to interest you."

"I doubt that he will."

Mrs. Jacobs made up her mind. "Let me see your drawings, will you, please?" Viola was surprised but surrendered her book open to the sketch of the school. "These are quite finely drawn, I must say. And do you sing or play an instrument?"

What was this? "I can sing and I do play the piano and the violin," Viola heard herself replying to this haughty woman. "I also speak four languages."

"Unless one is Apache, the other Navajo and the third a Puebloan dialect, those skills will not be necessary." She actually laughed a little. "You might be just the arts teacher the school needs, however." Viola was stunned at yet another stranger telling her she should be a teacher, and this stranger had the power to make it happen. "If you are interested in joining our faculty, do stop by the office near the front entrance and give them your information. You may tell them Mrs. Jacobs approved you and that you are to start next Monday." Viola felt rooted to the floor. "Oh, and please do something about your appearance before then." Mrs. Jacobs left Viola standing in the classroom with a thousand thoughts swirling through her mind. Do *what* about my appearance? Teach a classroom of Indians who don't speak English? Monday? Monty's wife?

Mrs. Jacobs returned to her office, closing the door before putting her head down on her desk. She may have stopped her philandering husband this time, but there would be others, and he certainly would be quite cross with her when he learned of her actions today. She couldn't even muster up any excitement about the inevitable piece of jewelry she knew she would receive.

Chapter Sixty-Five

Viola let herself be drawn through the employment process, filling out forms about her education, her employment history, and her current living situation. When the school secretary perused the forms she made no comment about Viola's nonexistent work history, but she did raise an eye about her address. "That simply will not do," she said, pointing a fingernail at the Hotel Alvarado. "A young woman, a teacher who is expected to be a model of virtue for the community, cannot be living in a hotel." Viola started to complain, but the secretary cut her off. "By Monday, you will have moved into a proper boarding house for young women."

Ugh, Viola thought, but after being dismissed with orders to bring pencils, notebooks and whatever other supplies she thought her students might need on Monday, Viola trudged to the train station. She'd have to speak to the train conductor about his sister's various lodging options. Monty saw her emerge from the school and suspected the game was up but felt compelled to give it one more try. He pulled his buggy up next to Viola. "Care for a ride, miss?"

"Mr. Jacobs. Why don't you turn your buggy around and offer your wife a ride home from school!" Viola glared at him and kept walking.

"I could do that, but I suspect your company would be a mite more entertaining than my wife, given the current situation."

"And just what situation is that?" Viola asked despite herself.

"You needing a house and all. I'm sure they told you that." He could see by the look on her face that they had indeed.

"I won't be living in one of your houses, and I'm sure you know why."

"I sorely hate to lose the rent," he laughed, "but I expect I'll survive." Viola continued to scuff her way along the dusty street. "Actually, I know just the boarding house for you."

"Another one of your questionable enterprises? Is a boarding house really necessary to house your harem?"

Monty laughed so hard he could have fallen out of the buggy. "Miss McDougall, you over-estimate me. A harem? No, I have quite enough on my hands with my estimable wife and a little gal here and there." Viola was red in the face with exhaustion from the heat, anger and frustration. "No, another friend runs just the kind of boarding house I expect you'd enjoy. Now, we're a far enough distance from the school. Hop in and I'll take you there."

Viola couldn't believe she climbed up into the buggy, but the events of the day had already overwhelmed her. She wasn't used to being swept along without carefully planning her decisions. What was one more bad one? Monty clicked the reins and the horses took off at a trot. They stopped at a rambling quasi Victorian shaded by oaks. A sign out front identified it as "Lolly's Love Nest." When Viola read the sign she nearly grabbed the reins herself. "Why, Mr. Jacobs! It's a whorehouse!"

"It is nothing of the sort," he grinned. "Now step down and come meet the proprietor." He couldn't help but add, "And mind your manners."

They walked up the wide staircase, Viola with her head up and chin stuck out, but before they could reach the landing the door was thrown open. "Monty Jacobs, you scoundrel! How long has it been?" The woman issuing the greeting was drying her hands on an apron. She was about medium height and size for a woman with curly brown-turning-gray hair and crows' feet. She smiled broadly at Viola and hugged Monty before pushing him away. "You're still a handsome devil, I'll give you that." She took both Monty's and Viola's arms and led them into a spacious parlor where Monty made the introductions.

"Lolly Thompson, may I present Viola McDougall, a new teacher for the Indian school."

The two women formally shook hands, but Viola couldn't help notice Lolly's mouth turn down. "So, a teacher. I expect you'll be wanting to share a room, given a teacher's salary."

Salary? Viola hadn't even thought about it. "Actually I have...other funds, so I would like two rooms, in fact." The potential landlady looked at her askance. "I'm an artist and would prefer to use one as my studio." Viola thought back to her days in Cheyenne and almost teared up.

"Oh, Monty, how fun, a school marm and an artist to boot!" Lolly laughed and Viola could see that the crow's feet were formed from a life of laughter. "I think I have just the place for you. Come, come!" She grabbed Viola's hand and led her out through the kitchen. Several girls were lounging about, some just in their slips, something Miss Marshall would never have allowed, and a good many exchanged greetings with the charming Mr. Jacobs. When they reached the back of the large house, Lolly threw open the back door and led Viola out into the most amazing space she had ever seen.

The yard was filled with every kind of tree that could flourish in the Albuquerque climate, and from every branch hung a birdhouse. A cacophony of bird calls greeted them, and now Viola did tear up. Birds. How long had it been since she had heard their calls? Lolly saw Viola's reaction and put an arm gently over her shoulder. "So now you see why we call it the Love Nest?" She led Viola and Monty to the back of the yard where a cottage awaited, a smaller one-story version of the main house with its own wide porch. "This here's a two-bedroom house with everything complete. You can paint back here with no one bothering you," at which point she shot a pointed look at Monty.

Viola was speechless when she saw the tall, broad windows and the beckoning rockers on the porch. "It's absolutely unbelievable. I'll take it." She turned slowly and felt at home for the first time in years, if ever. "I don't even need to see the inside." She reached in her purse, but Lolly stopped her.

"Rent's due first of the month. I'll give you some paperwork you can take to the school." She looked at Monty and laughed again. "You'll have to prove you're an upstanding young woman, after all." Monty tipped his hat to the ladies and left, going back through the house. There was no gate to the yard, something Lolly had thought of years ago.

Chapter Sixty-Six

"It's haunted, you know?" The other women boarders were gathered around a large rough-hewn dining table, some in dresses, others in light chemises, hair in disarray, a couple even smoking cigarettes. "Sometimes the rockers just start rockin' when nobody's in 'em." The young woman who was telling the story looked to the others for confirmation.

"Oh, I know. I've seen the curtains pull back all of a sudden, too," added another woman, in a low, conspiratorial voice. They all looked at Viola for her reaction.

"Well, then I shall have some company, won't I?" She knew they were teasing her. It was such a relief from the forced politeness of her last boarding house experience.

Lolly (no one called her Mrs. Thompson) came in with a steaming plate of pork chops and baked apples. "Now don't be telling Viola those silly ghost stories of yours!" She acted like she was upset but a smile broke out. "Let her meet the ghost for herself." The women dug into the food and ate like cowboys. Between bites Lolly told the others, "Viola is going to be teaching art and what-all at the boarding school, starting Monday." A murmur of appreciation passed between them. "I'd say it'd be nice if she could teach the bunch of you something, too, but I think she'll have plenty on her hands out there."

"Why do you say that?"

"Those children have never been in any school before, and they're pretty strict on them out there from what I've heard." Lolly picked up a chop and chewed the last remaining meat off the bone. "And away from their families and all."

Viola had so much on her mind, but not so much that she couldn't be shocked at the sight of a woman picking up a pork chop with her bare hands. This boarding house might be exactly what she needed. The women were raucous and fun, something Viola had never experienced in all her various boarding schools. Even with Kathleen, they could be silly but they were always proper, even with each other.

Over the next few days, Viola settled into her cottage which proved to be as perfect inside as out. Monty was good enough to lend his assistance in transporting her trunks from the hotel to the cottage, and he appeared amused at Viola's descriptions of life at Lolly's. The women all worked, a couple as barmaids who teased Viola that her salary for a month wouldn't equal theirs for a weekend. There was a seamstress who worked in the town's millinery. Several of the women were nannies who left the house early each morning in starched uniforms and returned at the end of the day vowing to never have children. They all had a common goal, and that was to get married and stop doing whatever job it was that they had. This was perhaps the only similarity to Miss Marshall's as the girls there pined for husbands and talked endlessly about what kinds of weddings they would have. When Viola was pressed on the issue one night, she was at a loss for an answer. "I have had men in my life," she began, only to be interrupted by a chorus of "oooohs" from the women and bawdy laughter. "But my true passion, I suppose is my art. I don't know if I would have enough of myself left over for a man." The women seemed to consider her response but then rushed to reassure that she just hadn't met the right one yet and would. She wasn't *that* old.

When Monday morning dawned, Viola was up and dressed, stuffing her satchel with paper, pencils, erasers and anything else she could think of that the students might need. It wasn't lost on her, however, that all of these supplies were coming out of her salary, an amount she hadn't even heard of yet. Lolly was up to see her off, holding a small sack in her hands. "You've got to eat. There's a little lunch for you." Viola was so grateful she nearly cried, but Lolly shooed her out the door with the admonition to just do her best and let the Lord sort out the rest.

Viola found her way to her classroom and emptied out the quite-dead flowers, replacing them with roses she had culled from Lolly's garden. She threw open the windows to get some air circulating. The room didn't let in as much light as she would have liked but there was nothing she could do about that. She sat at her desk and waited. At exactly nine o'clock a group of a dozen young men shuffled in, eyes downcast as they took their seats. There was none of the jostling and joking Viola expected among teenage boys.

She stood slowly. "I'm your teacher, Miss McDougall." She waited a few seconds. "And I hope you'll come to love art as I do." In unison the boys began the Lord's Prayer, something she had been told to begin each class with. In truth, they knew it better than she did. After the prayer concluded they stood awkwardly and looked around the room. The flag! She had forgotten to retrieve a flag from the school office and each class was also to start with the pledge of allegiance. She put her hand to her breast and led them in the pledge anyway. She would do better tomorrow, she told herself.

She motioned them into their seats and began, "Many think study of the arts is superfluous, but of course, art allows us to see things more clearly, and so..." What was she doing? These boys didn't speak English, much less care a whit about art theory. They looked up at her, a dozen blank faces. "Hmmm, so, let's get started." She held up her pencil and turned to face her sketch pad set up on an easel so all could see. She gestured toward the roses in their vase and began to sketch in their outline, motioning the boys to do the same. Utter silence pervaded the classroom other than the scratching of pencils. Viola was surprised by the knock on the classroom door.

"A word, Miss McDougall?" It was her friend, Mr. Burnham, the English teacher. "I would advise you not to turn your back on your students." He could see her classroom through the glass in her door, her room being directly across the hall from his. "Some of our guests are not as happy to be here as others." He looked to her sharpened pencil. "They might be willing to demonstrate their contempt of our hospitality." She blushed and was near tears, but Mr. Burnham simply patted her shoulder. Tomorrow was another day.

When had an hour ever seemed so long, Viola wondered, as the boys shuffled out of her classroom? She thought to make a list of all the things she had to improve on when another sullen group of boys filed in. The prayer and the pledge were done in rote. She moved her easel to a different angle, allowing her to watch the classroom. The roses in the vase were wilting as fast as she was.

Mr. Burnham waited outside her classroom when the midday bells were rung. Finally a short reprieve. "Well, you haven't flung yourself out a window," he laughed, "although a first-floor window would have been rather anticlimactic wouldn't it?" Viola laughed despite herself. She fervently hoped Lolly had put whiskey in her lunch sack.

Chapter Sixty-Seven

Each day of teaching became a little easier, of course. After each class Viola collected the students' pencils and their drawings to find that a few of the students showed genuine talent. She pinned those pictures on the walls and hoped that the artists would be pleased, but she was wrong. The boys who had done exceptional work became even more sullen seeing their drawings on display. Pride, it seems, was another trait that the boarding school system was eradicating. She talked about it at lunch one day with Mr. Burnham. "Why do they shun any attempt at recognition?"

The English teacher considered her question. "I think their cultures are more communal than ours, so that, aside from the tribal elders, everyone is more or less an equal." Viola still looked frustrated even after hearing his answer. "By singling one or two students out from the others, you set them apart, and really they're quite apart already."

"I suppose you're correct, but what reward is there for any of them?"

"I daresay there will be no reward. If the Bureau of Indian Affairs is successful in stifling and denying their cultures and forcing them to become little white men, there will be no home for them anywhere."

The bell sounded signaling the end of the lunch period. "You know, when I was younger I was a friend of the writer, Samuel Clemens." Mr. Burnham raised his eyebrow. "And he told me that soap and education would be the end of the Indian. I fear he was correct." They set off for their classrooms with a certain air of resignation.

When Viola entered her classroom she was surprised to hear some of the boys talking, although they immediately stopped when they became aware of her presence. She smiled to let them know a little conversation was permissible, but at that moment the administrator, Mrs. Jacobs, chanced by the classroom and immediately entered. "You, you and you," she said, pointing at the boys who had been talking, "Out, come with me!" She gave Viola a withering look. "They know, obviously better than you, that they are not to speak in their native language." Viola had heard that corporal punishment or long marches were meted out for any infraction of the rules, but one look at Mrs. Jacobs told her that any attempt at intervention on her part would be futile. The boys left the room, heads down.

That night at dinner, Viola listlessly pushed her food around on her plate until one of the boarders noticed. "Are you missing our dashing Monty?" The other girls tittered. "Or is there a new beau, maybe the ghost of the carriage house that's got you blue?"

"I most certainly am not missing Mr. Jacobs," Viola defended herself. "And I have yet to make the acquaintance of the ghost you talk about."

Lolly came in from the kitchen. "What's this talk about the ghost? Didn't I tell you to let up on that?" The other girls just laughed. "Is she bothering you?"

"She, who?"

"The ghost."

Viola looked at the boarders who were trying to contain their laughter. "They had just suggested to me that the ghost was a man, in fact."

"Oh, no. The ghost, if there is one, and I say, if, is definitely a woman." Lolly took her seat at the head of the table. "She's supposed to have been the maid to the man who built this house years ago. She worshipped the ground he walked on, but he never so much as said a kind word to her." The young women had all stopped eating to hear Lolly tell the story, even though many had heard it before. "His wife died and the maid thought maybe that would bode well for her being able to step up in the world, so to speak, but the master of the house went out and married another young woman who was a hateful creature and made the maid's life hell. I guess it went on like that for years until the maid couldn't take it anymore and she hanged herself right out there off the balcony." The women gasped. "When those rockers move on their own, it's her toes just grazing them, hoping to save herself from her own doing."

"We've all done stupid things over men," one of the women said, "but I damn sure wouldn't waste the rope on any one of 'em." Everyone went back to eating, and although the story was sad, it did lighten Viola's mood for the rest of the evening. She and some of the other women played hearts until well after dark.

The next day when the boys filed in to class, Viola motioned for them to remain standing after the prayer and the pledge. She stood by the door and indicated they should leave, taking a pencil and a few sheets of paper from her as they did. When everyone was in the hall, she led the way out the front door to the stand of pine trees just outside the gate. She sat on the bench and indicated the boys should sit in a semi-circle in front of her. She closed her eyes for a moment then began sketching a mountain scene with a stream bubbling over rocks, an eagle flying overhead. The boys were confused, but she addressed one who she knew spoke a little English. "Use your imagination. Draw anything you like." He relayed her message to the others. Mr. Burnham watched the tableau from his window. More trouble for Miss McDougall, he feared. The drawings that day were some of the best the students had produced.

Mr. Burnham wasn't the only one who had seen Viola march the students out the front gate. When she was leaving school that afternoon Mrs. Jacobs was waiting for her. "A word in my office, please, Miss McDougall."

Viola knew what was coming. "Before you admonish me about this afternoon, let me say, these boys simply cannot be confined here all the time other than to go on ridiculous, punishing marches around town."

"I believe I will decide what is ridiculous and what is not!" Mrs. Jacobs was angry with the fledgling teacher yet knew that what Viola was saying was probably true. Nevertheless, it set up a pattern that would go on between the two women for years to come. Viola would take a step toward giving the boys more freedom and Mrs. Jacobs would reprimand her and tighten the reins even tighter on the students. Viola was determined to bring some light and joy to her students, but after six years of teaching, it was becoming more and more difficult, and it was distracting from Viola's true passion of painting. She was so drained every night when she got home from school that she did little more than eat and perhaps play cards with the boarders.

Finally, the proverbial straw broke the camel's back. Viola had enlisted Lolly's help in making sack lunches for each of the boys, and she led them to a small bluff behind the school where there were trees and a long view of the countryside. The boys turned in excellent drawings, even making a distant yucca look like an Indian scout. When they returned to the school, however, Mrs. Jacobs was waiting for the boys. "There will be no dinner tonight for any of you, and I expect you to wash the dormitory floors — on your hands and knees!"

Viola completely lost her patience. "I wish I *had* slept with your husband years ago, you miserable bitch!"

She was shocked she had said it out loud and she could see that it wounded the older woman, but she felt no desire to apologize. She walked home in tears that night and confessed to Lolly, who had become her dearest friend, "I don't think I can do it anymore. I feel like ultimately I'm contributing to the destruction of their culture, too." They had had this discussion many times before, but tonight Viola seemed more serious about leaving the teaching profession she had reluctantly embraced some years before. "I just feel like I'm betraying them."

What Viola didn't mention and what ate at her soul even more, however, was the special form of torture that occurred every time a new crop of boys and girls was brought to the school. Viola studied every face and wondered, "Was Silver Wolf their father?"

Chapter Sixty-Eight

Finally Viola could put it off no longer. She had been in Albuquerque for more than six years and her life had settled into a pattern that was doing nothing to advance her art or her enjoyment of teaching, or anything else, for that matter. And she had noticed that Lolly was perhaps ready to stop being a landlady. When the boarders moved on, either to marriage or to try their luck in another town, Lolly didn't fill their rooms, and soon it was only Viola and one other woman, Minnie, a confirmed spinster who helped Lolly around the house.

She and Lolly sat in the rocking chairs on the porch of Viola's little cottage, sipping the remains of a bottle of wine Lolly had opened at dinner. The stars were close enough to touch in the clear desert sky and the birds were settled down for the evening. A few frogs could be heard chirping out beyond the fence. "I don't know how to bring this up, Viola began uncertainly, "but I really think it's time for me to go."

Lolly had heard dozens of conversations with Viola start this way. "Now what did that old witch do to you?"

"No, it's nothing to do with Mrs. Jacobs or the school. It's just that I've begun to feel that I too am exploiting the Indians and neglecting my own life in the process."

Lolly shifted in the rocking chair. "Well, it's true that you do live like our other spinster guest here, and I haven't seen you paint much of anything in, I don't know how long."

"That's just it." She poured herself another glass. "And I don't see it changing unless I move on." She looked at Lolly to gauge her reaction but it was already too dark on the porch since they hadn't lit the lanterns when they first settled in. "I'm thinking of going to the Grand Canyon. I've always wanted to see it."

"It's pretty impressive, I've heard." Lolly knew Viola was waiting for her to give her permission to leave but Lolly found it hard to give. She knew Viola was having a hard enough time though and finally relented. "Well, it's probably for the best, your leaving and all." She set her wineglass down. "You know I've had a few offers to sell this place. That widow Corcoran seems to want every boarding house in town, and I'm thinking of selling it to her. Minnie can go live with me in town somewhere if she wants."

"Oh, Lolly, that's just like you, always thinking of everyone else." Viola was nearly in tears but also felt a weight had been lifted from her shoulders. "The school term ends in a few weeks, and I think I'd like to leave right after that, but I'll pay an extra month's rent if you need it, or whatever."

Lolly patted her knee. "I'm fine. You know I've put by quite a bit over the years and I'm not selling this place cheap either." She laughed. "Maybe I'll be so rich that the gents will start calling on me again." She laughed even louder. "And it'll be a lot easier without all you young girls around to distract them!" They clinked their glasses in a mock toast then settled back to enjoy the rest of the evening. There would be no teary goodbyes as both women were quite settled in their decisions.

The next few weeks flew by as Viola made preparations to leave. Any books she had acquired in Albuquerque she gave to her friend, Mr. Burnham, who said he would continue teaching until he could no longer do it, or until the Bureau of Indian Affairs did away with the boarding schools, something he hoped he would see in his lifetime. He and Viola still harbored the belief that the boarding schools and other efforts to eradicate Indian culture were not necessarily positive, although they had to grudgingly agree that the world was changing and maybe in the long run...

When Viola told Mrs. Jacobs she would not be returning for the next term, all the woman could say to her was to be sure she left her classroom clean for the next teacher. Viola wasn't sure what she expected but she nevertheless felt a little let down by her nemesis' reaction. Monty at least showed a little sadness at her leaving but said he'd do what he could to help her move her belongings. Over the years he'd become something of a friend but never a romantic interest.

Viola bought train tickets from Albuquerque to Williams, Arizona, and from there would take a spur line up to the South Rim of the Grand Canyon. The stationmaster, still being the biggest gossip in town, let it be known that she was leaving and on the morning the train arrived, Viola was dumbstruck to find a small crowd waiting to see her off. Many of the former boarders were there, those that hadn't left town, with children on their hips or clutching their skirts. The manager of the Hotel Alvarado waved goodbye, and in the most poignant moment of the day, a troop of students from the boarding school marched past the train station, although they kept their eyes straight ahead as had been drilled into them.

The train ride to the Grand Canyon was pleasant enough as the elevation brought more pine trees and cooler mountain breezes. Viola tucked a shawl around her shoulders and wondered why she didn't feel the excitement of being on the move to a new place, something she had always experienced in the past. It had been years, but she still thought about Silver Wolf and realized this destination would take her even farther away from him, but it was more than that. She had an almost indefinable sense that this was the last such trip she would make, but rather than being apprehensive, she felt a certain contentment.

The flurry of activity at the Williams train station dispelled Viola's calm in no time. As soon as she stepped off the train she was met by a man with a ledger who inquired her name. "McDougall, McDougall, I don't have any record of that," he said, looking her up and down. "I don't know what group you're supposed to be with. Are you going to be a Harvey girl supervisor?" Viola had heard of the Harvey girls and realized he thought she was too old to be one.

"I don't believe I have anything to do with the Harvey girls. I'm simply here to change trains to go to the South Rim." The man looked relieved and turned to a group of young women exiting the train behind Viola. Fred Harvey had become rather well-known as a restauranteur who often as not built his establishments next to the train stations and who also provided meals for the train passengers. Already some five thousand Harvey girls served as hostesses or waitresses in his restaurant empire and were housed dormitory-style next to the restaurants. Those who were judged to have the right "look" could also be cast in the "Indian Detours" staged by Harvey. The chauffeured, guided tours had become popular with tourists who were taken to roadside depictions of "real" Indian life. Viola shook her head thinking of yet another way the Native Americans were being exploited, although, in fact, few of the productions involved any actual Indians.

Harvey and his minions also reportedly visited any Indian Pueblo or reservation they could find in search of Indian crafts which were then marketed at the Harvey restaurants in the West as well as those back

East. The Harvey empire grew rich exploiting the Indians in still another way.

Viola had become familiar with Harvey because of another concept he had refined, postcards of the West. A newspaper interview had quoted him as saying he was educating people about their own country, and Viola had to admit there was a kernel of truth to his claim as few people had any real experience in the West. Once I get settled, perhaps I'll draw some postcards for him, she thought idly, waiting for her transfer. The steam engine glided to a stop at the station, interrupting Viola's thoughts. A two-hour ride would deposit her at the Grand Canyon Lodge and perhaps the start of the next chapter of her life.

Chapter Sixty-Nine

When the train at last arrived at the South Rim, the passengers hurriedly disembarked and made their way to the lodge. Viola lingered behind, taking in the fresh pine smells and hearing the wind rustle through aspens just turning gold. Rather than join the others, she followed signs to a look-out point where there was a stone bench and terrace. She sat down and spread before her was the vista captured in the painting she had accepted from Signor Malatesta so long ago. This was the dream she had been chasing, the vision she had been seeking. This was why she was drawn west. If anything could fill the void in her soul, this was it. She was breathless from the altitude but also from the colors of the canyon walls being transformed in the fading sunlight. The golds, russets and peach colors she had admired for years in her precious painting were all right here. She probably would have sat there until darkness had not a lodge employee come by and asked her to accompany him to the Lodge before it got too dark, and therefore dangerous, to be on the narrow pathway. Visitors had fallen to their deaths, he warned her.

The registration desk had already checked in all of the other tourists. When Viola presented herself, the clerk seemed relieved. "We were hoping you didn't get lost!" She handed Viola a registration card. "How long do you plan to stay with us?"

"I hope forever," Viola replied. She signed the card and took out her purse to pay for the first two nights in advance, as a sign on the desk requested.

"Forever? I've never heard anyone say that before," the clerk chuckled, handing Viola her key. "Your bags have already been sent to your room." Viola was too lost in her own thoughts to even thank the woman, although she did find out what time the dinner service began.

The lodge, known as El Tovar, was newly-opened in 1905 and billed as one of the fanciest hotels west of the Mississippi, so Viola should not have been surprised by how elegant and formal the dinner was, with sparkling silver, starched white tablecloths and crystal glasses. She was content to dine alone although several groups of tourists asked her to join them. The room buzzed with conversations about the best viewpoints, the tours available and the ease of reaching the South Rim via the train which had largely supplanted the former stage coach service. The Fred Harvey Company managed the hotel, of course, due to Harvey's relationship with the Santa Fe Railroad which had come to the canyon four years earlier. Viola was interested to learn that the Hopi House next door to El Tovar was actually designed by the architect of the Hotel Alvarado in Santa Fe, Mary Colter.

Viola didn't migrate to the soaring hotel lobby after dinner as most of the guests did, preferring instead to go to bed early, although she doubted if she would sleep very much, if at all. She intended to see the sunrise over the canyon. True to her prediction, she barely closed her eyes that night but at dawn she had her satchel packed with an empty sketchbook, colored chalks and freshly sharpened pencils. It was too early to even inquire about having a lunch packed. She had studied the map of trails the night before and knew she had to find Lookout Point to be facing east as the sun rose. She found the trailhead easily enough and hurried along, completely oblivious to the wolf who trotted along next to her, only a few feet off the trail. The trail forked but a sign pointed toward the lookout and Viola found it just as the first rays of the sun began to hit the canyon walls. She was so mesmerized that she nearly forgot to draw and shade in the colors as they unfolded.

The hours flew by and gradually more and more tourists found their way to the lookout, so many that they began to annoy Viola with their questions about her drawings. "Have you ever been here before?" "Does the rest of the canyon look the same?" And on, and on. Viola would have to come up with a place where she could view the canyon but be undisturbed in the process. Later that afternoon she spoke to the El Tovar manager. "I wonder if there is lodging available along the canyon, other than here at your lovely hotel?"

"I don't know why you would want to forsake our hospitality, but yes, there are a few cabins," he said, reaching under the counter for a map. "Fellow by the name of Buckey O'Neill built a place ten or fifteen years ago, right on the rim."

A thousand ideas flooded Viola's mind. Maybe she could buy land and build her own cabin. Maybe this O'Neill gentleman would rent his out for a year. "How might I arrange to meet with him?"

"He's usually out adventuring one place or the other," the manager offered, "but I've got the keys to his place if you'd like to see it."

"You don't feel that he would be offended by our trespassing, so to speak?"

"Oh, no, he lets people stay there from time to time, and we just manage it for him." They arranged to meet the following afternoon after lunch had been served but before the train was due to arrive.

Viola repeated her early morning journey to Lookout Point but was back at the hotel in time for lunch, eager to not only eat but also to be sure the manager remembered their plans to tour the cabin. As soon as the last diner finished his lunch, Viola sought out the manager who surprised her by having a buggy already out in front of the hotel. "Good day, Miss McDougall!" he boomed out the greeting. Viola smiled broadly and allowed one of the nearby porters to help her into the buggy seat. She had a pang of sadness thinking of all the times Billy had done the same. "So, Miss, tell me again what it is that you do?"

She had never told him, or anyone else at El Tovar, what she did, but felt the question was innocent enough. "I am an artist. My intention is to capture some of the canyon's grandeur in my paintings."

"Well, it is grand, as you say."

The cabin itself was not so grand, however. It was a timbered structure half the size of the cottage she had lived in at Lolly's, but it did have at one end a massive stone fireplace encompassing nearly the entire wall, and there were windows on all sides. "It does have a certain...charm, I guess one might say," Viola said, "although it was clearly built for only a man to live in, and only occasionally at that." She noted the outdoor privy.

"Oh, Buckey gets a woman up here now and then," the manager replied, then blushed deeply at having said such a thing to a woman, an Englishwoman at that. He could think of nothing further to say that wouldn't add to his embarrassment so simply tied the horse up and helped Viola step down. He unlocked the door and then used his hat to knock a bit of the dust off the table. "So, here it is."

Viola was uncertain, but as she looked out the window she spied a bird's nest in the pine tree at the edge of the property. "I'll take it. Perhaps you can make the buggy available tomorrow to bring my things over here."

"Well, I really should try to ask Buckey first," the manager said, quite astounded, "but I suppose it'll be okay for a few days anyway."

Chapter Seventy

A few days turned into a few years as Buckey never returned to the Canyon to reclaim his home. As soon as she moved in, Viola set about cleaning the cabin from top to bottom but stopped often during the day to walk out to the canyon rim. At night she painted, often until well past midnight, closing her eyes and remembering the canyon. She found that if she took her easel to the canyon's edge during the day she was too distracted by the canyon's beauty, particularly on a day when billowy white thunderclouds built up, to paint. She simply sat and stared. She had fallen into a comfortable, satisfying routine, although her first few years at the canyon had been nearly overwhelming in their difficulties.

Viola recalled the day the first snowflakes coated the pine trees in the morning. By the time they had melted, the El Tovar manager was at her door. "Please, Miss McDougall, do close up the cabin and come with me back to the lodge. It's truly not safe for you here in the winter." She dismissed him casually, not really understanding what it would be like to be stranded, buried under six feet of snow, or more. When there were breaks in the storms, she could count on him riding out on horseback through the drifts, to bring her supplies and to check on her. He even helped rig up an indoor toilet. The following spring he brought laborers to build an addition onto the cabin, a real bathroom, even with the luxury of a claw foot tub.

From time to time in the long winter nights Viola would set down her paint brush and walk to the windows, pulling aside the curtain to see the moon lighting up the snow crystals. And, often, she would see the wolf, always just at the tree line, never any closer, and she wondered. Could it really be some manifestation of Silver Wolf keeping watch over her?

She had the fright of her life one afternoon when she had been dozing near the fire and there was a knock on her door. The manager had been there not two days earlier, so she doubted it would be him returning so soon. She opened the door to find a young Indian man with an axe. She opened her mouth to scream, but he stepped aside and pointed to a pile of wood near her door, wood he had chopped apparently. Viola was astonished. She stepped back in the doorway and invited him in, pantomiming that she could offer him some food, at least, but he declined and went back to chopping wood, something he did every few weeks when her supply began dwindling. Was it another sign or had she simply been out in the woods alone for too long, her fantasies taking over her judgment?

When the winter at last came to an end, heralded by wildflowers poking up through the remaining patches of snow, the El Tovar manager rode up to the cabin. Viola had heard the horse approaching and threw open the door to greet him. He was clearly relieved to see that she had survived the winter, as there had been long stretches when he wasn't able to get through the snow.

"Oh, Mr. Brooks, you're a sight for sore eyes, as they used to say in Cheyenne!"

He jumped down from the horse and bent to kiss her hand. "And you, Miss McDougall, you're lovelier than ever." She blushed but accepted the compliment and invited him into the cabin. Her paintings covered every wall and others were stacked on top of each other. "Oh, my! These are, well, they are wondrous, Miss McDougall, simply wondrous."

"So, you see I've been busy this winter." She bustled about setting out a plate of beans and biscuits for him and a glass of the cool spring water she'd come to enjoy so much. "I wonder if you can help me transport these down to the lodge. I might stay for a day or two to prepare them for shipping back East, that is, if you don't mind and there's room for me."

"I would put the President of the United States out in the street to make room for you!" They shared a good laugh and made plans to have him return with a buggy or enclosed carriage at the end of the week. Viola would be ready to go by then. As it happened, the restauranteur and promoter of all things Western, Fred Harvey, was also scheduled to visit El Tovar at the end of the week, something the manager debated about sharing with Viola. When the day came, however, he decided it might be best to warn her. "There's likely to be a little extra activity at El Tovar for a few days," he began. "Mr. Harvey himself will be staying with us, looking things over, so I might be pretty busy attending to him."

"That's quite all right, Mr. Brooks. I will have plenty to attend to myself." Viola wondered if the opportunity to meet Mr. Harvey might present itself, and if so, would she congratulate him on his promotions or castigate him for his exploitation? She didn't have long to ponder the question as the man was standing on the steps of El Tovar when their carriage pulled up. Mr. Brooks opened the door for Viola, offering his hand to help her out, and they both saw Mr. Harvey immediately become interested in this newest guest. Viola was happy she had worn one of her older, yet still stylish, gowns, and she had taken pains with her hair that day. The purple and lavender gown set off her violet eyes and chestnut hair, increasingly streaked with gray.

"Fred Harvey," he said, offering his arm to Viola at the base of the stairs. He looked over his shoulder at the manager. "Attend to our guest's baggage will you?" The manager winked at Viola then saluted Mr. Harvey, who had by now turned his back and was waltzing Viola into the lobby. "So is this your first visit to our grand hotel?"

"No, I was here nearly a year ago for several days until your very accommodating manager found lodging for me in a cabin on the rim."

"A cabin? You mean you've been out there through the winter?"

"Yes, I have indeed. Mr. Brooks has been most helpful with that as well."

Harvey was clearly astounded. "But why? What would you do out there? And you were by yourself?"

"I was indeed. I am an artist, Mr. Harvey, and wished to have the canyon all to myself, I'm afraid." Viola considered her next words carefully. "I am aware of your efforts to promote the West to people from other parts of the country…"

"From the whole world, miss."

"Yes, I'm sure. But, it's also a rare and fragile place, as formidable as it may seem at times, and I believe we also have to protect it, and the people who live in it. Perhaps through my paintings people can enjoy the Grand Canyon and other places without trampling it and destroying it."

"Well, I don't know what to say about that. I don't see any destruction," he said, waving his arm around the spacious lobby.

"That's just it, I'm afraid. Now, if you will excuse me, Mr. Harvey, I'd like to see to my paintings." She left him standing in the lobby looking totally adrift.

Chapter Seventy-One

Viola enjoyed a several-course dinner and was surprised to find that even though she was quite a bit older, her appetite showed no sign of diminishing as often happens with older people, though, she recalled, never with Aunt Vivian. While Viola accepted a second helping of roast pheasant, Mr. Harvey had found his way to the storeroom where her paintings had been placed. He knew the artist lady had insulted him in some way, but he couldn't define exactly how she had done it. What he saw in the storeroom, however, made him forget everything about their earlier encounter. Each painting was more impressive than the last, and he felt he was qualified to judge, having hired hundreds of artists to create postcards and murals for his restaurants. What to do? Should he buy the whole collection himself and do with the paintings as he wished? Or let her sell them to the galleries in the cities he saw on the list next to the crates—New York, Chicago, Paris, London, even Barcelona—and let the paintings promote the Canyon all on their own? He would have to decide tonight before the paintings were crated and shipped, although he could "conveniently" determine that the train had no room for extra crates. He slept poorly that night and was up at dawn, smoking a cigarette on the hotel's porch.

"Good morning, Mr. Harvey. I wouldn't have taken you for a person who enjoys the early hours." He strained to see where the voice was coming from and finally spotted Viola standing in the shadows, a large bag slung over her shoulder.

"Good morning to you, Miss McDougall. You're quite right. It is rare for me to be up and about so early in the morning."

"When the sun comes up over the canyon, it's quite lovely. Perhaps you'll come to enjoy it if you stay here a while."

"I'm sure that's true." He had at least made up his mind during the sleepless night. He'd let her ship the paintings out, but he'd also take advantage of the exposure without putting out a dime of his own money. "And where are you off to?" She told him and he admonished her to be careful out in the woods on the narrow trails. Perhaps they could have an early dinner together? She told him she would consider his invitation and leave word at the desk when she returned. That would give him plenty of time to set his plan in motion.

Harvey spent the morning and half of the afternoon contacting every gallery Viola had on her shipping list. He asked each gallery owner the same question, "How long have you been working with Miss McDougall?" to which all of the replied they didn't know the name. Puzzled, Harvey went back to the storeroom to examine the paintings. Clearly they were not the works of an amateur, but finally he noticed how the paintings were signed with the cryptic V McD. His second round of calls yielded more information. Some of the galleries had been representing her for more than thirty years, from her time spent in Europe, others only for her "western period." They all agreed that her work was greatly in demand and fetched top dollars. Harvey was happy he hadn't made an offer to buy all the paintings, quite confident his offer would have been laughed off the table. So, when to spring his little surprise, after she had returned to the old Buckey's cabin or while she was still a guest at El Tovar?

He called his manager in late in the afternoon and reviewed the reservations log. El Tovar was nearly completely full for the remainder of the summer. Good news, to be sure, but frustrating that the hotel wasn't twice as large. He'd talk to his fellow investors on the Santa Fe Railroad to see about expanding it, perhaps with a slightly lower-cost option. As he and Brooks walked around the grounds he spotted a few tourists with sketchbooks, although clearly their work was amateurish in comparison to Viola's. Still, it reinforced his instincts at promotion. He was onto something, he was certain. He thanked his manager, really a very competent young man, for the tour. "Oh, and will you send the man who works in the sign shop over to my office?"

For the next half-hour he was closeted in his office with the sign painter giving him explicit directions about what he wanted, and a very tight deadline. The man was in awe of meeting the actual Fred Harvey but seemed confident he could paint the sign the boss wanted and have it in the lobby before the lunch hour tomorrow.

Viola, meanwhile, was conducting an impromptu art class at Lookout Point. As always, most of the tourists who ambled by wanted to talk to her about her work, but in today's group there were several with sketchpads of their own. "How do you make it look like the rocks are stacked just so?" Or, "Why does my tree look like it's about to fall off the cliff?" Finally she culled the artists out from the other tourists and had them sit on the ground in a semi-circle in front of her, much as she had done with her students at the Albuquerque Indian Boarding School. She proceeded to give them a lecture on perspective and for some of the more ambitious students, pointers on shading and symmetry. She was annoyed to have been distracted from her own work, but she had enjoyed her time as a teacher and this was a somewhat poignant reminder of it.

By the time she returned to El Tovar she was exhausted, but a note under her door reminded her that she was an invited guest of Mr. Harvey's that evening, if her schedule so permitted. Which would be more tiring, avoiding him, pretending to agree with him while he pontificated about promoting the West, or arguing with him about his selfish use of the West and everything in it? She ultimately chose to respond with a note declining his kind invitation and ordered prime rib from room service. Of course, it would be nothing like the beef and bread pudding she remembered from her days as a child in England, but at least it would be filling. She wondered that she hadn't burst out of the seams of her clothing!

Viola slept soundly but still awakened in time to catch the dawn, tiptoeing out of her room and down the stairs. She doubted Harvey would be up early two mornings in a row, and she was correct. Her escape to Lookout Point was noted only by her unseen wolf companion. A storm was clearly brewing with the thunderheads climbing just as rapidly as the sun, so Viola's day was cut short. She had been warned by the guides numerous times about the danger of lightning on the high shelfs around the canyon. She hurried back to El Tovar, idly wondering what would be offered on the luncheon menu. She was unprepared therefore when she entered the lobby and saw a crowd gathered around a large sign, Mr. Harvey standing next to it.

"Announcing the Grand Canyon's 'Artist in Residence' program." The sign showed a woman, looking suspiciously much like herself (although Viola noted, without the gray hair), poised in front of an easel at Lookout Point. "Come to the Grand Canyon and discover the artist in YOU," the sign urged, "while learning from the biggest talents in the art world today." She stood transfixed, reading the sign and looking at Harvey's smug grin. The other tourists turned to look at her and made the natural connection. Some who had been in her 'class' the day before exchanged knowing looks.

Viola was furious. "I see you're doing what you do best," she spit at Harvey, "exploiting whatever you can!"

"Oh, Miss McDougall, did you think this referred to you?" He acted incredulous that she would have such a thought. "No, I expect we'll get some real artists to come out here and teach our workshops."

There was nothing she could say without escalating her anger and frustration even further. She went to her room and tried to relax, missing lunch. By dinner, she had resigned herself to the situation, but the final indignity was still awaiting her.

Chapter Seventy-Two

Viola's largest painting of the canyon was hanging in the dining room. Harvey had bought it from the New York gallery before it even went on sale there. The triptych was a diorama of the canyon at sunset and had taken Viola months to paint. When the host slid her chair in for her, she saw Harvey watching her from across the room. All she could do was look up at the painting and smile. She would contact the New York gallery the next day and assure herself that he had paid top dollar for her work, since it now felt like he had virtually stolen it—and her anonymity, something she had worked very diligently to maintain over the years.

Surprisingly, however, by the time the waiter had set the roast chicken dinner before her, she had already put the incident behind her and tucked into the chicken with gusto, even asking the waiter to bring a bottle of chilled white wine. She raised a glass to Harvey and couldn't help but notice his surprised reaction. If he was waiting to get a reaction out of her, he would be waiting a good long time indeed.

Viola had intended to spend a few days at El Tovar, but the next morning when she got to her favorite spot at Lookout Point, the tourists were already waiting for her. The solitude of the early morning was broken by their chatter and she returned to the lodge in despair. She sat in her room listlessly thumbing through magazines until she finally decided to take the bull by the horns, another saying that had always made her chuckle when she lived in Cheyenne. She freshened up and headed for Harvey's office, not bothering to knock before she entered. He was poring over ledgers but quickly put them aside. "To what do I owe this unexpected pleasure?"

"I have a proposition for you, Mr. Harvey." She made herself comfortable in a chair opposite him. "I will conduct a seminar such as an 'artist in residence' as you call it might do tomorrow afternoon."

"Splendid."

"And I will also be paid the entire proceeds plus have my bill here at the hotel covered in its entirety."

He looked aghast. "That's highly unusual, Miss McDougall, but..."

"There is no alternative. Elsewise I shall have my solicitor contact you and begin preparations for a lawsuit based on you misappropriating my identity for your latest campaign."

The threat got his attention, as Viola knew it would. "I don't think any misappropriation was intended," he tried. "I think it was just a happy circumstance that you and your artwork were here when I happened to visit, and..."

"There has been nothing happy about it," Viola said in retort, "but there will be an end to it tomorrow afternoon." She stood to leave. "Set the seminar for two o'clock. I must have my lunch first."

By the time Viola took the stage the next afternoon, the lobby was filled to capacity. Even the guests who had never drawn so much as bowl of fruit in their lives were eager to hear a "celebrity." Harvey, true to his nature, had virtually papered El Tovar and Hopi House next door with flyers about the seminar, and he had set the price of admission higher than Viola would have thought possible to produce such a crowd. She introduced herself and gave a brief background of where she had studied, then said she would open the floor to questions.

An earnest-looking young man in the front row began, "How do you know, I mean, how do I know, we know, if we have any real talent?"

Viola was surprised at how difficult the question was. "Well, of course, your friends will tell you how talented you are, and your mum will want to hang up your drawings, but I think you do need to subject your work to a more critical eye." She took a sip of water from the pitcher provided to give herself time to think. "I would look for an art class and start there, and if your teacher is encouraging — but critical — then perhaps take your work to a gallery." The crowd murmured. "It is difficult to lay your soul bare in your work and have it rejected or only received in a lukewarm way, but certainly if you believe in yourself and your craft, you must persist."

Another question followed on the heels of her reply. "But what if you do persist and still nothing happens?"

"I find myself at a loss to answer that, unfortunately, or rather fortunately, I would have to say." The group looked confused. "I personally enjoyed success from an early stage in my career." She hesitated. "I don't know if that is because of any talent I had as a young woman or if the timing was right for the sorts of work I was producing at the time." She laughed a bit, "And, of course, there's always luck involved."

Some of the further questions were more mundane, but a woman in the back of the room stood to get Viola's attention. "You're clearly a very accomplished artist, Miss McDougall. But what do you base your success on, personally?"

Viola had a ready answer for this question, although she hadn't expected to be asked. She had spent many afternoons at the edge of the canyon pondering it. "I believe you have to love and respect your subject." She thought back to her time watching Silver Wolf's band and of her recent years watching the canyon change minute by minute. "And you also must respect your own talent. Your talent, like your love, is nothing to be squandered." She turned away for another drink of water to mask the tears that had suddenly appeared. "I think on that note, I will thank you for attending today and encourage you to enjoy the West but to respect it as well." The crowd applauded enthusiastically, and Viola was grateful that Harvey immediately came to her side and escorted her off the stage and away to a side corridor. A secretary had been transcribing her comments and Harvey expected to send them to every newspaper in the country.

Viola left El Tovar the next morning to return to her cabin before one of the tourists could ambush her with more questions or ask for a critique of their work. The seminar had been emotionally draining and she yearned for the solitude of her remote part of the canyon. In the weeks that followed the manager of El Tovar often drove out to see her. One such morning they were sitting on the porch and Viola took a long look at him. He was no longer the eager young man who had pleaded with her not to stay the winter in the cabin. He had become a middle-aged man and now had a family of his own. When had that happened, she thought to herself? He told her about the other artists who were coming to El Tovar, names she dismissed as "lesser luminaries," bringing a chuckle to them both.

She enjoyed his visit and when he left decided to take her paints and canvas down to the canyon edge, something she rarely did. She picked up a brush, but this afternoon she felt content to just sit and look, letting the afternoon drift away. She no longer felt the urgency she once had to capture every moment. She also felt a great sense of forgiveness—for Aunt Vivian who, after all, had been thrust into a situation she was wholly unprepared for in caring for a little girl; for Kathleen not accompanying her on her grand adventure to the west; even for Silver Wolf not taking her with him. She had known great passion in her life, both love and sorrow, and now she knew peace. She leaned back against a rock and let the sun warm her face. The paintbrush slipped from her hand and she stayed that way until she could feel the sun no longer. The great silver wolf padded silently to her side, laying down with his head in her lap. She would not die alone.

The End

About the Author

Arline Fisher was raised in Carson City, Nevada, and is a journalism graduate from the University of Nevada, Reno. She has worked as a managing editor on several national magazines and on book-packaging projects, in addition to doing direct-mail marketing and public relations projects. She makes her home in St. George, Utah, but will always be a Nevadan at heart.

Thank you for your support

I have the best group of friends who were happy to read a chapter every time I finished one—and nagged me when I was a few days late. I took all of your comments to heart. So, as always, thank you to Vicki Lund, Claudia Reek, Kirsten Ball, Lonna Burress, Lolly Seal and Kathleen Halpern. This would have been impossible without you.

If you've enjoyed what you've read here, write a favorable review, tell your friends to buy a copy, and send me an e-mail at arlinefisher@centurylink.net. And, keep an eye out for my next novel. I'm sure I've got at least one more in me.

Publisher: Arline Fisher
arlinefisher@centurylink.net

Copyright @ Arline Fisher, 2016

ISBN-13: 978-0692742723 (Arline Fisher)
ISBN-10: 0692742727

www.ingramcontent.com/pod-product-compliance
Lightning Source LLC
Chambersburg PA
CBHW071150250626
47159CB00001B/50